Praise for Me[...]
The Dressmaker's Dowry

"With mystery, romance and a slice of history from San Francisco's infamous Barbary Coast, Jaeger's debut, *The Dressmaker's Dowry,* is sure to captivate. Comprising both a historical and contemporary story, Jaeger spins a tale of love, loss and a city divided by social class. Whether you read romance, mysteries, or historical or contemporary fiction, there is something in the novel for everyone."

—Sally Hepworth, author of *The Secrets of Midwives* and *The Things We Keep*

"In this deliciously satisfying tale of love and resilience, Meredith Jaeger sweeps us into nineteenth-century San Francisco, painting harrowing images of poverty alongside excesses of wealth, weaving a multigenerational novel impossible to put down."

—Lori Nelson Spielman, *New York Times* bestselling author of *The Life List* and *Sweet Forgiveness*

"Meredith Jaeger deftly intertwines two tales of love and loyalty and the vast lengths to which some will go to protect those they hold dear. A compelling debut novel that sent me racing to its final, revealing pages."

—Kristina McMorris, *New York Times* bestselling author of *The Edge of Lost*

"Jaeger's debut sends readers quickly and completely into San Francisco's history. Hanna, Margaret and Sarah are the perfect storytellers, young women determined to find their place in the world. This gripping read is a satisfying exploration of the timeless nature of love and resilience."

—*Booklist* (starred review)

"Jaeger weaves her mystery over two timelines, luring the reader into a riveting tale of intrigue and suspense. Blending the past and present together through strong descriptions and colorful, exciting characters, Jaeger creates an engrossing novel. Readers will be captivated by her voice, that of a good old-fashioned storyteller."

—RT Book Reviews

Boardwalk Summer

Also by Meredith Jaeger

The Dressmaker's Dowry

Boardwalk Summer

A Novel

Meredith Jaeger

wm
WILLIAM MORROW
An Imprint of HarperCollins*Publishers*

P.S.™ is a trademark of HarperCollins Publishers.

HarperCollins books may be purchased for educational, business, or sales promotional use. For information, please email the Special Markets Department at SPsales@harpercollins.com.

FIRST EDITION

Designed by Diahann Sturge

Library of Congress Cataloging-in-Publication Data has been applied for.

ISBN 978-0-06-274806-5

18 19 20 21 22 LSC 10 9 8 7 6 5 4 3 2 1

For Hazel Luna, I love you to the moon.

Boardwalk Summer

CHAPTER 1

Violet Harcourt

Summer 1940

My heart hammered as I stood on the bandstand, in front of the swelling crowd. *Cripes.* How many people had gathered on the beach today? Possibly thousands. The sun beat down on my tanned shoulders, warming them. Onions sizzled on the hot dog grill, mingling with the salty air, and a choir of seagulls cawed overhead.

Evie stood to my right, her hand placed on a cocked hip to show off her fire-engine-red nails. She tilted her head, her shiny dark hair swept up in perfect rolls. Winking at the crowd, Evie dared to bare her midriff in a tight two-piece. Mother found the new swimsuit fashion scandalous, but I wished I had Evie's confidence.

Out of the fifteen women who'd entered the Miss California pageant, three of us stood at the forefront, vying for a shot at the crown. I took a deep breath. Getting a Hollywood screen test was a dream I'd held tightly, knowing it could slip away at any second. This was my opportunity to be discovered.

"Ladies and gents," the emcee spoke into the microphone, "this is the moment we've been waiting for."

I wasn't going to win. With her luminous pale skin and amber eyes, Evie looked like Olivia de Havilland, and I looked like, well, me. Clearly, her beauty eclipsed mine. But the pin curls in my auburn hair stayed put, and my polka-dot swimsuit with its flared skirt complemented my slight curves. I'd lacquered my lips red as Evie's nails. Perhaps today would be my turn to shine in the spotlight.

When I'd sung Billie Holiday's rendition of George Gershwin's "Summertime" for the talent portion, my voice had come from deep within my soul. Mother thought my dreams of stardom were a childish phase, admonishing me every time she'd caught me using her hairbrush as a microphone. But my desire to perform had only grown stronger.

If Charles saw me onstage right now, he'd . . .

I pictured my husband's handsome face contorted with rage, and my stomach squeezed sharply. I tamped down my fear, remembering the lie I'd told the pageant officials. Yet I hadn't stopped myself from filling out the Miss California contest entry form, my hands shaking as I'd signed my name.

One of the Atlantic City judges for the Miss America pageant was Artie Schmekel, the financial backer for all of Broadway's biggest musicals. If he watched me sing, play piano or dance, perhaps I'd see my name in lights on a theater marquee—and then on the silver screen. Plenty of gals went to Hollywood after their pageant wins. Would a film director take a gamble on me?

The announcer cleared his throat. "Three beautiful ladies stand before me. Let's give them a round of applause."

My cheeks hurt from holding my smile, and I tried not to squint. *Jiminy Cricket,* could the sun be any brighter? A sea breeze ruffled the colorful beach umbrellas, cooling my sweaty skin. But it did little to ease my nerves.

"And the runner-up for the Miss California bathing beauty contest is . . ." The emcee paused. It seemed to stretch for an eternity. "Miss Evelyn Hastings of San Francisco, California!"

I let out the breath I didn't realize I'd been holding. Evie's dark brows knit together, but within seconds she'd put on a winning smile. She waved at the crowd, swishing her hips in her outrageously daring two-piece. Though her eyes held disappointment, she wouldn't stay down for long. For Evie, life was always coming up roses. She smiled as if to say, *This isn't the last you'll see of me.*

Evie had convinced me to enter the pageant. Two years ago, a new rule had been put into place: contestants had to be single women, never married, never divorced. But to that Evie had declared, "Hogwash! My Frank would be over the moon to see me with a crown on my head. Come on, Vi. What's a little white lie?"

A petite blonde stood to my right, a contestant from

Orange County. I swallowed, pushing the lump of guilt down my throat. She had a wholesome, all-American look about her, and sweet dimples framed her smile. The gal had done a fantastic tap dancing routine, and I figured it was her turn today. I prepared myself to lose as gracefully as Evie had. Perhaps it was for the best. Then neither one of us would get into trouble.

The emcee ran a hand through his oil-slick hair. "And the grand prize winner of the 1940 Miss California bathing beauty contest is our very own Miss Violet Sweeting of Santa Cruz, California!"

Once the shock of hearing my maiden name wore off, happy tears sprang to my eyes. Were they playing some kind of gas on me? I stepped forward in my peep-toe heels, barely able to contain my surprise. The brass band played "In the Mood."

Swinging my hips in time to the music, I waved at the crowd. Fleetingly, my heart went out to the blonde, as the emcee congratulated her on her third-place win. But I was floating.

The crowd roared. I didn't need Mother, Father or Charles to make decisions for me. How could they possibly understand? Onstage I was electric, burning bright as the marquee lights. Jazz made me feel more alive than Mozart ever had. My music degree from Mills College had pleased Mother, but I was ready to do so much more than play piano in the parlor for houseguests. I belonged in the pictures.

The emcee handed me a bouquet of fresh pink roses.

"Congratulations, Violet. Ladies and gentlemen, I present to you Miss California, 1940."

"Thank you very much."

I straightened my sash, my ring finger bare where my Tiffany diamond solitaire and matching wedding band should have been.

"Good luck, fellas," the emcee said, winking. "This bathing beauty sure is a looker! She won't be single for long."

The crowd laughed, and I forced a smile, but my stomach churned. I touched the strand of pearls around my neck, another lavish gift from my husband. The Cartier necklace caused Evie's eyes to bulge with envy. I knew without asking it was worth a fortune. Charles came from old money, inheriting a trust fund from a successful shipping business, long sold, and also the Oceano Golf Club, the finest and most prestigious course west of the Mississippi. Like me, Charles had been born and raised in Santa Cruz, but he mingled solely with the area's elite. Even celebrities traveled here to Monterey Bay for the stunning views along the Oceano's magnificent green.

"Give us a big smile for the camera," the emcee said.

I nodded, trying to shake the uneasy feeling that had settled over me. I focused on the quaint shops dotting the boardwalk and the children holding sticks of cotton candy. Laughter carried on the breeze with the whoosh of the wooden roller coaster. Peaks and valleys; it was normal to have those in a marriage, wasn't it?

Men played with their tots in the sand, scooping handfuls of it into makeshift castles. Charles would make a good father. He had an easy way with children, delighting them with tricks, like producing a dime from thin air. I'd glowed on every date during our courtship, feeling positively smitten. With his dark hair, long-lashed eyes and dazzling smile, Charles had the charm of Clark Gable.

On our early dates, we'd spent hours necking at the drive-in through double features. At night, I'd often slept in the cardigan I'd worn, to savor his cologne until it faded. We'd enjoyed our weekends at the boardwalk, and Charles had laughed as he'd rammed my bumper car at Auto Scooter, delighting in mischief like a young boy. But not long afterward, he began to question me constantly about my whereabouts. And I hadn't told him I would be participating in the pageant today.

The photographer crouched before me, his camera in my face. I looked down at his wingtips, overcome by a wave of dizziness.

"Miss Sweeting," he said. "Big smile. Eyes up here, please."

The shrill whistle of the *Suntan Special* blared. Passengers poured from the train coaches, men in fedoras and women in wide-brimmed sun hats. Children squealed, set free to release their energy on the beach. In spite of the summer heat, an icy chill ran through me. I saw him there in the crowd.

The notes of "In the Mood" swelled from the beach band, welcoming the new arrivals. I watched my husband's broad shoulders as he made his way past the beachgoers, holding his briefcase. His dark hair shone in the sunlight;

he stood a head taller than most of those around him. *Oh Jesus.* Hadn't he meant to arrive this evening?

Cool fingers squeezed my hand. I whipped around.

Evie smiled. "Why'd ya have to steal my chance? I heard the Miss America crown is made of real diamonds. It's an ugly shame it won't be on my head."

I tried to laugh.

Evie's doll-like eyes filled with concern. "Good grief, Vi. What's the matter?"

I swallowed, my throat dry. "Evie, I don't think I should have—"

"Excuse me, Evelyn?" The emcee stood between us. "Sorry, darling, but we need a picture of Miss Sweeting alone. Then we'll photograph you gals together."

Evie dropped my hand as he shooed her away.

"Okay," he said. "On three. One, two . . ."

Before the bulb flashed, my gaze settled on Charles. Those warm brown eyes of his had once crinkled at the corners with laughter, but now they were filled with a cruel look I knew all too well. Sweat beaded on my forehead.

What a stupid, stupid thing you've done.

This time, Charles's voice would hold no annoyance. He would remain silent, and his silence frightened me more than anything. The look in my husband's eyes was one of anger and betrayal. This was my fault. I never should have lied. Why did I crave the attention? I ought to have stayed home. Or clapped politely for the other girls while sitting underneath an umbrella, wearing something modest.

As the crowd cheered for me, I shivered. I no longer looked forward to the floats, the parade, the celebratory dancing or tonight's fireworks. Charles would feign pride in my pageant win, because what else could he do? We'd have chicken sandwiches for lunch with Evie and Frank, and then stroll together along the pier. But tonight, behind closed doors, I would pay dearly for my careless mistake.

CHAPTER 2

Marisol Cruz

Summer 2007

"Lily, honey. Put on your other shoe. It's time to go."

"I want my purple sneaker."

Mari looked down at her daughter's feet, one bare, and one clad in a silver-glitter ballet flat. Then she glanced at her watch. Her shift at the Jupiter Café began in exactly fifteen minutes.

"Okay, your purple sneakers? Let's put them on."

"No. *One* sneaker."

"But then you won't match."

Lily rolled her eyes and flopped on the bed; she was four going on fourteen.

"I *want* to mismatch."

Too tired to argue, Mari slipped the purple sneaker on her daughter's left foot and did up the Velcro straps. With her Belle T-shirt, plaid leggings and buns all over her head, Lily resembled a tiny Gwen Stefani, circa 1998.

"Are you taking me today?" she asked, her green eyes wide.

Mari's stomach pinched with guilt. "Not today. Mommy has to work."

With an exasperated sigh, Lily heaved herself off the bed and slipped her *Little Mermaid* backpack over her shoulder. "You *always* have to work." She glanced around the room. "Where's my tiara?"

Mari's eyes scanned the bedroom in the quaint 1940s beach cottage that had belonged to her grandfather. When he had passed away, her parents had inherited it, and now Mari lived with them. Lily's small bed with purple floral sheets, hidden beneath her stuffed animals, fit snugly in the corner, while Mari's modest twin sat beneath the open window, the ocean breeze ruffling the gauzy, white curtains.

Outside, the natural beauty of California's coastline stretched for miles. The sun through the window warmed Mari's face, and today would be another perfect seventy-eight degrees. Perched on the northern edge of Monterey Bay, Santa Cruz sat beneath the cool shade of the redwood trees, offering the most beautiful views in the world.

Atop a shelf on Mari's bookcase, Lily's tiara sparkled in the sunlight.

"Found it," Mari said, walking over to reach for the plastic crown.

Lily clapped her hands. "Hooray!"

A hard lump rose in Mari's throat as her gaze settled on her history textbooks, which she hadn't opened in years. She longed to trail her finger down their worn spines, remembering the words of Howard Zinn and W.E.B. Du Bois.

"Let's go," Mari said, placing the tiara atop Lily's head. Lily beamed as she adjusted it, like the rightful winner of the Miss Universe pageant.

Stepping into the tiled kitchen, Mari found her mother putting together Lily's lunch box. "Oh Ma, I was going to do that."

Paulina shrugged, her thick chestnut hair reaching her shoulders. Even in her late forties, she still turned heads. "I wanted to help." Looking down at her granddaughter, Paulina opened her arms. "*Buenos dias,* sweetie!"

Lily ran to her *abuela,* tripping over her mismatched shoes.

Raising an eyebrow, Paulina looked at Mari. "*Mija,* what is she wearing?"

"She's four," Mari mumbled. "Look, it's only shoes."

"Look at this stuff, isn't it neat?" Lily belted out, freeing herself from Paulina and twirling around the kitchen. "Wouldn't you think my collection's complete?"

"Oh great." Paulina shot Mari a look. "Is this going to last the whole car ride?"

Mari smiled. "Sorry."

She snuck a quick glance in the hallway mirror, smoothing her waitress uniform—a short blue dress with square front pockets. The Jupiter Café encouraged its employees to look "funky," but this morning Mari had put on tiny gold hoop earrings in defiance of the tacky plastic jewelry rule. Wearing no makeup, she could still pass for a college student—except she felt about a hundred years older.

"Come here," Mari said, scooping Lily into a hug and kissing her face until she erupted into giggles.

Mari breathed in the scent of Lily's apple shampoo, her heart aching when she thought of her little girl entering kindergarten in the fall. How was that possible? She liked having Lily at Green Frog Preschool, where Paulina worked as the director of the bilingual school. Santa Cruz housed a mix of open-minded, eco-friendly families, eager for their children to learn Spanish. Mari loved that about her community.

"I *love* you, Mom," Lily said, blowing a kiss.

"Love you too," Mari replied, watching her daughter scamper out the door.

Grabbing her lukewarm, half-finished mug of coffee off the counter, Mari took a swig, wondering if she should reheat it in the microwave. Instead, she put Lily's empty cereal bowl in the dishwasher, finished loading the machine, and turned it on. Her stomach growled, but she had no time for breakfast.

In the hallway, Mari paused to look at a framed black-and-white photograph of her *abuelo*, the famed Ricardo Cruz. Her young grandfather plunged headfirst from a trapeze into the Pacific Ocean. He'd been a Santa Cruz

Beach Boardwalk performer in the 1940s, a stunt diver who delighted the crowds with his daring act.

Mari swallowed, remembering all the times she'd strolled hand in hand with her *abuelo* along the wooden slats of the boardwalk. He'd bought her cotton candy and ice cream, taken her for endless rides on the carousel, and let her sit on his shoulders when she'd gotten tired of walking.

He'd told her stories—so many stories—about his adventures as a young man, bringing the sights and sounds of the boardwalk to life. The bands that had played, the people he had known, they danced in Mari's mind like images from a vintage movie reel.

She blinked back tears and twisted the door handle.

"Bye, Abuelo," she whispered. "I miss you."

BY THE TIME she reached the Jupiter Café, Mari had broken a sweat, even though the scenic walk from Beach Hill, overlooking the sparkling blue ocean, took less than ten minutes. Tourists on beach cruisers zipped past, their tanned legs pushing bicycle pedals as they made their way toward Pacific Avenue's shops and restaurants.

Mari slipped in the back entrance of the café, donning her planet-covered apron with one hand and punching her time card with the other. She was already looking forward to picking Lily up from school, so they could collect seashells at Natural Bridges Beach, dip their toes in the water, and admire wildflowers along the footpath.

"There you are."

Wanda appeared from around the corner, her gaze like an owl's behind her rhinestone 1950s cat's-eye glasses, her bleach-blond hair stuck up in spikes.

"Oh!" Mari said, putting a hand to her chest. "You scared me."

Wanda scrutinized Mari's face, then looked down at her bare arms and clucked her tongue. "What's this? I want *funky*! You're young, Marisol. You're a pretty girl. Where's that Latin flair? *Arriba*!"

"Sorry." Mari shrugged. "I guess I didn't bring it today."

"You want my red lipstick?" Wanda offered, digging into the pocket of her apron. The alarming crimson shade had worked its way into the wrinkles above Wanda's mouth, enhancing the yellow tint of her teeth.

"No thanks," Mari said, dodging Wanda's outstretched arm. "Looks like table four needs coffee. I'll bring them some."

Putting on a bright smile, she approached the red vinyl booth in the corner. Two girls sat slumped over, wearing hooded UC Santa Cruz sweatshirts and tight yoga pants, their blond hair tied up in messy buns.

"Good morning," Mari said, holding up a steaming pitcher. "Coffee?"

"God yes," one coughed, her voice as hoarse as a chain-smoker's. Rings of mascara were smeared around her eyes. "Give it to me."

"Ugh," the other moaned, rubbing her temples. "I think I'm still drunk."

Mari poured two cups, smiling sympathetically. It had

been years since she'd woken up with a hangover. As a working, single mom, she had enough to worry about without the added pressure of nausea and a headache.

Chewing her lip, Mari remembered the last time she'd been *really* drunk . . . the summer of her graduation from UC Santa Cruz. She'd aced all her finals, made the dean's list, and hadn't seen the harm in throwing back a few (okay, several) tequila shots. That was the night she'd wound up pregnant.

Mari shook her head to clear away the memory. "I can bring you both some water too if you like. It's good to stay hydrated."

"Sure," one of the blondes said. "Thanks."

"Do you know what you'd like to order, or do you need a few more minutes?"

"Hash browns and eggs," the hoarse girl barked.

"And I'll have the pancakes," the other answered.

"Sure thing," Mari said. "They'll be coming right up."

She made her way around the room to other tables, carried steaming plates laden with food from the kitchen, refilled coffee, wiped down countertops and called out orders to the cooks. When she returned with the order of hash browns, eggs and pancakes for the blondes, they were in the midst of a heated argument.

"Santa Cruz became a city in 1900," the bossy one said with a flick of her fingernails. "A Spanish guy discovered it. He built the missions."

"Are you sure?" the other blonde asked. "Because this test is in an hour."

Setting down their plates, Mari counted to ten in her head. *Don't say anything you'll regret. Let these two party their education away.*

"There were just, like, a bunch of Indians here or whatever," blonde number one continued. "The Spanish brought them culture."

"Actually," Mari said, her words tumbling out as she refilled both mugs of coffee, "Santa Cruz became a city in 1866. In 1848, following the Mexican–American War, Mexico ceded the territory of Alta California to the U.S. in the Treaty of Guadalupe Hidalgo. California was the first portion of the territory to become a state, in 1850."

The college students sat there slack-jawed, staring at Mari like she'd spoken in a foreign language. Her cheeks heating, Mari filled the awkward silence by spouting more facts. *What was she doing?* She didn't know how to stop herself.

"And before the arrival of Spanish soldiers and missionaries in the late eighteenth century, Santa Cruz was home to the Awaswas people. They're *Native Americans,* not Indians. The misnomer Ohlone is often used to describe the native people of the Santa Cruz area, but really it's a generalized name for the many diverse tribes who lived in the region. They were also referred to by the Spanish as Costanoan."

The blonde who'd seemed so sure of herself rolled her eyes, while the other pulled her slumped body upright and grabbed Mari's hand.

"Can you take my test for me?"

Mari sensed Wanda watching her—or rather, felt the heat of Wanda's glare.

"I wish I could," Mari said, her voice quiet. If only she could rewind time to that night after finals . . .

But then she wouldn't have Lily, her greatest joy in life. And wasn't Lily the reason she worked as a waitress? Mari's flexible schedule allowed her to pick Lily up from preschool and to be there when her daughter needed her.

In the bustling heat of the kitchen, Mari stuck meal orders on tacks and wiped the sweat from her brow. Wanda appeared, strong hands placed on thick hips.

"What did I tell you about talking to the customers?" Her eyes narrowed behind her pink cat's-eye glasses, the rhinestones glinting menacingly.

"Keep the conversation light." Mari lowered her head. "Wanda, I'm sorry."

"If you're not happy here," Wanda said, leaning in so close that Mari could smell stale cigarettes on her breath, "just say so. I've got other employees who want more shifts. They would be happy to take your mornings."

"Oh no, I—"

Mari's cell phone vibrated in her apron pocket, and she resisted the urge to pick it up. But what if it was her mother, and something had happened to Lily at school?

"It's okay," Wanda said. "Take fifteen. You're due for a break."

Stepping outside into the sunlight, Mari took in a deep breath, letting the salty sea air fill her lungs. Pulling her phone from her pocket, she looked at the unfamiliar number flashing on screen. Mari sat down on a bench in the parking lot behind the café and kicked a cigarette butt away with the toe of her sneaker.

"Hello?"

"Is this Marisol Cruz?"

The woman's voice was polished and crisp.

"Yes, this is she."

"Hello, Marisol. This is Jane Anderson, lead curator at the Santa Cruz Museum of Art & History. I'm responding to your application for the customer service position working at our exhibit during the Beach Boardwalk Centennial Celebration."

Mari sat bolt upright, her heart pounding in her chest. "Yes?"

"We *loved* learning that your grandfather, Ricardo Cruz, was one of the famed Beach Boardwalk performers of his time. Of course, we were impressed by your résumé too, especially your graduating with honors in history from UC Santa Cruz. We would be thrilled to have an actual descendant of Ricardo's teaching tourists about the legacy of the boardwalk. Do you have time for a quick phone interview?"

"Yes." Mari swallowed, her mouth dry. "Of course."

"Wonderful," Jane replied. "Just to clarify your job duties, you would be selling raffle tickets and operating our museum booth showcasing the history of the Beach Boardwalk. This would be every Saturday and Sunday from June through August. According to your résumé, you currently work as a waitress . . . can you tell me more about that?"

Mari winced at the confusion in Jane's voice. *What was someone who graduated cum laude doing working in food service?*

"I have a daughter," Mari explained. "She's four. I wait tables at Jupiter Café so that I can spend more time with her. I have a flexible schedule. And it won't affect my ability to work at the exhibit. I have extensive customer service experience."

"Well," Jane said. "Fantastic! Can you come by at noon next Saturday? You'll meet with the boardwalk archivist, Carol, above the Cocoanut Grove Ballroom on Beach Street. She'll let you know more about getting started."

"Absolutely," Mari said, even though Saturdays and Sundays were her best-paying shifts. "Thank you so much." She dug her nails into her palm, thinking about her lost tips. But hadn't she wanted this job—gone out on a limb to apply for it?

"Great. We look forward to seeing you then. Please bring your driver's license, and we'll have you fill out the employment paperwork. Goodbye, Marisol."

"Bye." Mari brought her fingers to her lips.

Working for the Santa Cruz Museum of Art & History had long been her dream job. Yet in the last four years, Mari's dream had gotten derailed. She'd lost her confidence to the responsibilities of being a mother—dealing with fevers, dirty diapers, dirty dishes and dirty laundry.

What about the girl who'd studied late into the night, who thought about going to graduate school, who wanted to work in the heart of a museum? She'd had a big smile and even bigger aspirations. Mari's throat tightened, wishing she could hug her grandpa or hear his voice just one more time. She'd been thinking about him when she filled out the online application to work the Centennial Celebration, proudly telling his story.

She looked up at the sky and whispered, "Thank you, Abuelo."

Wiping her hands on her apron, she walked back toward the Jupiter Café. Taking this weekend job was a big risk—one that probably wouldn't pay off in the way she hoped. The summer would end, and then what? Jane Anderson would see how smart she was and offer her something permanent and full-time? *Ridiculous.*

But hadn't Mari's grandpa always told her to be brave?

She closed her eyes, imagining the courage it took him to release his knees from the trapeze, and to plunge headfirst into the ocean. It had to be terrifying, but exhilarating too. Abuelo had always told her to reach for the stars. And she was going to try.

CHAPTER 3

Violet Harcourt

1940

Soapy water sloshed over my rubber gloves as I washed the dishes, my insides wound tighter than a music box. Last night, after the pageant, Charles squeezed my hand hard during the celebratory fireworks, and I'd been too frightened to breathe.

But Frank and Evie had been there with us, and Charles would never raise his voice to me among company. At home, after I'd taken off my girdle and put on my dressing gown, I'd braced myself for his words, sharp as shards of glass: *stupid, selfish, whore, embarrassment.* But they hadn't come. Instead, Charles had turned his back to me in bed, lying stiff as a board, impenetrable. I'd gotten lucky.

I removed my dishwashing gloves, wiping my hands

on my floral apron. Turning to the window, I watched as a burst of sea spray shot upward, while a large wave crashed against the cove. A bicycle bell jingled on the footpath. Our lovely Spanish-style bungalow on West Cliff Drive, overlooking the ocean, was the safe haven I had longed for. Yet, this home had become my prison.

The door creaked behind me as Charles entered the kitchen. He took his seat at the breakfast table. I swallowed, turning my gaze to the bacon sizzling in the skillet.

"Good morning," I said, imbuing my voice with cheer. I turned off the gas and transferred the hot food to my husband's plate. I touched the hollow at the base of my neck, then picked up the plate and carried it toward him. Charles unfolded the morning paper.

When I set down his eggs and bacon, he said nothing. But I felt something in the air, like an electrical charge before a thunderstorm. *For crying out loud!* I'd set the radio to a jazz station, and Charles would rather listen to the morning news. I ought to have known better. I wiped the perspiration from my temples.

My husband sipped his coffee, a deep crease dividing his brow. His voice came out harsh as he stared at the newspaper headline. "Norwich has been bombed. Civilians were killed."

I felt it then. In my stomach. A tiny squeeze. But perhaps he was only upset with Hitler and the atrocities of the *Luftwaffe*? I looked at the photograph on the front page of the newspaper. In the grainy picture, Nazi planes flew against a darkened sky.

"That's terrible," I said, eyeing Charles's untouched breakfast. I'd taken extra care to make the bacon crispy and the eggs soft, just the way he liked them.

Swift as lightning, he gripped my wrist. Hard. His eyes narrowed. "You don't give a damn about politics, you stupid cow. What were you thinking, parading in front of those men in your bathing suit like a common whore?"

"Charles," I breathed. "Let go of my arm. Please, you're hurting me."

His nails dug into the soft flesh of my forearm. He pulled me close, so I could feel his hot coffee breath on my neck.

"You are *my wife,*" he hissed. "You belong to *me*. Do you know how foolish you looked? How you've embarrassed me?"

"I'm sorry," I whispered. "I'm so sorry."

When I'd learned that Charles's first love, a woman named Caroline, had broken off their engagement, my heart had ached for him. Who could hurt such a kind, wounded man? Now I wondered if Caroline had understood something I hadn't.

His deep brown eyes shone with rage. It was too late. My muscles tensed in readiness.

"You know my dream is to perform," I said quietly. "You knew that when you met me. You used to like watching me sing."

My mind conjured up a picture of that fateful summer day two years ago, the afternoon I'd been riding my bicycle up and down the boardwalk with Evie. We'd been carefree in our culottes and blouses, and we'd giggled when we'd noticed the handsome fellas who'd disembarked from the *Suntan Special.*

I'd turned my head, to make sure Charles was watching me. Then I'd sung along to "Heart & Soul," while the beach band played the tune. He'd approached me afterward. *"What a beautiful voice. May I have your name, little songbird?"*

"Violet Sweeting."

Charles had laughed. *"An appropriate name for a sweet girl. May I take you out?"*

My little songbird . . .

"Shut your mouth," Charles said, rising from his chair so quickly it fell over. The crash brought me back to the present—popping the memory like a balloon with a pin. He pushed me hard, and I stumbled backward.

His hands clenched into fists. "Your duty is to serve me, and only me. And yet you stood up there half naked, without your wedding ring. You will let go of these ridiculous notions that you can flit off to Hollywood and let other men appraise your body. You never ought to have entered that goddamned pageant!"

My insides crumpled. I'd dreamed of doing a screen test for years. Success was so close I could see the Hollywoodland sign rising from the golden California hillside. Every pageant winner got an audition. How could I make my husband understand that this was the chance of a lifetime? I had the talent to sing and act in front of a director, to make an impression.

I braced myself against the countertop. "Charles, I'm

terribly sorry. You see, it was Evie's idea—only to get around the pageant rules. In no way does it diminish my commitment to you. I'd only be gone for a few days. You can come with me if you'd like. It'd be a nice vacation for both of us. Wouldn't you like to travel to Los Angeles and then to Atlantic City?"

Charles grabbed the handle of the heavy iron skillet. He flung the pan at the wall with all his might. Droplets of hot bacon grease seared my flesh, burning the inside of my wrist. I screamed in pain. Splatters of fat covered my apron and pinafore. I shielded my face with my hands as the pan clattered to the ground.

"You will *not* go to Atlantic City," Charles yelled. "Nor will you go to Los Angeles, to entertain your delusions of becoming an actress. You will never perform on any stage, anywhere. Do you understand? Now clean up this mess."

Tears pushed against my eyelids. Throbbing, the skin on my wrist bubbled into a blister. That would leave a scar.

I turned on the tap, sticking my arm beneath the cool, running water, and winced as it cleansed the wound. As I felt the tension in the air slip away, I pictured Charles's eyes unclouding and regaining their focus. *Caring eyes.* The eyes I had fallen in love with. He put his arms around my waist and I flinched.

"I'm sorry," he whispered. "It was an accident. You know I'd never hurt you." He let his arms fall by his sides. "I'll get the broom and dustbin."

I turned off the tap and placed both of my hands on the

edge of the basin. My breath shuddered as I let it out. Why did he have to wrench my heart from my chest? I loved my husband. And he loved me. But I was frightened for my life.

Lately, I had been able to sense when his episodes were coming. The air between us would crackle with static. Anything could set him off. I'd say the wrong thing, cook the wrong food or place a household item in the wrong spot. *Careless,* he called it. *Absentminded.* Or worse—I'd ask him how business was doing at the Oceano. This made him incredibly angry, as if I had intruded on a private matter.

And it was my fault. If only I'd been more patient or learned to hold my tongue. Yet, sometimes, I got so tired of stepping on eggshells around Charles that I'd deliberately set him off. *I wasn't Caroline!* How could I prove to him that I wouldn't ever leave him? But entering the pageant had been far too dangerous.

After our spats, when Charles felt remorseful, weeks would go by without incident. Heartbroken, he'd promise it would never happen again, and purchase beautiful gifts, like the pearls I'd worn yesterday. That necklace was more than an anniversary present. It was an apology for the broken rib no one could see.

This was only a bad fight. All couples fought.

I looked at the cream-colored walls, stained with bacon grease. *Baking soda.* I reached into the cabinet and removed the box, stirring three tablespoons of powder into a glass of warm water. I dabbed the corner of a tea towel into the mixture and began to scrub. The blister on my arm throbbed. Scrubbing harder, I clenched my teeth. Charles returned with the broom and the dustbin.

"Well," he said, leaning against the wall. "I'll take breakfast at the club. I trust this will be clean when I return."

His eggs and bacon sat untouched on the breakfast table. With a war on in Europe, I'd heard about the bacon, butter and sugar rationing in England. Charles dumped the contents of his plate into the trash bin. All that good food wasted.

He placed his fedora atop his head. "Violet," he said, stroking my cheek. "I love you, darling. Please don't give me that look."

When the door shut behind him, I wept, picturing Charles driving the winding road to the Oceano in his gleaming black Cadillac. He had the freedom to soar through the verdant countryside, to his palace on the hill, away from our problems. A waiter in a crisp, white uniform would be waiting, handing him a Bloody Mary.

And I was left here, alone, to clean up this mess. My burn stung, and I rubbed the rag against the wall as hard as I could. But nothing would remove the stain from our marriage. It was stuck forever, a dark, dirty secret.

CHAPTER 4

Marisol Cruz

2007

Mari smoothed her blouse, pausing a moment before she knocked on the door to the offices above the Cocoanut Grove Ballroom. She looked down at her dark jeans, nervously wondering if they were appropriate for her first day on the job. At least they were *clean*. Last week, Lily had thought it was funny when she placed her paint-covered hands on Mari's back, leaving two sticky palm prints on Mari's favorite shirt.

With a deep breath, Mari rapped on the door. A grandmotherly woman pulled it open, her blue eyes sparkling from behind her glasses.

"You must be Marisol," she said, extending her hand. "I'm Carol."

Mari shook it. "Nice to meet you, Carol. You can call me Mari."

"Come on in."

Mari entered a cramped office stacked with binders and boxes. Vintage posters, handbills and photographs papered the walls. Mari's eyes were drawn to a black-and-white photograph of young women lined up in old-fashioned bathing suits, their wavy chin-length hair framing their faces, which hung above Carol's desk.

"That's the first-ever Miss California pageant," Carol said. "It was held right here on the Santa Cruz boardwalk in 1924."

"That's wonderful," Mari replied, though she was tempted to point out she was already well familiar with Santa Cruz's history. The girls in the picture looked real, nothing like today's beauty queens with their fake teeth and spray tans. *Much better role models.* Mari thought of TLC's *Toddlers & Tiaras,* and the moms who entered their daughters, some younger than Lily, in cutthroat beauty pageants. It was horrible, but oddly fascinating. Why couldn't they let their kids be kids?

Carol clapped her hands together. "Let me show you around. We have everything here ranging from nineteenth-century newspaper clippings to a nine-foot-long neon sign from the casino souvenir shop. Only a handful of people have access, and normally everything that leaves has to be signed out. But we're displaying our most treasured artifacts for the Centennial Celebration."

"That's great," Mari said, glimpsing a frayed white towel with the words "Property of Seaside Company" draped over the side of a cardboard box.

"This is a relic from the Saltwater Plunge," Carol said. "It was a boardwalk attraction for fifty-five years. It closed in—"

"Nineteen sixty-two," Mari said with a smile. "I happen to know a few things about the history of our town."

"Of course," Carol said, laughing. "I'm sorry for rambling on. I've been working alone here in the archives for so long, I fear I might be going a bit batty. Feel free to interrupt me anytime."

Carol gestured to some larger boxes. "In there you'll find a flügelhorn and bass drum from the Hastings Band. It was a popular beach-era attraction at the turn of the twentieth century. You can help me carry them downstairs."

Mari reached into the box and removed a paper parasol.

"Do you know what that is?" Carol asked.

Mari nodded. "These were sold to hundreds of complexion-conscious beachgoers in the early nineteen hundreds. Unlike today, women did not want to be tan."

"Correct, indeed."

Mari smiled, though her heart sank, thinking about how little progress had been made in the last hundred years. Brown skin was still considered a setback in life. The racial taunts Mari endured as a child—*beaner, spic* and *coconut*—were harsh words she hoped Lily would never hear. *Coconut* had offended her the most. Just because she was articulate implied she was brown outside and white inside?

With her light skin and dazzling green eyes, Lily likely

wouldn't experience the same level of discrimination that Mari had. In fact, most kids at Lily's preschool thought she was white. *Your father is white,* Mari had offered to Lily in explanation. Her whole body tensed whenever Lily asked about her dad.

Mari put the parasol back into the box, shaking the memory from her mind. Following Carol, she walked down the office corridors, where the items got larger: antique arcade games, a carousel horse, a wicker beach chair and a machine with escalating electrical shocks that said, "Electricity—The Silent Physician!"

"Ah," Carol said, stopping in front of a box marked "1940." "Here we are. Do you mind carrying this one downstairs? I'm afraid it's a bit heavy for me."

"Sure," Mari said, lifting the box. "Where is the museum booth set up?"

"On the boardwalk, right across from the old gazebo. You'll see the museum banner hanging over the tabletop. I'll meet you there in ten minutes. I have to find our reel of raffle tickets. I know they're somewhere in this mess!"

WITH HER ARMS straining beneath the weight of the box, Mari's stomach rumbled at the scent of garlic fries. Though she'd managed to eat half a sandwich before heading over to the beachside amusement park, the last time she'd sat down and enjoyed an uninterrupted meal had been before Lily was born.

A number of food stands dotted the boardwalk, their colorful awnings tempting Mari to buy something unhealthy: caramel apples, a hot dog on a stick, funnel cake, pepperoni pizza or a churro, her favorite Mexican pastry, rolled in cinnamon and sugar. It was a sad imitation of *real* churro, but smelled delicious nonetheless. Mari's heart ached for her *abuela,* who made the best ones from scratch.

The memory of her grandmother rolling out the dough with her wrinkled, papery hands was punctured as Michael Jackson's "Thriller" gave way to the sounds of hair metal. Passing the beach bandstand, Mari smiled, thinking of the musicians who had come to play in Santa Cruz during the jazz era—Benny Goodman, Duke Ellington. How romantic the boardwalk must have been, back when her grandparents danced beneath the fairy lights strung along the historic gazebo.

Sky glider chairs passed overhead, with tourists dangling their legs. Though its attractions had aged, the boardwalk still held a certain kind of magic. Beneath the faded paint of the buildings, Mari could imagine it exactly as it had been in its heyday—a lively place for dancing, carousel rides, bumper cars and kissing beneath the stars. Not that *she* would be kissing anyone. This wasn't her grandparents' era. Men today were boys, not gentlemen, completely unable to handle adult responsibility.

A few shirtless teenagers ambled past with their pants sagging over their boxer briefs. One wagged his tongue at her, then grabbed at his chest like he was feeling a large breast. What a little *pendejo!* And they only got worse as they got older.

The history museum's green banner came into sight as Mari located the booth. She set down her heavy box, admiring the Victorian details of the old gazebo, which stood alone in the sand. The historic structure leaned slightly to one side and was badly in need of repair, but Mari pictured her grandmother in a fitted blue dress, Abuelo's hands circling her waist as they danced salsa.

When her grandparents were alive, they would put on old records and dance sweetly around the living room. Mari loved knowing that even though they were gone, she could still picture them here in the gazebo, forever young.

Shielding her eyes from the sun, Mari looked for Carol. People congregated around the main stage. Maintenance workers adjusted microphones and lights, getting ready for Mayor Harcourt to deliver his speech. A balloon arch bobbed against the bright blue sky, framing a banner that read 100 YEARS OF FAMILY FUN!

With Carol nowhere to be seen, Mari fanned out the museum pamphlets and tried to make herself useful. Reaching into the box, she lifted out a wooden frame. Behind the glass was a yellowed *Santa Cruz Magazine* article, accompanying a photo of a beautiful young woman. Even though she smiled, her eyes held so much sadness.

"There you are. You found it."

Mari set the framed article back inside the box. "I did."

"Sorry about that," Carol said, wiping perspiration from her brow. "I wasn't kidding when I told you I'd misplaced the raffle tickets. It took me ages to find them."

She plopped a wheel of purple tickets on the table.

"Money goes in here," Carol said, handing Mari a large plastic jar. "The tickets are ten dollars each. Our prizes range from a romantic dinner for two at Trabocco to a private tour of Santa Cruz's historic homes. We have quite a few prizes. Do you think you'll be able to memorize them all?"

Mari smiled. "I'm a waitress, of course I can."

"Great! Now, let's see here, we can get started with this box—"

Feedback from the speakers cut Carol off with a loud screech. Mari brought her fingers to her ears. A man in a black uniform rushed to the stage, adjusted the microphone, then disappeared into the shadows.

Cheers rose from the audience as Mayor Thomas Harcourt ascended the stairs. Mari clapped half-heartedly. For someone in his sixties, the mayor still had a handsome charm with a head of salt-and-pepper hair and a thick mustache.

"Good afternoon, Santa Cruz," he said, waving at the crowd. The applause grew louder. "Welcome to the opening ceremony of our Beach Boardwalk Centennial Celebration. One hundred years of family fun!"

Taking the microphone in one hand, the mayor strolled across the stage. "While we treasure our town's past, we are equally committed to its future, one that we can share with our children. We cherish our memories of riding the Giant Dipper and taking a spin on the Looff Carousel, but we're also committed to progress and innovation."

The mayor's words faded into the background as Mari's

eyes drifted to the framed magazine article poking out of the box. She thought about the woman in the photograph. Who was she, and why did she look so sad?

The applause died down.

". . . And with that, I am proud to introduce my son, Travis Harcourt. With my full endorsement, we'll be building luxury condominiums right here on the beach."

Mari's eyes darted to the stage.

"Unfortunately, we will have to demolish the gazebo; however, the wood will be made available to local artisans. Here's to building the future of Santa Cruz!"

Bracing herself against the table, Mari felt as if someone had dumped a bucket of ice water over her. Her skin pricked with needlelike pain.

Travis Harcourt took the stage. He'd been in Mari's graduating class at UCSC, a trust fund kid. His million-dollar smile beamed at the beachgoers, his thick brown hair perfectly coiffed. He shielded his eyes from the sun as he addressed the audience in his casual outfit of a button-down shirt and jeans.

"Hello to all the beautiful people of my hometown! How are you doing? I am so happy to see all of you here with your families today. Santa Cruz is where I grew up, and it will always be a place of strong family values."

Mari balled her fists, her nails biting into the flesh of her palm.

"Today, I am proud to say that with my father's support, we're building luxury condos, right here overlooking the ocean. This is a passion project of mine, and I'm finally making it a reality. Santa Cruz is not only known for its beaches, but as a hub of innovation and discovery. We're not that far from Silicon Valley. Let's attract the best minds in the country to live here. Commerce is sure to follow!"

Carol narrowed her eyes. "The nerve of that young man. We don't need luxury condos. The gazebo is a *historic* structure."

Mari wanted to speak, but she couldn't find her voice.

"Honey, are you all right?" Carol touched Mari's arm with a soft hand. "You look nervous."

"Do I?" Mari looked down at her hands, which she rubbed as though they were cold. "I'm sorry, it's just—my grandparents, they loved that gazebo. They danced there all the time in the 1940s. It was where they held their wedding reception."

She swallowed the lump in her throat. Sadness turned to anger as she clenched her jaw. Her first day working for the museum was supposed to be the beginning of a new chapter in her life—moving forward toward something better. Instead, she'd been dragged into the past . . . a painful reminder that men like Travis Harcourt could do what they wanted with no repercussions.

She imagined a shiny glass tower dominating the skyline, the bones of the gazebo buried in the sand beneath it. If the historic boardwalk disappeared piece by piece, what memories would she have left to share with her daughter?

CHAPTER 5

Violet Harcourt

1940

"I'm withdrawing from the Miss America pageant."

I felt numb as I uttered the words. But I couldn't go to Atlantic City. Charles had made sure of that. He'd sent me a bouquet of roses after our incident, with a card that read, "I love you." Now I was expected to play my part of the dutiful wife.

Evie stared at me openmouthed.

"Have you lost your mind?" she whispered. "You've dreamed of stardom as long as I've known you."

The pageant organizer looked at me over his horn-rimmed glasses. The placard on his desk told me that he was Henry Warner. Two damp patches bloomed beneath his armpits.

"Miss Sweeting," he said, his dark eyes meeting mine.

"Are you certain you wish to withdraw from the pageant? Once you do, you can't change your mind."

"Yes, Mr. Warner. I'm awfully sorry to tell you this, but my name is Mrs. Harcourt. You see . . . I'm already married."

Evie narrowed her eyes in a silent threat, though she ought to have known I'd never dare reveal her secret as well. Henry Warner's face sagged, and then he shook his head. "That's quite a shame. You lied on your application?"

My cheeks burned. "Yes, sir."

I squeezed Evie's hand. "Why don't you go in my place? You're a far better dancer than I am, and with your jitterbug routine, you'll blow the judges away."

Henry Warner fixed his gaze on Evie. "And you're not married?"

I held my breath, the air seeming to vanish from the room. But Evie, without missing a beat, gave him a dazzling smile. "Of course not! Single as a gal can be."

Bless her heart. This had been Evie's harebrained idea in the first place. Let her go to Atlantic City instead.

"All right, then," Mr. Warner said. "Miss Hastings, as the runner-up, you're our new winner. Can you travel to New Jersey to compete for the crown?"

Her eyes sparkled with mischief. "Absolutely. Yes, sir."

In spite of the fact that I ought to have been relieved, my stomach felt sour. How I wanted to impress Artie Schmekel, the judge with ties to Broadway, to show him I had what it took to become a star. And now I would never get the chance.

Evie grabbed my hands, smiling like she would burst from happiness. "Oh Violet, thank you!"

I flinched as she gripped my wrist where the ugly blister had formed, but I grinned through the pain. "You better knock their socks off."

When Mr. Warner bent his head, reaching into his drawer with his eyes downcast, she dropped her voice to a whisper. "What's the matter with you? I thought we agreed not to utter a peep. We pinky swore!"

"Not now," I hissed.

"Ain't that swell?" Evie said, releasing her grip as Mr. Warner sat upright in his chair. "I can't wait to tell Frank. He'll be over the moon!"

Mr. Warner lowered his glasses. "Frank?"

"My uh . . . uncle," Evie said, giggling. I refrained from rolling my eyes. Evie's husband, Frank, owned a car dealership. Despite Frank's booming business, Charles didn't like him. He found Frank's jokes to be crass—a shame, because I thought Frank was a gas. Frank would be so happy for Evie, he'd likely pack their luggage for Atlantic City himself. He'd laugh at how she pulled the wool over the eyes of the pageant organizers. And with a hat company agreeing to pay the pageant winner two thousand dollars to endorse its merchandise, he'd be thrilled.

I pictured Frank cheering, *Atta, girl. That's my girl up there!*

Mr. Warner pushed a paper across his desk. "Miss Sweeting—or shall I say Mrs. Harcourt?—please sign here. This states that you've voluntarily withdrawn from the pageant, acknowledging yourself to be ineligible."

Evie babbled to herself, something about needing a new wardrobe. She jitterbugged toward the open window. With a lump rising in my throat, I scrawled my name across the bottom of the page. As I did, the sleeve of my cardigan hiked up, revealing the nasty burn on my arm, and the purplish bruises from Charles.

Henry Warner's eyes met mine. "Everything all right?"

I tugged my sleeve down. "Everything's fine. Thank you. I'm a clumsy cook, that's all. I had a little accident with some bacon grease."

He clucked his tongue. "Cooking takes patience. You'll get the hang of it." His bushy brows pinched together as he studied my face. "You know, you're a gifted soprano. But rules are rules, I'm afraid. Your friend sure is flipping her wig over there. I guess we won't have a problem sending her to Jersey."

". . . and a ball gown!" Evie said, twirling in the corner. "I must have Uncle Frank buy me a new one for the pageant. A green one!"

"So everything's settled, then?" I asked.

Mr. Warner beckoned Evie toward him with a hooked finger. "Almost. Come here, Cinderella. I need you to sign the papers too."

I SUCKED MY strawberry milkshake through a red and white straw, while the waves crashed heavily against the shore. Children shrieked as they scampered about the beach. The wet sand sank beneath my bare feet, and the wind ruffled the hem of my calf-length dress. It was a beautiful, warm summer day, but there might as well have been thunderclouds overhead.

"Here," Evie said, handing me the maraschino cherry from her vanilla shake. "I know you love these."

I popped it in my mouth. "Thanks."

Even as I chewed, the sugary sweetness couldn't erase the bitterness on my tongue. We'd gone to Marini's soda fountain on the boardwalk after our visit to Mr. Warner's office, but it hadn't cheered my mood in the least.

The zip line whirred overhead. Donny Pierson hung from a trapeze by his knees, dangling Ricardo Cruz by one ankle and one wrist. I gasped as the muscular stuntman and the lean teenager launched from the balcony of the Boardwalk Casino, hurtling toward the ocean. The zip line was 750 feet long, spanning the length of the beach and pier.

I didn't dare breathe as Donny and Ricky sped over the spectators on the sand, in the direction of Pleasure Pier. Seconds before the trolley slammed into the wooden pilings, both men let go of the trapeze, diving headfirst into the choppy waves. The beachgoers erupted into applause. The "Slide for Life," Donny and Ricky's stunt act, was one of the boardwalk's most popular attractions and had been immortalized on a postcard.

"Those two could kill themselves," Evie said, as the crowd went wild.

I shook my head. "I don't know how Ricky does it."

Ricky emerged from the water, his brown skin shining in the sun. He waved at the women, men and children who'd gathered to watch the stunt. Donny followed behind him, strutting the beach in his tight swim trunks. He smiled at two pretty girls, and they dissolved into giggles. Ricky waved at me, and then began to approach.

"Here comes the Mexican," Evie whispered.

I elbowed her in the ribs. "*Evie*. He's my friend."

"Hi, Violet," Ricky said, stopping in front of me and toweling off his wet hair. "Did you see my drop? Pretty bonkers, huh?"

"It sure was," I answered. "You're going to give me a heart attack. Say, don't you think that stunt's far too dangerous?"

He waved his hand. "I've practiced it loads. Besides, I'm a strong swimmer. Did ya know I can hold my breath underwater for two minutes?"

"Hot diggity dog," Evie said. "That's impressive."

"Thanks." Ricky smiled, his brown eyes squinting behind his freckled cheeks. "I gotta run, but we're having a party tonight at the bowling alley if you gals wanna come. It's a goodbye shindig for Harry Goodman. He's moving to Hollywood."

"*Hollywood*," I said, unable to hide my shock.

"Yep. Doing stand-up at the Cocoanut Grove ain't enough for him anymore. He wants to try his hand at making it big, going to the movie studios and all that. He says he knows some director. He's leaving in the morning."

"Well, I'll say." There was that bitter taste in my mouth again.

"Eight o'clock," Ricky said, winking at me. "There'll be

rum punch and plenty of dancing. It'll be a gas! I hope you'll join us."

"No thanks," Evie replied. "Vi and I have a prior engagement."

"That's too bad," Ricky said. "Another time, then."

I watched Ricky's slender build shrink into the distance, then I turned to Evie. "You didn't have to turn the fella down so quickly."

She shook her head. "Violet, I'm only looking out for you. What would Charles do if he saw you socializing with Ricardo Cruz? You know how he feels about Mexican immigrants. And going to a party with entertainers and service workers? It's not proper . . . even if we would have one hell of a time."

"You're right," I said, curling my toes in the sand. "But I don't always agree with Charles. Besides, I *was* a service worker . . . remember? I used to wait tables at Mary's Chicken Shack, right here on the boardwalk."

I held my breath, fearing I'd said too much. Part of me longed to tell Evie the truth. *What would she say if she knew?*

"Vi," Evie said, her expression suddenly serious. "Is everything all right? I don't want to compete in the Miss America pageant if it's still your dream. That'd be a crummy thing to do. Why did you tell Mr. Warner you were married?"

My throat tightened. I couldn't let Evie suspect a thing, or heaven knows what Charles might do.

"I'm not sure the limelight is for me after all," I said,

giving her what I hoped appeared to be a genuine smile. "Especially when my leading man is right here at home."

She grinned. "You're ready for a bun in the oven."

A twinge of discomfort worked its way down my spine, then a spike of dread. I'd wanted children with Charles. Yet he'd become so unpredictable lately . . .

I forced a laugh. "I'm a rotten liar. Thinking about keeping up the charade for the judges made me woozy. *You*, my dear, have the best poker face I've ever seen."

Evie nudged me in the ribs. "A little white lie never hurt anybody."

My eyes settled in the distance on the green and white awning of Mary's Chicken Shack and my heart sank. How I missed the fun I used to have with my waitress pals, Stella and Dot, and listening to the jukebox at the soda fountain after work, laughing and joking with Ricky. I didn't have much, but I had my freedom. Then Charles asked me to leave my job. And of course I did.

The white lie I'd been telling myself, that everything would be all right, wasn't working anymore. My marriage was a sham. I touched Evie's hand.

"I ought to visit Mother for lunch. Sorry, I've got to skedaddle. Give me a ring tomorrow, will you?"

"Will do," she said, blowing me a kiss. "Take care, honey."

IN THE OLD-FASHIONED kitchen of the farmhouse where I'd grown up, I patted the last of Mother's porcelain plates dry, running the dishcloth along the chipped edges.

"You've made the right choice," Mother said.

Her suit-dress hung around her narrow frame. Neither one of us had been lucky enough to inherit Grandma's curves. But at least I had some, whereas Mother's legs were twigs and her breasts mosquito bites. My belted dress gave me the illusion of a waist, though my figure was too boyish for my liking.

"Yes," I said, staring out the window at the sagging porch. The blue paint had faded, giving the old Victorian a sad and neglected look. And the damp, salty air had been harsh on the aging wood. Father didn't have the money to fix it.

"You're lucky to have him," Mother said, her gray eyes weary. "The rest of us have to be frugal. You've got a man who can provide."

Like a figurine inside a snow globe, I was enclosed in a bubble of comfort. Mother constantly reminded me that I had married up. If only she knew the true cost of my shiny life. Mother, with her pale lips and cropped curls, rarely spoke about feelings. Yet, right now, I could desperately use some motherly advice.

"Did you ever sacrifice your dreams for Father?" I asked.

Her mouth turned down at the corners. "Dreams are for fools. We live in an unfair world, Violet. You're fortunate to have a man to protect you."

Lucky. Fortunate. I should be so grateful.

I stepped into the sitting room and trailed my fingers along the keys of Grandma's piano. The notes made a ghostly sound. Our antique grandfather clock ticked dutifully in the corner. It had served as a metronome when

Grandma sat next to me on the piano bench, teaching me to play scales.

I touched a framed photo of my grandmother, which sat atop the piano. Her deep blue eyes twinkled, the same shade as my own.

"Your eyes are bewitching," Charles used to say. "I never want to look at anything else."

Sadness hit me all at once, and I longed for my grandmother's soft embrace. She had to die, as elderly people do. But that didn't make her passing any easier. Suddenly, the dark old house felt suffocating.

"Goodbye, Mother," I said, walking through the kitchen. "Thank you for lunch."

"Violet, where are you—"

Before she could stop me, I hurried down the porch steps and ran around the side of the house. Beneath the ramshackle awning, my old blue beach cruiser leaned against the clapboard siding. I brushed off the cobwebs and hopped on my Schwinn.

Pedaling toward the ocean, my legs pumped as I climbed the hill. Sweat beaded on my brow and the wind tangled my hair. I rolled downward, toward the endless Pacific, shimmering blue. Exhilaration filled me at the freedom of it.

Charles wasn't here to admonish me or to control my every move. Tears stung my eyes. White-hot panic blossomed in my chest.

What if the next time was worse?

My breath came in deep gulps. I turned onto a path, my bicycle hurtling down it. Then I squeezed the brakes, coming to a screeching halt. Letting go of the handlebars, I swung my leg over the seat. My Schwinn clattered against the ground.

I let out a sob. My perfect life was a lie. Leaving my bicycle on the ocean path, I walked toward the cliff's edge, my saddle shoes crunching the ice plant, which burst with purple flowers. The tide rushed in violently, and the ocean spray touched my face, inviting me to come closer.

I took a hesitant step forward. Loose pebbles toppled over the brink and fell into the choppy water below. I swallowed. The slippery rocks at the mouth of the cove jutted out of the ocean with slick, sharp edges.

My heart pumped harder. If I didn't break free I'd lose my mind, or die at the hands of my husband. I shut my eyes. I needed to be fearless.

CHAPTER 6

Marisol Cruz

2007

Mari sold raffle tickets with a smile, but inside she seethed with anger. The locals who lived in this town deserved to enjoy waterfront views. Instead those would belong to rich vacationers who'd stay in their million-dollar luxury condos for only half the year. And the historic gazebo was beloved by so many people.

Did Mayor Harcourt really want to take away the integrity of the boardwalk, trading it for a homogenized and sterile look? Santa Cruz's funky Victorians and Art Deco structures lent the town its character.

After the hours of her shift passed, Mari put away the last of the museum brochures. Other vendors had already shut down their booths. She surveyed the artifacts, which she'd packed and organized.

Her fingers trailed along the edge of the framed magazine article. Curiosity compelled her to lift the frame from the box. There was something about that beautiful girl, her hair done up in pin curls, smiling with a sad, far-off look in her eyes. Mari read the text.

A BEAUTIFUL SUICIDE: LOOKING BACK AT THE TROUBLED LIFE OF MISS CALIFORNIA
September 25, 1940

On Friday, September 24, around 7:30 in the evening, 20-year-old Violet Harcourt walked to the edge of the bluff on West Cliff Drive overlooking Natural Bridges. Through the mist she gazed at the ocean, 30 feet below.

In her desperate determination, she leapt, hitting a ledge before plunging into the choppy waters. Several eyewitnesses recount watching her red dress billow in the breeze, and her slender frame disappear beneath the waves.

Police immediately sent a search party to the scene, but Harcourt's body never resurfaced. The authorities have determined her death a suicide, and the cause of death, drowning. However, Harcourt left no suicide note behind.

Harcourt (née Sweeting) is survived by her husband, Charles Harcourt, and her parents, Mary and William Sweeting. Why would a young woman with so much potential take her own life? This is the question that Harcourt's grieving friends and family are struggling to answer.

Two months prior to her death, Harcourt, recently crowned Miss California, withdrew from the Miss America pageant, admitting her marital status rendered her ineligible to compete. Runner-up Evelyn Hastings took her place, inheriting the title of Miss California.

Harcourt, an auburn-haired beauty, had sought the silver screen of Hollywood, according to Hastings. She had landed a minor role as "the vixen at the bar" in a John Huston film. Harcourt was a gifted soprano, and a graduate of Mills College in Oakland, where she majored in music.

Her lead role as Belle Stark in the Santa Cruz stage production of *Rocket to the Moon* will be remembered fondly as a moving performance. The beautiful young woman with the voice of an angel now rests among the clouds.

As Mari looked at the photograph of Violet, it felt as if Violet were trying to tell her something—but what? The name Harcourt wasn't very common in Santa Cruz. Could she be related to the mayor? Mari mused. Sliding the framed article back inside the box, Mari felt sad for the aspiring starlet who'd taken her own life.

She turned to look at the gazebo. It leaned slightly to the left, empty and forgotten. But what if its wood floors were sanded and waxed until they shone, and globe lights strung across its rafters? A muralist could touch up the faded image of a starry night sky painted on the ceiling and bring its magic back to life.

This gazebo had once been a gathering place where shy young men and women made eyes at each other from across the dance floor. Mari swallowed the sour taste in her mouth and turned away. Soon the gazebo would be nothing but dust.

"**ORDER UP FOR** table seven!"

Mari wiped the perspiration from her brow as she picked up a hot plate of huevos rancheros. Her mouth watered looking at the fresh slices of avocado and the big dollops of salsa and sour cream. Rumbling loudly, her stomach reminded her that once again, she'd forgotten to eat breakfast. But that was being a mom, right?

Last night, Lily had climbed into Mari's bed, tearful and afraid. She'd had another nightmare about a faceless man. Mari stroked her daughter's hair until her tears dried, and Lily fell asleep. But Mari lay awake, her mind spinning. Could these dreams of the man with no face be Lily's interpretation of not knowing who her father was?

Mari was willing to talk with Lily about her father, but not right before bed. She didn't turn off the TV when Dora the Explorer talked to her daddy, but Mari usually tried not to place a deliberate emphasis on "dad" in Lily's life. She'd changed every reference of "Daddy" to "Mommy" in Lily's favorite bedtime story, *Mr. Pickles Says Goodnight.*

She'd brought up her concerns with Lily's pediatrician.

Dr. Marlow assured her it was okay not to overly expose Lily to "daddy" movies or books. She said to answer Lily's questions about her father kindly and simply. Mari tried her best. She reminded Lily there were all types of families, and what really mattered was love: *Abuelo, Abuela and I love you more than the moon and stars, you know that.*

Covering her yawn with her hand, Mari approached table seven, hoping she could change Lily's bedtime routine, maybe add in an extra story, anything to prevent the nightmares. She looked up expecting an elderly citizen eating alone on a Monday morning. But instead she found a guy her age, his thick brown hair tousled as he hunched over a copy of *The Kite Runner*. His eyes met hers, chocolate brown and warm.

"Huevos rancheros," she said, setting the plate down in front of him. "Is there anything else I can get you? Coffee, tea?"

He smiled, his grin disarming. "I'd love some coffee. Do you have a dark roast?"

"We have Java. It's from—"

Without warning, Wanda swooped down upon them. She smiled from behind her cat's-eye glasses. "The Java is from Latin America, just like Marisol here. You'll love it. Enjoy your breakfast, handsome."

Mari's cheeks pricked with heat. Thankfully, Wanda bustled over to the next table, to flirt with other unsuspecting patrons.

"It's from Indonesia," Mari said, voice lowered. "And I'm from California, born and raised in Santa Cruz."

The young guy chuckled, extending his hand. "I'm Jason, nice to meet you."

"Mari," she said, startled by the warmth of his palm. It had been a long time since someone cute had touched her.

"This is a silly question," Jason said. "And I don't want to sound like a coffee snob, but do you know if the coffee is fair trade?"

Mari smiled. "It's not a silly question at all. Offering better trading conditions to coffee bean farmers is important." She dropped her voice to a whisper. "Unfortunately, Wanda is in the habit of replacing our fair trade coffee with regular. It's cheaper."

"Ah," Jason whispered back. "Thanks for the tip."

"That's a great book, by the way," Mari said, glancing down at his worn copy. "I love the complicated friendship between the wealthy boy and the son of his father's servant, and the intimate look at the history of Afghanistan. It's beautiful, and sad."

"Do you enjoy history?"

"Absolutely. History was my major, back in college."

Jason raised an eyebrow. "You make it sound like you graduated a long time ago. But that can't be possible . . . unless maybe you were a child prodigy?"

Mari laughed. "I'm twenty-six and not a wunderkind of any sort. Though I did graduate with honors."

"Nice," Jason said. His brows drew together. "Is this, like, a part-time job while you write the next great historical novel?"

Mari clenched her jaw. Why had she even bothered to tell him about herself?

"No, it's my everyday job."

"Oh," Jason replied. "That's cool. Everyone's got to make a living. In fact, I took a new job at UC Santa Cruz only a week ago. I moved here from Chicago, so I don't know anyone yet." He smiled again, his brown eyes sparkling. "I could really use someone, like an impressively knowledgeable local, to show me around. Would you like to get lunch together sometime?"

Mari's stomach tensed. It was hard enough to explain to Lily why she didn't have a father—that some daddies weren't ready to be daddies yet. She remembered Lily as a newborn, her chubby little face with a Cupid's-bow mouth, alert eyes and rosy cheeks. Who couldn't love such a perfect baby? But Lily's father chose not to share those heart-melting gummy smiles. And she still resented him for it.

The last thing Mari needed was to confuse Lily. It was pointless to start a relationship. Why get her daughter's hopes up just to smash them?

"Sorry," Mari stammered. "I can't—I better get to my other tables. Enjoy your breakfast."

She turned her back to Jason and her shoes squeaked against the linoleum as she walked away. It was safer to keep things as they were. No one would get hurt that way.

"HOW WAS YOUR first day working for the museum?" Paulina asked, rinsing the last of the dinner dishes. "I forgot to ask you about it yesterday."

Mari reached for the plate, rubbing the edges dry with a towel. Their dishwasher had broken last week, much to the horror of Mari and her mom. The culprit had been one of Lily's hard plastic toys—a pony, lodged in between the spinning gears. A replacement dishwasher would cost four hundred dollars, which they couldn't afford right now.

"It was good. I like talking to people about the museum artifacts and telling them about our local history. I sold a lot of raffle tickets too."

"*Mija,* that's great! So tell me, why do you look so sad?"

Mari threw the dish towel on the counter. "The mayor made an announcement at the centennial celebration. He's approved a development of luxury condos to be built on the beach. They're going to tear down the old gazebo, where Abuelo and Abuela had their wedding reception. Didn't they meet there, at a community dance?"

Paulina wrinkled her brow. "Yes, they did. Luxury condos? What kind of people does the mayor think live here? It won't get past city council."

"It already has. He gave a speech about bringing in money from the tech industry—making Santa Cruz some kind of hub of innovation. The condos will block the view of the ocean for all the locals. Just one more thing they're taking away from us."

Paulina sighed. "That's why we can never stop fighting."

"What are we fighting for?" Lily asked, skipping into the kitchen. Her brown hair, streaked with honey blond, had come free from her ponytail. She clutched a Barbie doll in her right hand.

"To get this dishwasher working," Mari said, tickling her daughter. "Did you apologize to Abuela for sticking your pony in there?"

Lily hung her head. "I'm sorry, Abuela. You can use my allowance to fix it. But he wanted to go swimming!"

Paulina smiled, guiding Lily by the shoulders. "It's going to take more than your allowance to fix, *mi amor*. You have to be careful with our things. They aren't easily replaceable. Now why don't you get ready for bed, and we can give your mama a little break? She's had a long day."

After Lily had scampered down the hallway, Mari frowned, meeting her mother's eyes. "Once the gazebo is gone, I won't have anything to remember Abuelo and Abuela by. It's like their history is being erased."

"Marisol," Paulina said. "I've kept Abuelo's things upstairs in the attic. If you feel like poking around up there, you'll find pictures from their wedding reception. That way you can always remember them."

"Really? Thanks, Ma."

Pulling down the hook to release the trapdoor, Mari found the rickety ladder leading to the dusty crawl space that served as their attic. Climbing the ladder rungs, she sneezed, and then let her eyes adjust to the darkness.

A leather trunk sat wedged beneath a pair of stilts that had belonged to her grandfather. He'd taught Mari how to walk on them when she was a little girl. How she loved to hear his stories about the boardwalk and the performers who'd been his friends. Walking on those stilts, Mari pretended she'd been a boardwalk performer too.

She tugged the trunk from the corner, disturbing a cloud of dust. She sneezed again, and then wiped her nose. Prying the lid open, Mari looked inside. Though the leather exterior had peeled with age, the faded red silk lining had preserved all of Abuelo's things as they'd been nearly seventy years ago.

Mari lifted a black-and-white photograph. Her grandparents stood in front of this very house, both so young. Abuelo's hair shone with pomade and Abuela's fell to her shoulders in perfect curls. Abuelo's face lit up with pride. It meant a lot for a Mexican family to put down roots here, to own something of value.

Beneath the photograph, Mari found a postcard of a funny-shaped restaurant, like an old-fashioned hat. The caption read, "The Brown Derby, Hollywood CA, 1940."

Mari turned it over and looked at the neat cursive—a woman's handwriting.

Dear Ricky,

I've made it here safely. I have to pinch myself to believe I'm really in Hollywood! I've never done something so reckless, and I'm a bit terrified. But you're the reason I was brave enough to come here. Sure, I'm a fool for trying to make it as an actress, but I'd be crazier not to try, isn't that right?

I apologize for heaping my troubles on you that night at the party. You're wise beyond your years, and I'm lucky to have you as a friend. Thank you for giving me the courage to follow my dreams. Oh, and did you know, Clark Gable and Carole Lombard have been spotted here at this restaurant? They really do have the best Cobb salad. If you come to visit, you have to try it. I'll write again soon. Take care.

—V

Mari scrunched her brow. Did Abuelo have a sweetheart before he met Abuela? If so, he'd never mentioned her. She smiled. Her grandpa had inspired this unknown woman to pursue her dreams—a dream of stardom in Hollywood. That was so like him, always helping others. Whether this "V" had been a previous girlfriend or just a friend, Mari hoped Abuelo had helped her find a better life.

CHAPTER 7

Violet Harcourt

1940

"So it's done, then?"

"Yes. I told Evie to go in my place. She's quite excited."

Charles locked his eyes on mine and I stayed as still as an animal caught in a bright light. Beneath the covers, I gripped my thumb.

"Good," he said, his dark brows pulled together. "You were never meant to enter that pageant in the first place."

"It was very foolish of me," I said, pulling my thick cotton nightgown more tightly around my body. If he so much as touched me, I would be done for. My heart began to beat faster.

Charles yawned, his eyelids heavy. He placed his tumbler of scotch on the bedside table, the ice cubes rattling in the glass.

"Turn off the light, will you?"

"Of course," I whispered, reaching for the switch. With one click, darkness enveloped the room. I lay on my back, rigid as a board. Then I turned my head, watching the soft rise and fall of Charles's chest. He was a sound sleeper, and after a few scotches, not even an air horn would wake him.

I swallowed, hard.

Withdrawing from the Miss America pageant had been my apology. Tomorrow, the old Charles would return. He'd compliment me on my cooking, and we'd dance slowly in the living room while we listened to Bing Crosby on the Victrola. I'd bury my face in his sweater, drinking in his bergamot-scented cologne.

Perhaps Charles would humor me and we'd get lunch with Evie and Frank at Miramar Fish Grotto, enjoying the view of the ocean from Fisherman's Wharf. We'd have cocktails and laugh at Frank's off-color jokes, while Evie would say she wanted a floral gown identical to the one Vivien Leigh wore when she accepted the Oscar for *Gone with the Wind*.

But as much as I wanted a life in Santa Cruz with Charles as my doting husband, I knew he would hurt me again. Which is why I'd already made my painful choice.

My eyes darted to the clock on the bedside table: 10:03 P.M. I needed to act now, before I lost my nerve. Leaning slightly toward Charles, I stared at my husband's face in the darkness. Stubble peppered his square jaw, and a snore escaped his mouth, which hung open, relaxed. He looked so peaceful like this. I felt the urge to wrap my arms around him one last time, to hug the man I married.

Blinking back tears, I slowly eased the covers off. Carefully, I set one bare foot down on the carpet, and then the other. I stood, placing my hand over my racing heart. If Charles were to wake . . .

I clenched my hands. By golly, I could do this. Being told that I couldn't, that I wouldn't amount to anything, only made me more determined. I would prove Charles and Mother wrong. I was meant to be somebody.

Carefully reaching into my robe, I pulled out the note that had been tucked against my breast. With shaking fingers, I unfolded it, placing it on the bedside table. I'd deliberated for months now about leaving this message for Charles, but I'd always lost my nerve. After tonight, there would be no repairing my marriage.

I'd tried to find the right words so many times. Fear told me to burn this letter, as I had the others. Instead, I left the note for Charles to find in the morning, my cursive sure to carve a mark on his heart, sharp as a razor blade.

Charles,

I cannot pretend to be happy any longer. I've tried to be the best wife I can, but my best isn't enough for you. I want a divorce. I have given this careful consideration. I do not want your money. You may keep the house, your car, and your assets at the Oceano. All I ask for is my freedom. Please do not search for me. I will have a lawyer mail you the divorce papers. I am so sorry to leave you this way. Forgive me.

Love,
Violet

Tiptoeing toward the door, I stopped abruptly when I heard a change in Charles's breathing. Was he coming to? My own breathing came in rapid gulps. If he woke, I would be done for. My stomach tightened, imagining his rage after reading the note. But within a moment, Charles's snoring grew louder. It was now or never.

Placing one foot in front of the next, I walked out of the bedroom, then through the kitchen, until I stood at the front door. The kitchen clock ticked down the minutes, puncturing the silence. Would Harry's party still be going at this hour? I let out my breath in a shudder. If I stepped over that threshold, there would be no turning back.

My eyes lingered on the cast-iron frying pan. Once again I felt the bacon grease burn my skin, and saw myself crying on the floor. It was all I needed. Taking a deep breath, I twisted the door handle and stepped outside.

The cool damp air, carrying the scent of ocean brine, heightened my senses. I crouched among my red roses, which had come into full bloom. I couldn't risk being seen by the neighbors. I admired the rose petals, illuminated by the moonlight. Their beauty disguised the ugliness that took place inside this house.

Carefully scooting the terra-cotta flowerpots to the side, I retrieved the duffel bag I had packed earlier. How I'd wished to take more of my things—my dresses, jewelry and shoes. But that wasn't possible. Instead, I'd packed my favorite green gown, hopefully to impress a casting director, my saddle shoes and my best pair of heels.

Slipping my bathrobe from my shoulders, I stashed it inside the duffel bag. I smoothed my blue dress over my stomach, noting that the belted waist had become a bit tight. I would need to lose a few pounds to have a real shot at Hollywood stardom. Retrieving my saddle shoes from my bag, I slipped them over my stocking feet. Thanks to the loose fabric of my robe, Charles hadn't noticed my dress beneath it.

"Goodbye," I whispered to my rose plants. "Wish me luck."

Without a second glance, I hurried down the path, making my way along West Cliff Drive. If I walked fast enough, I could be at the Boardwalk Bowl in fifteen minutes—in time to catch the tail end of Harry Goodman's party.

THE CRACK OF bowling balls against the pins caused me to jump. I clutched my duffel bag tightly against my chest.

"Violet, you made it!"

Ricky walked toward me, a grin on his face. "What are you doing here so late? Your fella let you out of the house to see us lowlifes?"

I couldn't manage a smile. Immediately, Ricky's eyes grew concerned. He gently touched my shoulder.

"Is everything all right?"

I shook my head. "I need a drink."

"Sure thing," Ricky said, turning toward the bar. "I'll bring you a cup of rum punch. Take a seat. The party's winding down, but Harry's over there in the corner booth. You missed Stella, but Dot's still here."

"Thanks," I said, my palms sweaty. Beneath the bright lights of the bowling alley, I felt exposed. There would be no turning back now—too many people had seen me here. What if I'd made a terrible mistake?

"Vi!" Dot cried, spotting me from across the room. Her drink splashed on the floor as she stood. Pushing her short blond curls out of her eyes, Dot hurried toward me, still wearing her waitress uniform. She wrapped her arms around me, the scent of fried chicken clinging to her clothing. My shoulders sagged with guilt. After I'd taken up with Charles, I'd dropped my waitress pals like a hot potato.

"By golly, I never thought I'd see you here tonight, Violet. Ever since you got married, you've all but disappeared. Then yesterday I watched you win the pageant, and you should've heard my cheer! I turned to Stella and said, 'Told ya Violet would be famous one day.' You ask her. We miss you, doll. We're so happy for you."

"Thank you, Dot," I said, holding back my tears. "I'm so sorry I haven't stopped by Mary's Chicken Shack to see you and the old crew. Married life has kept me busy."

Dot smiled. "It's all right, doll."

She looked so much older than her twenty-six years, and so thin. She was probably scraping to get by. And yet she managed to remain upbeat, bringing smiles to customers' faces with her jokes. She gestured toward the booth.

"Sit down, why don't ya? Harry will be over the moon. We never expected you'd come to the party, but we're sure happy you're here."

She ushered me into a leather booth, oblivious to the duffel bag I clutched in my hands. I looked beneath the booth, eager to stash it out of sight.

"Violet!" Harry exclaimed. "Holy cow!" His jolly face shone even redder than usual, and he lifted his Hawaiian shirt, fanning himself. "Whew. It's hotter than Hades in here. Or maybe it's just the company?"

Dot rolled her eyes. "I hope the Los Angeles crowd is kinder than we are, because your jokes stink."

"Oh hush," Harry said, jiggling his gut. "I'm like Santa Claus, sweet and harmless. Now who wants to sit on my lap?"

"No, thank you," Dot said. "Santa has had a few too many martinis."

Ricky appeared, holding a cup of rum punch garnished with a paper umbrella. He handed it to me.

"Thank you," I said, gratefully taking a sip. The sweet mixture tasted mostly like fruit juice, but with the pleasant burn of alcohol.

"Look who's here," Harry bellowed, turning to Ricky.

"Soon we'll be listening to the radio, to see if this old gal of ours has won the Miss America pageant. And to think she started as a waitress, right here on the boardwalk."

"Say," Dot said, narrowing her eyes at me. "Where's your fella? Isn't it awfully late for you to be out alone?"

"He's—uh, a bit under the weather with a dreadful cold," I stammered. "But he told me to catch up with my old pals. He didn't want me to miss the party."

"Ain't that swell," Dot said, slurping the rest of her drink. "I wish I could find myself a nice fella like that. Does he have any friends?" She shook her head. "Never mind. Those folks from the golf course wouldn't give a girl like me a second glance."

"Oh Dot," I said, placing my palm atop hers. "That's not true." I dug into my purse. "Here. Put on a swipe of my crimson lipstick."

I handed her my powder compact and watched as she tried the shade on. It brightened her face considerably, and she beamed at herself in the little mirror.

"Look out, Vivien Leigh." Harry whistled. "There's a new star in town."

Dot punched Harry on the arm, but she held herself a little straighter.

"Keep it," I said. "It looks lovely on you."

"You sure?"

"Absolutely."

"Thank you!" Dot said. "That's awfully kind. Now if you'll excuse me, I need to use the ladies'."

"Good idea," Harry mumbled, hoisting his hefty body

upright. "I've got to piss like a racehorse." He braced himself on the edge of the booth.

As he and Dot disappeared toward the loo, I turned to Ricky, who'd been eyeing me silently while the others chatted.

"I don't mean to pry," he said. "Does your husband really know you're here?"

Taking a deep breath, I let it out with a shudder. "No, he doesn't. I withdrew from the Miss America pageant today. Charles didn't want me to compete."

Ricky's eyes held mine without any judgment.

Finding his silence encouraging, I continued, "He doesn't think it's proper for me to dream of stardom. Perhaps he's right. But I've tried to quench this fire inside me and I can't." A tear slipped down my cheek. "I'm leaving him, Ricky."

Ricky handed me a napkin.

"Thank you," I said, dabbing at the corner of my eye. My gaze darted to the doorway; I was expecting Charles to walk through it. I didn't want to tell Ricky the truth of how bad things had gotten. I buried my face in my hands, fear and shame washing over me. "Oh, I'm so foolish. I ought to go home and burn that note before he wakes."

Ricky placed a comforting hand on my back. His eyes locked on mine. "Breathe . . . Tell me something. How many years have we known each other?"

When I first started working at Mary's Chicken Shack, Ricky was newly arrived at the boardwalk, fourteen years old and scrawny—a year younger than me.

"Five."

"And how long have you been talking about how you'd make it in Hollywood as an actress someday?"

"But I was merely a silly teenage girl . . ."

"How long?"

I sighed. "Five years."

Ricky smiled. "Sometimes we have to follow our hearts, even if it means leaving those we love behind. Did I ever tell you how I came to the boardwalk?"

"I don't think so."

In my memory, Ricky had just suddenly appeared. With his infectious smile and daredevil acts on the trapeze, he'd always been part of our Beach Boardwalk family.

"My parents and I came here from Mexico when I was ten years old in search of a better life. We found work on a strawberry farm in the Central Valley." He grimaced. "In the burning-hot sun we worked ten-hour days, sometimes twelve, without bathroom breaks, food or water. My hands bled from picking the berries. Instead of being paid fair wages, we barely made enough to eat."

"Oh Ricky," I said. "I had no idea."

"Every night, I'd look up at the stars and dream of running away to join the circus. I'd seen the circus once in Mexico City, and the tightrope walkers and tigers mesmerized me. But when I saw the trapeze artists, I felt something inside me light up. That was exactly what I wanted to do—I wanted to fly."

"Did you tell your parents about your dream?"

Ricky nodded. "They thought it was nonsense and told

me to get my head out of the clouds. Instead, I found an old rope, strung it up between two tree branches, and practiced swinging back and forth."

I smiled, picturing little Ricky, tired after hours of relentless work on the farm, refusing to let exhaustion crush his spirit.

"What happened?"

Ricky got a faraway look in his eyes. "When I was fourteen, I couldn't take it anymore. I hitched a ride to Salinas, where other farmers went looking for work. Then from there, I hitchhiked to Monterey, then Santa Cruz, where I'd heard of the Beach Boardwalk and the performers who worked here."

"Have you spoken to your parents since then?"

Ricky shook his head. "I hide money inside a bag of corn flour with a note saying it's for my ma's tortillas and mail it to the farm. I hope that Mama is getting it." He smiled wistfully. "I sent her a postcard with me performing the 'Slide for Life' so she'd know how far I've come."

I'd seen the photo of Ricky and Donny dangling from the trapeze. It was one of the most popular postcards sold at the souvenir shop.

"It must have been terribly hard to leave," I said softly. "But I'm sure your mother is proud of you."

His eyes were sad. "I got my own box at the post office in case my ma ever writes me back. Number seven-seven-seven."

I smiled. "Lucky number."

"Look," Ricky said, lowering his voice as Harry emerged

from the men's room. "If you're in trouble, I can help. And if you want to go to Hollywood, I'll get you there." His eyes narrowed. "Violet, if your husband ever lays a finger on you . . ."

Charles would kill Ricky if he found out we were in cahoots.

My voice dropped to a whisper. "I have enough money for a ticket to San Jose on the *Suntan Special.* I can take a Greyhound bus to Los Angeles from there. But I'm frightened someone will recognize me at the station."

Ricky looked at me. "Ask Harry to drive you. That's why you're here, ain't it?"

I bit my lip. I hadn't thought my escape plan through beyond getting on the midnight train. But in my heart, I'd hoped Harry Goodman would be my salvation.

"Please don't tell Harry the truth about Charles. He'll never agree to take me to Hollywood unless he thinks my husband has allowed me to go."

"My dear friends," Harry said, slapping a hand on Ricky's shoulder. "It's time for me to hit the hay. That was one hell of a party."

"Harry," I said, gathering my courage. "Could I hitch a ride with you to Hollywood? I've only brought a small bag, and I won't be a bother, I promise."

"Ha!" Harry said. "Good one, Violet."

"I'm serious. You said you know a casting director? It'd mean the world to me if you could introduce me."

Harry stroked his cleft chin with a meaty hand. "What about your fella? Surely he doesn't want you traveling all the way to Los Angeles with a grumpy old fart like me."

"He trusts you," I lied. "Everyone who's ever met you knows you're decent to the core. Besides, with business booming at the Oceano, Charles doesn't have time to drive to Hollywood. You'd be doing us both such a large favor."

"I don't know," Harry said, shaking his head. "Something doesn't feel right about this. Why don't you sleep on it, and your fella can talk to me in the morning?"

My shoulders sank. I couldn't go back to my old life—*I couldn't.*

"Charles sent Violet over here," Ricky said, giving Harry a winning smile. "Didn't I tell ya? He's proud as can be of Violet. Said to me he can't wait to see his wife take on Hollywood. She's going to be a star."

I held my breath. Was Harry drunk enough to believe Ricky?

"All righty, then," Harry said, a puzzled look on his face. "The more the merrier! Should I pick you up tomorrow 'round noon? My car's already packed to the brim, but I suppose I've got room for another bag."

"We leave tonight," I said, surprised at the firmness in my voice.

Harry laughed. "Honey, I'm in no state to drive."

"I can drive." In truth, it had been over a year since I'd driven. Charles forbade it, like he controlled every other aspect of my life.

"Why the rush?" Harry asked. "It's nearly midnight, for Christ's sake."

"Think of how we'll beat the awful Los Angeles traffic. Aren't you as eager to get to Hollywood as I am?"

Ricky slapped a palm on Harry's shoulder. "Come on, Harry. Listen to the gal!"

"Okay," Harry said, waving his hands in surrender. "To hell with it! I hope you're an excellent driver, Miss Violet, because if you so much as scratch my Oldsmobile . . ."

I batted my eyelashes. "I wouldn't dare."

Ricky placed a comforting hand on my back as he guided me out of the bowling alley, through the parking lot and into the driver's seat of Harry's car. I stuck the keys in the ignition, my nerves rattled as I looked around the empty lot. Fog hung thick over the street lamps, and the ocean waves crashed against the shore.

Harry mumbled something, then tilted back his seat and dozed off.

"You *do* know how to drive, don't you?" Ricky asked.

I pushed in the clutch and shifted into first. "It's been a while."

"That's it," Ricky said. "Now let the clutch out slowly so you don't rev the engine too much."

I did as I was told. The car sputtered to life.

"Ricky," I whispered. "I'm scared. Look at this fog."

"Trust yourself," Ricky said. "Even if you can only see as far as your headlights, you can make it the whole way like that. Keep your eyes on the road in front of you. And shift into second gear before you stop."

"Thank you," I said, fighting the knot of fear in my stomach. "I'll send you a postcard as soon as I arrive, so you know that I'm safe."

Ricky rapped the window with his knuckle. "You're braver than you think."

He held my eyes for a meaningful second, as if he sensed my resolve wavering. His voice softened. "I'm sorry about Charles. I really am. If there's anything you need, I'm always here for you. You promise you'll come to me if you're in trouble?"

"I promise."

With both hands clutching the steering wheel, I navigated Harry's Oldsmobile out of the parking lot and onto the Pacific Coast Highway. Slowly, I wound along the coastline in the dark, the cliffs to one side and the ocean roaring beneath me. My heart pounded with exhilaration and fear. For the first time, I was in charge of my destiny.

CHAPTER 8

Marisol Cruz

2007

Mari stood next to Carol, a thought nagging persistently at the back of her mind. Mayor Harcourt came from a line of rich and powerful men—a prominent Santa Cruz family. So why hadn't anyone ever mentioned the name Violet Harcourt? If the young beauty queen was in fact related to the mayor, her death should have been town gossip. Mari and her friends had told plenty of ghost stories as children, but Violet Harcourt's name had never been mentioned as part of the local folklore.

"What do you know about Violet Harcourt?"

The rush of the Giant Dipper sounded overhead, and shrieks carried on the breeze. Mari waited for the rickety wooden roller-coaster cars to pass so that Carol could give her an answer.

Carol frowned. "It's a sad story. She was Miss California 1940 and had a promising life ahead of her. She tried to make it as an actress in Hollywood, but she returned to Santa Cruz a few months later, then jumped off a cliff."

"Is she of any relation to Mayor Harcourt?"

"She was his father's first wife. Charles Harcourt remarried a few years after her death. Most people only know of his second wife, Grace."

Mari nodded, figuring the mayor would rather not focus on this sad aspect of his family history.

Carol sighed, her eyes settling on the gazebo. "I shouldn't say this, but it really is *such* a shame what the mayor is doing. All of us at the museum feel that it's wrong to tear down a historic structure."

Mari furrowed her brow. "Then let's do something about it. What if we filed the paperwork to get the gazebo listed on the National Register of Historic Places? That would prevent the building from being torn down, wouldn't it?"

"I suppose we could try. The property must be at least fifty years old, which it is—and we'd have to prove its historic significance."

Mari smiled. "I might have photos of my grandparents attending community dances there. I'm sure other locals have photos too. We could submit them with the application."

"It feels icky to oppose the mayor. His son certainly seems like a determined young man. I'm sure he wants what's best for the town. Maybe the new construction will include affordable housing for families?"

"I highly doubt it."

Carol turned to Mari. "I admire you for showing such passion toward preserving a piece of our town's history. Perhaps we should put up a fight."

"Let's do it," Mari said.

Carol nodded. "I can print the forms for us to send to the state historic preservation office. Of course, there's no guarantee our request will be approved. They could reject the property, or ask for more information. Oh wait—here comes someone."

She beamed at the young man approaching. "Welcome to the Santa Cruz Museum of Art & History exhibit. Would you like to buy a raffle ticket?"

"I'd love to," Jason said.

Crap. Mari couldn't find her voice, her hands hanging uselessly at her sides as she met his warm brown eyes. Carol nudged her in the ribs.

"Raffle tickets are ten dollars each," Mari replied. "Our prizes include dinner for two at Trabocco, Beach Boardwalk season passes, a beach cruiser bicycle—"

"I'll buy ten of them."

Carol's eyes widened. "Wonderful!"

"That'll be one hundred dollars . . ."

"Great job," Carol whispered, as Jason handed Mari five twenties. "I'm heading out, but I'll check in with you tomorrow. Have a great evening."

After Carol left the booth, Mari smirked. "How did you find me?"

"Wanda was eager to tell me about your weekend job. You work for the museum. Why didn't you tell me?"

"Look," Mari said. "I don't mean to be rude. But it's complicated. I'm not looking to date anyone right now."

"*Okay*. But I think you're smart and cool. Is there a reason we can't be friends?"

Mari smiled. "Well, you did spend a hundred dollars on raffle tickets . . ."

STROLLING ALONG THE wooden slats of the boardwalk with a cotton candy in hand, Mari paused in front of the historic Looff Carousel.

"I used to ride this carousel with my grandpa," she said, smiling wistfully. "I loved the jewels on the horses. Did you know each animal is hand-carved? This carousel is from 1911. And the organ is a rare Wurlitzer."

Jason's eyes crinkled at the corners. "It's so cool that your family has lived here for generations. My grandparents moved to Chicago in 1945, but my grandmother never talks much about her childhood, or her life before the war."

"Really?" Mari took a bite of the sugary confection. "My *abuelo* always told me about how he immigrated here from Mexico, worked in horrible conditions on a strawberry farm until he became a stunt performer. He liked to talk about the past."

Turning to the neglected gazebo, Mari sighed. "He met my grandma at a dance there. It's such a shame the structure is being torn down. I want to get it listed on the register of historic places, like this carousel."

Jason smiled. "You have a bit of cotton candy on your chin."

"Oh," Mari said, bringing her hand to her face.

Jason laughed. "I love how passionate you are about saving historic structures. But it's hard to take you seriously when you have a pink beard."

"Very funny," Mari said, glaring.

Jason held up his hands. "Hey, I think it's wonderful that your grandparents met at a gazebo dance. But the bureaucracy of getting a structure listed on the register of historic places can take a while to work through. Have you thought of other ways to generate public interest in saving the gazebo?"

"I could post some of my grandpa's pictures on Facebook. Lots of girls enjoy doing retro-style photo shoots here at the boardwalk. It could be a great wedding backdrop if it were restored."

Jason raised his eyebrows. "That's definitely one way. Have you thought about applying for a Swanson Grant? I saw a flyer up in the English department on campus."

Mari shook her head. "I don't know anything about the Swanson Grant."

"Oh. The James Swanson Memorial Fund accepts proposals that promote understanding of the history of Santa Cruz. Like, intellectual research." He snapped his fingers. "How about writing a story, or making an art piece, or filming a documentary about the gazebo?"

Mari scrunched her brow. "So I could publish an article on the gazebo's history that would get people interested in the gazebo?"

He smiled. "You're the historian. You tell me."

She smirked. "Do you work in the English department? Sorry, I've been talking so much, I haven't even asked you what you do at UC Santa Cruz."

"I'm an IT specialist," Jason said. "I help professors in the English department."

"And you noticed a grant flyer which in no way relates to working with computers?"

Jason grinned. "I thought *somebody* might be interested."

"How much is the grant award?"

"Twelve hundred bucks."

Mari thought about what she could do with that money. She could construct a replica of the gazebo as it was in its heyday, maybe even an entire diorama with people dancing, and have it on display at the museum's booth at the boardwalk. She'd have to hire artists, but it was more than enough money. And Carol would give her permission to show it off. That would get people interested, wouldn't it?

Mari smiled. "I like that idea. Thanks."

Jason punched her lightly on the shoulder. "Any time, buddy."

Mari glanced at her phone. "Shoot, I better get going."

"Hot date tonight?"

Mari turned her phone outward so Jason could see the screensaver.

"This is my date. Her name is Lily."

"You're a *mom*?"

"Yep. My most important job of all."

"Wow, she's beautiful." Jason paused a beat. "And Lily's dad is . . ."

"Not in the picture."

Jason's eyes filled with understanding. "My sister's a single mom. I love my niece and nephew to the moon and back, but I see how hard it is for her."

Mari was taken aback by the directness of his statement. But he was right. It *was* hard. She found his openness refreshing.

"Hey, I really do have to go," she said. "But thanks for the cotton candy."

"I had a great time," Jason said. He pulled a business card from his wallet. "Here's my number. No pressure. Call me if you want to hang out."

"I'll think about it," Mari said, slipping his card into the back pocket of her jeans. Before she lost her nerve, she pulled a pen from her purse and scribbled her phone number on an old receipt. "Here's mine."

Jason's face lit up when she handed him the paper. "Cool."

He gave a friendly wave, and her shoulders relaxed. Since becoming a mom, she'd isolated herself. She was too young to connect with the other moms at the preschool, many of whom were in their late thirties. They had careers, book clubs and wine nights, which she was never invited to. Maybe once she had been, but she'd declined too many times. Today it felt possible to open her heart to friendship.

WHILE LILY SLEPT nearby, Mari's laptop screen illuminated the dark room. She typed "Swanson Grant" into the search engine and waited for the results to load.

Apply for a Local History Grant

Are you working on a local history project? Want to receive some funding and support for your passion for Santa Cruz's past and future? The History Forum, a group of Santa Cruz community members with a particular interest in local history, supports the annual Swanson Award competition for local history research. The award comes with public recognition and a grant of $1,200 to support original projects that promote the understanding of the history of the Santa Cruz/Monterey Bay area. These projects can be documentaries, studies, performances, art installations or publications. We care about the content, and we look forward to receiving applications that reflect innovative approaches to preserving local history. You don't have to be a professional historian to be an effective champion for local history.

Mari smiled. It was as if the grant had been written for her. The language was friendly and inviting—the site even stated she didn't have to be a professional historian. And building a diorama of the gazebo would certainly be innovative, right?

Maybe in addition to hiring artists, she could interview elderly members of the community about their gazebo memories, record those memories and then play them along with the diorama installation. It would be like a guided museum tour.

Clicking the link to the application, Mari waited for the file to open. Her narrative couldn't exceed five hundred words, but she had additional pages to upload her proposal material. Abuelo's photos would be perfect. She had to list who was participating, the location of the project, how it would be implemented and its timeline, and she had to explain its connection to Santa Cruz County history.

Her mind was already three steps ahead—she would be the sole participant, unless Carol wanted to join. She could easily find artists willing to build the diorama—Santa Cruz was filled with artists. And the timeline would have to be tight, before the destruction of the gazebo, so beachgoers and locals could witness the history of what was going to be destroyed. She'd have to get it done before August, in time to put her diorama on display during the Centennial Celebration.

Mari rubbed her temples. Would she be able to pull it off? Heck, she was waitressing, working weekends, and plus, she was a single mom. But she thrived under pressure. *She could do this.* Lily sighed in her sleep, and Mari admired how her daughter's dark eyelashes lay perfectly against her soft cheeks. Didn't she want to make her daughter proud? Every time Lily told her preschool friends that Mommy was a waitress, it stung. Mari had meant to be so much more.

Carefully setting her laptop aside, Mari opened the lid of her grandfather's leather trunk, which she'd hauled down from the attic. Reaching inside, she scraped along the bottom, removing a stack of photographs and postcards. She lifted a black-and-white photo to the light. Abuelo stood in front of a Beach Boardwalk diner with the sign MARY'S CHICKEN SHACK. He looked very young, perhaps no more than sixteen.

Grinning, he had his arms around two pretty girls in waitress uniforms. Mari brought her hand to her mouth. *That face.* She lifted the photograph closer, squinting at the girl on the right. She wasn't just pretty—she was beautiful. And suddenly Mari knew who she was: Violet Harcourt, the young beauty queen who had committed suicide.

CHAPTER 9

Violet Harcourt

1940

My heart swelled as I looked over the balcony of the Pink Flamingo Motel. Girls in two-piece swimsuits lounged under striped umbrellas by the kidney-shaped swimming pool. The pink and yellow motel walls shone bright in the California sunshine, and rows of palm trees stretched for miles. Wearing oversize sunglasses on a bright Los Angeles morning, I felt like a movie star.

"Hey," Harry called, waving at me from down below, dressed in Bermuda shorts and a straw hat. "I'd invite you for a dip, but I'm set to meet with my contact from RKO in an hour. You want to tag along?"

I curled my hands around the railing. Did I ever!

"You betcha," I called out. "Let me make myself decent."

One of the Big Five movie studios! RKO Pictures had

brought Ginger Rogers and Fred Astaire to fame, producing some of my favorite musicals.

Though I'd only slept a few hours since we'd arrived, I felt as though I could take on the world. Retreating into the cool motel room, I shut the door behind me. The place was a bit shabby, but clean. Harry had gotten us a room with two twin beds, and thankfully he hadn't tried any funny business.

I reached into my clutch, counting the dollar bills I'd pilfered from Charles. It would be enough for a short time . . . maybe a week at most. I closed my eyes, praying for my big break. Opening them, I practiced a winning smile in the hotel mirror—like I had for the Miss California beauty pageant. Charles wasn't here to hold me back, and *doggone it,* now was my time to shine.

WITH HARRY DRIVING us down Sunset Boulevard, I gawped at the colorful billboards and neon signs. Passing Grauman's Chinese Theatre, I nearly squealed with delight. The new nightclubs along this strip teemed with the rich and famous. Though supposedly the gangsters Mickey Cohen and Bugsy Siegel owned the places, I'd die to rub elbows with Judy Garland, Greta Garbo and Clark Gable. Mickey Rooney came to play golf at the Oceano once, but Charles commanded me to stay home that day.

I shuddered, picturing Charles waking up to an empty bed. *What would he do?* I rubbed the back of my neck. Would he call the police? It wouldn't take long for someone to say they'd spotted me at the bowling alley. But no one other than Ricky had seen me get into Harry's car. My stomach clenched, fearing what Charles could do to him. My friend had worked his way out of far worse pickles. Still—I feared I'd placed him in an awful predicament.

As we passed Sunset Tower, I shielded my eyes from the sun, gazing up at the Art Deco structure. Harry grinned at me. "Howard Hughes lives up there in the penthouse. Did you know he rents a bunch of other apartments in the same building for his mistresses? Can you imagine 'em running into each other?"

I pulled my cardigan more tightly around my shoulders. Plenty of girls used their feminine wiles to sleep their way into a picture. I hoped a film producer would sign me for my talent—and not for something else.

"I've heard he's handsome," I offered. "Maybe they don't mind sharing."

Harry guffawed. "Goodness Violet, you're a spitfire today."

I felt different here. Perhaps it was the air, or the freedom of my hand out the window of Harry's Oldsmobile. The old Violet was gone. I would do anything for a taste of fame. Once my star began to rise, Charles would never lay a hand on me again. But until then, I needed to be cautious. If Charles were to somehow find me and phone the motel, Harry would tell him everything. It wouldn't be wise to stay with Harry for long.

"WHERE ARE WE?" I asked, looking around at the expanse of flatland before me. We'd driven for nearly an hour, though traffic had slowed our progress.

"Culver City," Harry answered, swerving into a large parking lot. "This is the RKO back lot, otherwise known as the back forty."

"The what?"

"It's forty acres. All of the buildings from *Gone with the Wind* are here. You'll find Atlanta in the heart of California."

I covered my mouth. "This is where Tara is?"

"That's right. My buddy is a set designer. He invited me to come on down so I could have a chat with the boss. David O. Selznick might be here today."

Pulling my compact from my purse, I checked myself in the mirror. My crimson lipstick hadn't smudged, and pins held my auburn waves. If I were to meet the powerful producer today, I'd only have one chance to impress him.

Going to the movie palaces had been my escape from the looming threats of war. Watching the beautiful people on-screen while laughing along with a comedy or singing the tune of a musical transported me to another world. And entering the RKO lot felt like a dream I didn't want to wake up from. I pressed my face to the glass as the structures of *Gone with the Wind* came into view.

"There's the courthouse and the bank. And there's the train depot! Oh, isn't it wonderful?"

Harry chuckled. "It sure is."

As Harry parked his car, I crossed my fingers for luck. This was the home of Ginger Rogers, Katharine Hepburn and Fred Astaire. Fred Astaire had been balding in his thirties and a nobody. But Mr. Selznick had seen his charm. If I could attract the interest of even an assistant director, today could be my lucky break.

Stepping out of the car into the sunshine, I followed Harry across the parking lot and through the doors of the RKO Pictures building. The open and cavernous space felt like an airplane hangar. A ladder had been propped on the right side, and studio lights shone against the walls of the empty room.

"What is this place?" I asked.

"It's a soundstage," Harry answered. "Fully soundproof, so dialogue can be recorded here."

"Well, hello there! You made it."

I turned around to see a short, shiny-faced man strolling toward Harry. He'd combed his greasy hair back to hide a bald spot, but the pink skin shone through his thinning strands. He wore a plaid suit over his portly frame.

"Johnny!"

The two men embraced, slapping each other on the back. Johnny's eyes fixed on mine, then traveled down my legs and up again, resting on my décolletage. I shivered, wishing I could avert his gaze.

"Look at the gams on you. What's your name, sweetheart?"

"Violet," I said, forcing a smile.

"You here for a screen test too?"

I blushed. "Well, actually, I was hoping . . ."

Johnny laughed. "No need to be shy, sweetheart. If Harry thinks he can get his ugly mug on screen, you sure have a chance with a face like that."

Harry grinned. "Is the big boss here?"

Johnny shook his head. "Selznick's not in. But his assistant director is." He turned to me with a sleazy smile. "You heard of *Rebecca*?"

"The film? Of course."

The Gothic tale had been directed by Alfred Hitchcock and produced by David O. Selznick. I'd found it quite sad, and a bit frightening.

"Eric Stacey was one of the assistant directors. Now he's looking to cast the part of Selznick's next big film. We've got a handful of gals here for the reading."

"Oh," I said, standing up straighter. "Swell. Shall I join them?"

He placed a hand on my shoulder, and I tensed, wishing I could swat it away. Instead, I allowed Johnny to guide me from the soundstage into a dimly lit hallway. Ten or so girls sat on the floor waiting there, some whispering in pairs, others reading. A few looked up, eyeing me warily. I offered a shy smile, but no one returned it.

"Wait here," Johnny said. He turned to Harry. "Come with me. I want you to meet my buddy from the sound department. He knows a great Hollywood agent looking for a comedian for his next film."

"Break a leg," Harry called, waving at me.

I waved back, then took a deep breath. Was I supposed to have prepared a monologue? My eyes darted to the other girls with their reading material. I racked my brain, trying to recall a scene I had used in a previous audition.

"Nerves gettin' to ya?"

The girl who'd spoken was a bottle blonde, her voluptuous body nearly spilling out of a satin dress, so tight it looked sewn on. A faux-fur wrap hung about her shoulders. Heavy makeup made her striking features appear a little harsh. Yet perhaps that much rouge was needed to stand out on-screen.

I smiled. "Yes, afraid so."

She extended her hand. "I'm Roxy Marlow."

"Violet Sweeting," I said, taken aback by her firm grip.

"You're new in town?"

"Can you tell?"

Roxy chuckled. "You've got that wide-eyed look about you. I've been trying to get more than a bit part for years, still haven't caught my lucky break."

"I'm sorry to hear that," I said, fidgeting with my clutch. "Say, are we meant to have prepared a monologue?"

Roxy shook her head. "It's a cold reading. Someone else will read the dialogue with you. The assistant director wants to see how you play off the other person."

"Oh," I said, the tension between my shoulders lessening a little. "Thank you."

Fluffing her curls, Roxy grinned. "I always know the scoop. Word on the street is that Joan Fontaine has already been cast as the lead, but they're looking for a girl to play a nightclub singer. Do you sing?"

"Yes. It was my talent in the . . . ," I trailed off, afraid to give away my identity as Mrs. Charles Harcourt, "beauty pageant I entered."

"Aw shucks," Roxy said, tilting her head. "Another Miss

Pretty-face, trying to strike it big in Hollywood. Listen, doll, this town is cutthroat." She lowered her voice. "You see those girls?"

I nodded, glancing at the others.

"Most of 'em won't make it. Some will end up finding their meal ticket dating some bigwig bozo, and if they're lucky, getting a year's contract at Columbia. But if you have an affair with a studio boss, it will always be *all* about him."

"I don't expect to have any type of affair—"

"You don't *now,*" Roxy said, looking me in the eye. "But if you fall on hard times, you'd be surprised what you're willing to do. A girl's got to eat."

I swallowed.

Roxy smiled coyly. "I'm a cigarette girl at Tropical Gardens Nightclub. Lots of bigwigs meet there. It's where I hear all the Hollywood gossip."

"Really? How exciting."

"We're looking for a new lounge singer, if you're interested. The last girl quit as soon as she got a ring on her finger. You ain't married, are you?"

My palms began to sweat as Roxy's eyes darted to my bare finger. I'd left my diamond solitaire and wedding band in a jewelry box on my nightstand in Santa Cruz. Instead, I'd brought my diamond and sapphire earrings that had belonged to my grandmother. My left hand felt strangely barren without the large rock. *Divorce.* I hated the sound of it. But what choice did I have? I needed to find a lawyer.

"Not married," I said, fighting the tightness in my throat.

"Ladies!" a voice boomed. The girls sitting on the floor scrambled to attention, some dropping their papers as they stood. I smoothed my hands against my green dress, praying to stand out from the crowd of pretty faces.

A handsome man in khakis and a white shirt stood before us, his eyes appraising. Unlike Johnny's, his gaze didn't linger on my legs or my face. Perhaps in Hollywood I wasn't such hot stuff after all. Every gal here looked like a knockout.

"My name's Ed. Mr. Stacey is at the soundstage, awaiting your auditions. Line up, single file. I don't got all day."

My stomach dropped, like the time I'd ridden the Giant Dipper roller coaster. I stood behind Roxy, second in line.

Removing her faux-fur stole, Roxy winked at me. "Good luck, doll. Say, where are you staying?"

"The Pink Flamingo Motel."

"I know the place," Roxy said. "I live at the Tropicana, on the other end of Sunset Boulevard. It's a bit of a dive, but the rent is cheap. Come by sometime. I'm in room one-thirteen. I can help you get on your feet."

"Thank you," I said, as Roxy walked away with an exaggerated sway of her hips. "And good luck!"

Roxy laughed, calling over her shoulder, "My luck ran out a long time ago. If I get this part, it will be thanks to five years of waiting tables and selling cigarettes. This town will knock the stars right out of your eyes."

I resisted the urge to bite my cuticles while Roxy departed for her screen test. One of the other girls whispered in line behind me, "Did you know hundreds of actresses tested for the role of Scarlett O'Hara? The director found something wrong with every one of them. Too young, too beefy, you name it."

I smiled politely. "The leading lady needed to be just right for such an iconic role."

We locked eyes on each other. Unlike Roxy, this girl had lustrous dark hair, dark brows and a fresh, dewy face. I felt the heat of jealousy creep up my neck. Minutes passed like hours. I tried not to fidget.

"Next! Who's next?"

I nearly jumped out of my skin as Ed returned with his clipboard.

"I am," I said, raising my hand.

"Hurry along, then."

My heels clicked against the floor as I followed him to the soundstage. I looked around for Roxy, but she was nowhere to be seen.

A dark-haired man sat at a table in the corner, his chiseled features so similar to Charles's that my heart nearly skipped a beat.

"What'sa matter?" Ed asked. "Nerves getting to you already? Sit down. This is Jimmy. You'll be reading a scene from *The Wizard of Oz*. Your script is on the table."

"Thank you," I said, trying to hide the quiver in my voice. I looked over Jimmy's shoulder to catch a glimpse of the man sitting in a director's chair nearby. He wore spectacles and appeared to be in his midthirties. I put on my winning smile, but his face remained impassive. The knot in my stomach began to feel like a rock.

"Three, two, one, action!"

"Oh," I whispered. *Was there no warning before we began?*

"I haven't got a brain," Jimmy said, "only straw."

Quickly, I recovered. "How can you talk if you haven't got a brain?"

"I don't know . . . But some people without brains do an awful lot of talking . . . don't they?"

I projected sweetness into my voice. "Yes, I guess you're right."

"Cut!"

I looked up at the spectacled director. He'd yelled so loudly I'd cringed in fright. I tried not to pay any mind to the camera filming me, but it was difficult not to.

"Do it once more," the director commanded, his accent distinctly British. "More gently, more quietly, more mood."

"Right," I said.

After a second read through, the director cut me off, this time standing from his chair in frustration.

"Once more. Your face is so hard."

Heat rushed to my cheeks. "Is it?"

With my nerves rattled, I read again. Only this time I flubbed my lines more than once. "Oh nuts. I'm sorry."

The director dismissed me, and I held in my tears as I walked off the soundstage. Roxy's words rang in my ears. This town would knock the stars right out of my eyes.

CHAPTER 10

Marisol Cruz

2007

Lily stuck out her bottom lip as she walked hand in hand with Mari down the tree-lined street toward Green Frog Preschool.

"Anna went with her daddy to his work. And she said he works in a big, shiny building. Anna said her daddy is very important."

Mari smiled. "That's nice."

Lily's green eyes grew serious. "Mom, where does my daddy work?"

"I don't know where he works," Mari said, her jaw tightening. "But we can visit Abuelo at his work. Would you like that?"

Lily shook her head. "No! It's noisy and boring."

Mari's father owned a small construction firm, specializing in helping Santa Cruz families make their homes more eco-friendly. She felt proud of him for giving undocumented immigrants good jobs while making his customers happy. But the job sites often were noisy, and Lily had never shown much interest in the forklifts or cranes. She preferred her tiaras and baby dolls.

Tugging Mari by the arm, Lily picked up her pace. "Ellie's mom has a *boyfriend* and he's in a band. She brought him to show-and-tell and he played guitar."

Mari lifted an eyebrow. "She brought a boyfriend to show-and-tell?"

"He was funny and knew *all* of the songs. Why don't you have a boyfriend?"

Her daughter had no filter—an annoying four-year-old trait. "I don't have time for a boyfriend. I work at the Beach Boardwalk on weekends for the museum. And I work during the week at the café."

"The boardwalk with the rides and candy? I want to go!"

Mari smiled, feeling relieved Lily had dropped the boyfriend topic. "I'll ask Abuela to bring you next weekend. When I'm done working, we can ride the carousel together and eat funnel cake."

"With strawberries and whipped cream?"

"You bet."

"Yay!" Lily cried, skipping toward the doors of the preschool. She dropped Mari's hand, spotting one of her friends. Mari bit her lip. She'd lied to her daughter. She knew where Lily's father worked. And recently it had become a problem.

FANNING HER GRANDFATHER'S photographs and postcards across her bedroom carpet, Mari scrutinized the papers like a ship's navigator attempting to read a faded map. She'd found a wonderful photo of Abuelo and Abuela posed in front of the gazebo the night of their wedding. Mari placed that one at the top, admiring her grandmother's dark lipstick, and how beautiful she was, with her retro waves and bright smile.

The lights of the gazebo lent the black-and-white photograph a magical quality. Unfortunately, Mari couldn't find any other pictures with the structure in view. She would have to search the library archives, or reach out to members of the community, so that she could include more photographs of the gazebo with her grant application.

Below that picture, Mari placed the postcard of the Brown Derby restaurant in Hollywood and the picture of her grandpa with the waitresses at Mary's Chicken Shack. Putting the two together, Mari felt certain the woman named "V" who'd written the postcard to Abuelo was Violet. She'd sifted through her grandfather's things looking for more evidence of their communication, but had found nothing.

There were photographs of the boardwalk as it had been—Abuelo in tight swim trunks, a wide smile on his face as he posed with his arm around the large and muscular Donny Pierson, his stunt diving partner. She'd found a few other postcards, but unfortunately, they were blank. Abuelo had likely picked them up as souvenirs from the places he'd visited in his travels as a young man.

Mari looked at vintage postcards of the Empire State Building in New York, the Ferry Building in San Francisco and the Wrigley Building in Chicago. She'd found a few trinkets in the bottom of the trunk—a key chain from Texas, a blue ribbon from a diving competition, a deck of cards, a pair of dice, a matchbook. There was also a small brass key, dulled with age. What it belonged to, she had no idea. Mari sighed, disappointed she hadn't found any other connection to Violet, aside from that Hollywood postcard. She turned it over to check the postmark—July 25, 1940.

Opening her laptop, Mari searched Violet Harcourt's name, along with the word "obituary." Finding the link to the magazine obituary article, Mari reread the first few paragraphs.

A BEAUTIFUL SUICIDE: LOOKING BACK AT THE TROUBLED LIFE OF MISS CALIFORNIA
September 25, 1940

On Friday September 24, around 7:30 in the evening, 20-year-old Violet Harcourt walked to the edge of the bluff on West Cliff Drive overlooking Natural Bridges. Through the mist she gazed at the ocean, 30 feet below.

In her desperate determination, she leapt, hitting a ledge before plunging into the choppy waters. Several eyewitnesses recount watching her red dress billow in the breeze, and her slender frame disappear beneath the waves.

If the postcard was from Violet, she'd arrived in Hollywood in July (according to the date stamp) and yet in September, she was back in Santa Cruz. Two months wasn't a very long time to pursue an acting career, and Violet seemed determined to make something of herself—a feeling Mari could relate to.

Mari turned over the postcard of the restaurant shaped like a derby hat, looking at the neat blue cursive of "V."

Dear Ricky,

I've made it here safely. I have to pinch myself to believe I'm really in Hollywood! I've never done something so reckless, and I'm a bit terrified. But you're the reason I was brave enough to come here. Sure, I'm a fool for trying to make it as an actress, but I'd be crazier not to try, isn't that right?

I apologize for heaping my troubles on you that night at the party. You're wise beyond your years, and I'm lucky to have you as a friend. Thank you for giving me the courage to follow my dreams.

Mari felt a pit in her stomach as she read the words. It was almost as if the message were coded. *I've made it here safely. I'm a bit terrified. I apologize for heaping my troubles on you.*

What was Violet so afraid of? What troubles was she running from?

Looking at the picture of Violet and Abuelo standing next to each other in front of the diner, Mari saw the face of a carefree teenage girl. Her demeanor was so different in that photo from the later one. And yet it had only been taken a few years before her beauty pageant picture. What had happened in the years in between?

Mari returned to her computer, continuing to read.

> Two months prior to her death, Harcourt, recently crowned Miss California, withdrew from the Miss America pageant, admitting her marital status rendered her ineligible to compete. Runner-up Evelyn Hastings took her place, inheriting the title of Miss California.

Why did Violet lie about being married? Was she determined to compete in the Miss America pageant—or did she secretly long to leave her husband? The outdated pageant rule was still in place: contestants needed to swear they were unmarried, not pregnant and not the adoptive or biological parent of a child. Just one more opportunity single mothers were denied.

Mari continued to search Violet's name on her computer but came up short. She sighed, then clapped her hands together as she had a brain wave. The UC Santa Cruz library had an extensive online archive of materials.

Someone had gifted the university with their entire private collection of photographs and articles from the Second World War period, which had all been converted to microfiche. Mari had used these 1940s photographs before, for a history paper in college. Checking the time on her computer, Mari decided to catch the bus to campus. She still had a few hours to herself before it was time for her shift at the Jupiter Café.

IN THE QUIET comfort of McHenry Library, Mari suppressed the ache in her chest. How she *missed* this place—the smell of the books, the redwoods reaching their branches into the fog outside the floor-to-ceiling windows. Mari's four years as an undergraduate at UC Santa Cruz had been the happiest years of her life. And then everything had turned upside down because of one night of partying.

Exhaling sharply, Mari logged into the University of Santa Cruz search engine to access the archived materials on file. This time when she typed "Violet Harcourt, Santa Cruz 1940," a few different newspaper articles appeared. The first was a wedding announcement in the society pages of the *Santa Cruz Sentinel* from June 1939. In the accompanying photographs, Violet looked gorgeous in a fitted satin wedding dress with cap sleeves, an enviably narrow waist and a long train. Her hair fell in waves to her shoulders beneath a white veil. Her husband, Charles, looked dapper in a black tuxedo, posed with his arm around Violet's midsection.

Mari shifted her focus to the article's text.

HARCOURT NUPTIALS GAY AND GLAMOROUS

On Monday, June 10, at 4:00 P.M. Miss Violet Sweeting became the bride of Mr. Charles Harcourt. The wedding ceremony took place at the Church of Saint Peter. The bridal party then traveled by limousine to the Oceano Golf Club, owned by Mr. Harcourt. The lavish reception included 200 guests and a 10-piece orchestra. The bride's wedding band is adorned with 32 diamonds to complement her Tiffany ring. She wore custom diamond and sapphire swirl clip earrings as her "something blue." The bridal table held two lovebirds carved in ice next to the seven-tiered wedding cake. The glamorous affair was the talk of the town, and included such high-profile guests as the city chancellor and golf legend Gene Sarazen.

Upon being asked how he felt to be married, the groom responded, "Violet is my most prized possession." The bride smiled demurely and replied, "I am grateful for a husband who loves me so."

Mari shuddered. She would hate to be with someone who thought he owned her. Charles's words had dark undertones.

Mari typed "Charles Harcourt, 1940." Photographs and vintage postcards of the Oceano Golf Club filled the screen.

Charles looked confidently at the camera in every photo, strikingly handsome, like Leonardo DiCaprio.

The Oceano Golf Club had been sold prior to Mayor Harcourt taking office, but the family had benefited from generations of wealth. In Mari's family, her dad and her *abuelo* were self-made men. She admired them for their hard work, which had allowed her to go to college and live in a wonderful town.

Charles remarried a woman named Grace Vanderkamp, who also came from a wealthy family. She seemed the opposite of Violet, with a large blond, bouffant hairdo and a smile that didn't appear genuine. Scrolling through the links online, Mari gasped as she caught an offensive headline:

OCEANO BANS MEXICANS FROM EMPLOYMENT

With heat creeping up her neck, Mari read the 1942 article. Charles Harcourt had fired every Mexican employee from his resort. "I refuse to employ gangsters, murderers and thieves at my fine establishment. They have no place in this country and should return to Mexico."

The racial stereotypes never ended. Mexicans had historically been paid lower wages than whites and were forced to labor under unsafe conditions. But worst of all, the patriotic Mexicans who had fought for America during World War II had been denied funeral services by the military. Her *abuelo* had proudly served in the Philippines during the war, his fluent Spanish invaluable because he could communicate with Spanish-speaking Filipino soldiers as they fought together against the Japanese.

In fine print, the article had an addendum. "As a Quaker, Mr. Harcourt has declared himself a pacifist and unable to serve due to his religious beliefs."

A pacifist Quaker? Mari laughed out loud at the ludicrous statement. He owned a golf resort, for heaven's sake—he wasn't a missionary. His money and connections had gotten him out of serving his country. Clearing her search, Mari felt eager to rid herself of Charles Harcourt and the metallic taste in her mouth. She'd come here to find out more about Violet, but now would be a good time to look for gazebo photographs.

When the screen populated again, Mari smiled. Oh, these were perfect: images of the gazebo with smiling young couples at community dances, saddle shoes on their feet and flowers in the women's hair.

The more photographs she clicked through, the more Mari realized that many members of Santa Cruz's Chicano and Latino community attended these dances. The crowd was largely brown, with a few working-class whites sprinkled in. This gazebo had been a gathering place for her people, who were largely marginalized. Judging from the happiness on their faces, they felt safe there, and welcomed.

With attitudes like Charles Harcourt's pervading the public conscience at the time, Mexicans were denied entry to traditional dance halls and wedding venues. This public gazebo, though modest, had held a very special purpose.

Grabbing a pen, Mari scrawled the title of her grant application topic in her notebook: "A Place Beneath the Stars: Cultivating Community Among Santa Cruz's Mexican Immigrants."

She downloaded the images she wanted to use, including the link to the archive collection for proper copyright credit. She would ask Latino artists to create the diorama of the gazebo. Mari smiled, feeling she had made a good start on her grant application. The shabby old gazebo didn't matter to someone like Travis Harcourt, but it mattered to her. The Latino community had always found a way to transform urban spaces—street vendors pushing carts, neighbors chatting over fences, sidewalk artists painting colorful murals on concrete walls. Their modest beach flats that surrounded the boardwalk didn't look like much, but during Christmastime they boasted elaborate nativity scenes behind chain-link fences strung with colored lights.

After packing her bag, Mari inhaled the scent of the books as she walked through the library stacks. She wasn't a student anymore, but the thought of working on her grant application gave her the rush that studying used to. Mari smiled—it was a wonderful feeling, using her brain for something other than nursery rhymes. She'd been dulled watching kids' cartoons, washing dishes, doing laundry. For the first time in a long time, she felt like more than just a mom.

CHAPTER 11

Violet Harcourt

1940

"So, how'd it go?" Harry raised an eyebrow, his Oldsmobile cruising down Hollywood Boulevard.

I touched my fingers to the window glass, looking at the drugstores, ice cream parlors, boutiques and shops: Kress's, Newberry's, J.C. Penney and Woolworth's. There were furriers, florists, jewelry stores, hatmakers, perfume stores, dressmakers and salons dotting the length of the strip. If I didn't land a part soon, people would begin to notice I only had one dress. And judging by how terribly today's audition went, I didn't have much time to prove myself before I'd no longer be a fresh face in Hollywood.

"Not well. I'm afraid I let my nerves get to me."

Harry turned right, pulling into the parking lot of the

Pink Flamingo Motel. "Sorry to hear that. Did I tell ya I got a meeting with the bigwig agent?"

"You did? Oh Harry, that's swell."

"We're having dinner at Musso & Frank's tonight. Apparently it's the hangout of writers and playwrights—newspaper people, those types. This agent says they serve a good steak, and he wants to hear my stand-up shtick."

I smiled, genuinely happy for Harry. "I'm sure you'll tell wonderful jokes in such good company."

"Thanks," he said, wiping his brow. "Whew! This Los Angeles heat is something else, ain't it? Say—you oughta call your fella. Surely he'll want to know you arrived safely, and I don't want him hunting me down with a shotgun."

I laughed nervously. "He would never."

Strolling through the lobby, my eyes darted to the young woman behind the desk. She flipped through the pages of her magazine, engrossed in the photographs.

"Excuse me," Harry said, dinging the bell rather obnoxiously.

She looked up, her smile bright as a toothpaste advertisement. Now, *this girl* could be in the pictures. Was everyone in Hollywood so beautiful?

"How can I help you?"

"My friend here would like to use the telephone."

"Thank you," I said, looking at Harry. "Why don't you head on up to the room and I'll meet you in a minute?"

"I don't mind waiting."

Rats!

"What's the number?" the girl asked.

I glanced at the cover of her magazine, *Screen Secrets.*

Grinning conspiratorially, I leaned over the counter. “Please, allow me. I’d hate to keep you from the latest Hollywood gossip. You can give me the scoop later.”

She winked, pushing the rotary phone toward me. “Thanks a million. I’m trying to figure out the latest blind item. I think Bette Davis has a new beau.”

Watching Harry from the corner of my eye, I bit my bottom lip. *What number to dial?* I couldn’t risk calling Charles. But I couldn’t very well call Mother either. Those were the only two numbers I knew by heart.

Feeling Harry’s eyes on my back, I began to sweat. Without knowing what else to do, I placed my finger in the zero of the dial and rotated it all the way around to the right.

“Operator. How can I connect you?”

“Charles! Hello, darling, how are you?”

“Ma’am,” the operator said dryly. “You need to tell me the number you’d like me to connect you to.”

I laughed, turning toward Harry. “Thank you for asking. Everything is going just swell. We’ve arrived safely and Harry has a meeting with a Hollywood agent tomorrow. Isn’t that exciting? I’m afraid my own screen test didn’t go as well.”

“I don’t know what kind of pickle you’re in,” the girl hissed, “but I’m going to disconnect you now.”

“Thank you,” I said, a lump rising in my throat. “I *will* keep trying. Just like you said, I’ll knock ’em dead at the next audition. I love you too. Goodbye.”

Harry's face softened, seeing the shine of my eyes. "Aw shucks. It's only been a day. You miss him already?"

I nodded, blinking back tears. I hadn't realized what speaking to an imaginary Charles would do to me. Suddenly, I felt icy cold, imagining Charles reading my note and then smashing everything in our home. I shuddered.

Harry patted my back. "I'm taking another dip in the pool. I'm sweating like a pig. Want me to wait for you?"

I waved him away. "Go ahead."

After Harry disappeared, I turned to the receptionist.

"Can you please dial the Tropicana for me? I need to reach a guest in room one-thirteen."

"Sure thing," she said, setting aside her magazine.

I exhaled, watching Harry through the sliding glass door. I couldn't keep up my charade with him, or he'd catch on soon enough. But Roxy didn't know I was married. And I intended to make sure she wouldn't find out.

"THANK YOU SO much for meeting me," I said, following Roxy toward the Brown Derby, a popular restaurant on Wilshire Boulevard. EAT IN THE HAT! a sign atop the bowler-shaped restaurant boasted.

"It's no trouble at all," Roxy said, puffing out a ring of cigarette smoke. Her crimson nails glinted in the sunlight as she took another drag.

I eyed the shabbily dressed men leaning against the walls of the restaurant, tattered photographs in hand.

"Who are they?" I whispered.

"Gawkers," Roxy said, wrinkling her nose. "They can't

afford a meal, so they hang around the entrance, asking for autographs. Plenty of stars dine here."

My eyes lit up. "They do?"

"Sure," Roxy said, tossing her brassy blond curls. "Across the street is the Ambassador Hotel. The stars go dancing at the nightclub there, the Cocoanut Grove, and then come here for late-night bites."

As we stepped inside the restaurant, the scent of gravy and fried chicken hit me so strong it nearly bowled me over. Had I always possessed such a keen sense of smell? We made our way to a leather booth, and I admired the hundreds of celebrity drawings, paintings and caricatures hanging on the wall.

A waitress approached, handing us two menus. I looked mine over, but Roxy pulled it out of my hands.

"You wanna order the Cobb salad. Trust me."

"I do?"

"It's new. You'll love it."

I looked around the restaurant, drinking in the scene. Smartly dressed men and women shared plates of food, talking casually in the booths.

Roxy grabbed my hand, startling me. "Don't look now, but that's Louella Parsons over there."

"Who?" I asked, craning my neck.

"I told you not to look! She's a gossip columnist. She writes the blind items in *Screen Secrets*."

"Is that so?"

Roxy sipped her coffee, then set it down. "Louella always asks to be seated over there by the bar. You see these vaulted ceilings? The sound carries across the room. She knows where to sit so she can eavesdrop on private conversations."

I leaned over the table. "Do you think there are any celebrities dining here now? That man over there looks a bit like Charlie Chaplin."

Roxy chuckled. "Not him. You'll learn to recognize who's who. Sometimes they look different off screen." She stared at me, her blue eyes tough as steel. "Tell me straight. Who's this fella you're traveling with? Is he your beau or a meal ticket?"

My cheeks burned. "Harry? No. He's a friend. He drove me here from Santa Cruz. We took the Pacific Coast Highway. Thankfully the traffic wasn't awful."

Roxy smiled wryly. "Sheesh, I came all the way from Kansas."

"That's quite a distance," I said, relieved she didn't press me any further about Harry. "Do you stay in touch with family there?"

Roxy's eyes had a faraway look. "No, doll. They aren't very nice folks, to tell the truth. I don't ever want to see that dusty hellhole again."

"I'm sorry," I said, taken aback by her harsh language.

Roxy winked at me, her smile returning. "It's all right. Everyone has a past. I was once a sad little brunette named Mary Ellen Pigford. Is Violet your real name?"

"It is."

"And your hair, is it natural?"

"Yes." I laughed. "Do you think I ought to keep it?"

"The auburn suits you. Not too many redheads here in Hollywood. As for your name, keep it until you get a new nickname. Everyone around Tinseltown has one."

"What's yours?"

Roxy frowned. "The Mouth. I can't get rid of it. Unfortunately I have a habit of speaking my mind, even when it gets me in trouble."

I giggled. Then I spotted a postcard stand near the register. I dug in my purse for a nickel. Ricky ought to know I'd made it here safely, and he'd appreciate the postcard.

"Excuse me for a minute. I'm going to purchase one of those."

Roxy raised an eyebrow. "For a beau back home?"

"No. Just a friend."

She pursed her lips. "An awful lot of friends you have. Don't worry, I don't judge."

My cheeks burned. "It's not what it looks like. Actually, I need a place of my own. Are there any open rooms at the Tropicana?"

Roxy's eyes twinkled as she pulled out another cigarette. "You can stay with me. With the money we'd save on rent, think of the shopping we could do. If I could buy a dress from Betty Blanc's, that might be the ticket to landing a lead role."

"Oh, you're too kind," I said, my stomach fluttering. "But I hardly know you. I wouldn't want to put you out."

"You wouldn't," Roxy said, lighting her cigarette. "Get your postcard and think about it."

I PULLED MY cardigan more tightly around my shoulders as I followed Roxy down Hollywood Boulevard. The street had taken on a different character in the evening light, losing its luster as the sun dipped behind the Hollywood Hills.

Vagrants dug through garbage bins, looking for cans of food. Shady men in oversize suits whistled at us as we passed. Girls in dark lipstick eyed us warily, hiding in the shadows in fishnet stockings and tight dresses.

"Are those working girls?" I whispered, my eyes darting behind us.

Roxy shrugged. "Could be. Or perhaps they're chorus girls, out for a night on the town. You'll see everyone from directors to panhandlers on the boulevard here. Pimps and playwrights, kooks and weirdos, Hollywood has it all."

I dodged a man dressed as a walking billboard, wearing a large sign advertising a play over his dirty clothing. Passing yet another dingy storefront with a CHURCH sign in the window, I turned to Roxy. "Are people very religious here?"

She laughed. "You're a hoot! Those are fortune-tellers. They put the church signs up so they don't get in trouble with the cops. They've got crystal balls and tea leaves—you name it. So many poor schmucks have lost their life savings and their dreams, they flock to these dives praying that their luck will turn around."

"I see," I said, an uneasy feeling creeping up my spine.

"Boulevard of Broken Dreams," Roxy said. "That's what some call it."

I stood up straighter. My drive to make something of myself couldn't be squashed so easily. Perhaps I'd ask Harry to introduce me to his agent, or I'd find my own.

"Do you have an agent?" I asked Roxy.

She shook her head. "I got conned once, when I first arrived."

Roxy pointed to the offices above the shops lining the street. "You see up there? Plenty of shady characters rent the second-story offices on Hollywood Boulevard, pretending to be agents and movie producers. They'll take your cash and you'll never hear from 'em again."

"That's awful," I said, trying to glimpse one of these con men through the blinds. Good thing Roxy had told me as much, or perhaps I also would have been played for a fool. "How do you know which agents are reputable?"

"The bigwigs are in the Taft Building," Roxy said, cupping her hand as she lit a cigarette. "Powerful movie agents, talent agencies. I'd kill to get signed."

"Are there lawyers in that building too?"

"Sure," Roxy said, raising an eyebrow. "Why do you ask?"

"No reason," I said, trying to keep my voice casual.

Roxy winked. "You're not fooling me. Can't blame a gal for wanting to catch one. They sure earn good dough."

Notes of jazz music drifted onto the street, and I smiled, snapping my fingers in time to the melody. "This band is fantastic! Where is the music coming from?"

"The Blue Lagoon," Roxy said. "I have a friend who works there. Great blues singers perform at all the bars here on Hollywood Boulevard. You like jazz?"

"I love it, but my hu— I mean, former beau, hated it, so I couldn't play my Duke Ellington records at home. He wouldn't allow it."

I bit my lip to stop myself.

"Unmarried and living in sin?" Roxy smiled at me. "I didn't take you for the bohemian type. He sounds like a schmuck. Good thing you left."

I looked down at my shoes. Roxy thought I was some kind of loose girl, which couldn't be further from the truth. But I didn't dare tell her about Charles.

We stopped in front of a palatial white building with a neon sign and palm trees out front, the Florentine Gardens. "This club looks nice. Have you been?"

"Used to work there," Roxy said, stubbing out her cigarette. "But dancing in the nude gets tiring, you know?"

I gasped. "In the nude?"

Roxy laughed. "Don't look so surprised. A girl's got to eat."

"But it looks so upscale."

Roxy shrugged. "They've got a twelve-piece orchestra and the largest spring dance floor in the West. The rooms are done up like you're in ancient Italy. Men are all the same, no matter how much dough they earn. Even when they're sipping fine wine at an expensive dinner, they just wanna see some tits."

Crossing the street, Roxy beckoned me to follow her. "This way, we're almost there."

Turning down a side street, a green neon sign came into view, written in graceful cursive: "Tropical Gardens Nightclub."

Tucked in between a pharmacy and a tailor, the club didn't appear too dodgy. I breathed a sigh of relief. Passing beneath the green awning and through the doors of the building, I thought it looked almost like a chic Parisian café.

My jaw dropped as we entered. Palm trees stretched upward, touching the high ceilings, and colorful scarves draped from the carved wooden balcony. Round tables set with white tablecloths clustered around the stage. Green leather stools encircled a black marble bar, where a bartender poured cocktails garnished with little paper umbrellas. I removed my cardigan in the heat of the room, dazzled by the jazz band performing onstage. Men and women danced to the music, dressed to the nines.

"This place is neat!" I called over the noise.

Roxy smiled. "It ain't the Cocoanut Grove, but we do get some celebrities. Follow me. I'll introduce you to the manager."

I felt a wave of nausea in the heat of the room, and feared for a moment that I would vomit. Perhaps it was only my nerves—being in an unfamiliar place. Weaving through the crowd, we worked our way toward a back room. In the dimly lit hallway, the glamorous tropical feel of the nightclub disappeared. Roxy pushed aside a shabby curtain to reveal a dressing room with wall-to-wall mirrors. A few sequined outfits had been flung haphazardly over chairs, and scuffed pairs of heels touched the wall.

Roxy walked toward a door next to a costume rack and rapped it with her knuckles. "Tommy? You here?"

The door swung open and an Italian in a fitted pinstriped suit pulled it open. His black hair was slick with pomade, and his brown eyes appraised me. I felt myself blush at the directness of his gaze. He was dark and handsome—perhaps in his late thirties, but the way he held himself felt powerful and intimidating.

"Who's this?" he asked.

Roxy touched his arm. "This is Violet Sweeting, fresh off the bus."

The man extended his hand, wrapping it around mine in a grip that felt overly familiar. My toes tingled. No man had touched me since Charles.

"Tommy Ciccone. I own this joint. What can I do for ya?"

"Um, I heard you need a new nightclub singer. I sing, you see . . . perhaps I could perform for you sometime?"

Tommy laughed. "You and every girl in town want the same thing." He looked me up and down. "You got a pretty face and the rest of you ain't half bad. But if you want to work here, you start at the bottom. Then maybe I'll put you onstage."

"Oh," I said, my shoulders drooping. "I see."

Tommy turned to Roxy. "Does your friend here think she's too good to be a cigarette girl? I ain't got time for snobs."

"I don't think I'm too good. I used to work as a waitress. Please give me a chance. I'll sell all the Chesterfields you have."

"Excellent." Tommy grinned like a fox. A little twinge in my gut told me that perhaps I shouldn't trust him. "Roxy will show you where the uniforms are. And remember, the bigger your smile, the bigger your tips."

"Right," I said, smiling at him, though I felt uneasy.

After Tommy shut the door, Roxy nudged me toward the costume rack. "Here's what we wear. What size are you?"

I gawped as she lifted a strapless black number from the hanger, no bigger than a negligee. "That's the uniform?"

Roxy nodded. "Along with a pair of fishnets and garters. Don't act so prissy. Didn't you wear a bathing suit in your pageant?"

"I did," I said, looking at the short ruffled skirt. *But I wasn't standing within arm's reach of strange men.* "Give me a size small."

As I struggled to zip the uniform, I huffed in frustration. *Drat!* Was the sizing different here, to make ladies feel inadequate? I needed to lose a few pounds to fit in with this crowd. At least my weight gain had also gone to my breasts. They swelled nicely from my brassiere in a way I hadn't noticed before.

After zipping myself into a size medium and putting on a swipe of red lipstick, I gazed at my reflection in the mirror.

"A knockout," Roxy said, slapping me playfully on the bottom. "Flirt with the fellas for all the dough they're worth. The tips will add up."

But I hadn't come to Hollywood to sell cigarettes. I took a deep breath and put on my pageant smile. *Pretend it's an acting gig.* This would only be temporary. If I played my cards right, I might catch the eye of someone important in the crowd tonight.

CHAPTER 12

Marisol Cruz

2007

Mari walked the path through the redwoods from McHenry Library, emerging into the sunlight near the Bay Tree Bookstore. A crowd of students had gathered around a makeshift podium in the courtyard, listening to a presentation. There appeared to be a job fair going on, with booths sct up outside beneath blue tents.

Shielding her eyes from the sun, Mari peered up the hill to see if a shuttle was approaching. The speaker's voice carried on the breeze.

"And that's how you can become successful like me. Hustle hard, dream big, and work every day toward your goal. Don't take no for an answer."

Clenching her teeth, Mari recognized the speaker. Travis Harcourt stood at the podium in a pair of gray slacks and a polo shirt, his stage smile smug as ever.

"You know, I hate to say it, but that guy sounds like a douchebag."

Mari turned around, startled to see Jason standing behind her.

"Where did you come from?"

"I walked over from Kresge College, where my office is. I was about to grab some lunch. What are *you* doing here?"

"I went to McHenry Library for research," she said, her eyes homing in on Travis. The heat of anger began to creep up her neck. *"Hypocrite,"* she muttered.

"Do you know him?" Jason asked.

Mari nodded. "He was in my graduating class. He's the son of the mayor. Everything he's ever wanted has been handed to him. How can he talk about the value of 'hustling hard' when he's a trust fund kid?"

Jason smiled, running a hand through his messy brown hair. "This proves I have a good people radar. I knew he was a total bro from the second I heard him speak." His eyes twinkled. "And I knew *you* were cool the moment I met you at the diner."

Mari laughed. "You're a good judge of character. Not only is he a total *bro,* but he's also tearing down the gazebo to build luxury condos."

"So that's what privilege looks like," Jason said, looking Travis up and down. "Check out his shiny leather loafers. Who wears those on campus?"

Mari eyed Jason's old-school tennis shoes, poking out from beneath his black pants. He had on a T-shirt with some kind of graphic design, and a hooded sweatshirt. Not exactly work attire—though computer programmers were notoriously casual. His sense of style didn't seem to have evolved since the grunge era, but she found it endearing that he still dressed like the skater boys she used to crush on.

"About the gazebo," Jason said. "Are you applying for the grant I told you about?"

"I am. But that doesn't mean I'll get it."

"You will. You have more passion than most girls." His cheeks colored. "I mean more conviction . . . You know what I mean. Girls in my hometown don't want to be anything more than housewives."

"That would bore me to tears," Mari said, noticing how cute he was when he blushed. "And who says I'm not passionate? I'm Latina, I can't help it."

"Shut up," Jason said, smiling.

As the shuttle pulled into the bus stop, Mari's stomach sank. To her surprise, she didn't want her conversation with Jason to end.

"Well, this is my bus. It was nice running into you."

"You still have my number?"

"I threw it out," Mari deadpanned.

Jason looked like he'd been punched in the stomach.

"I'm kidding! Let's get lunch sometime. I know all the good spots on campus."

His smile returned. "I'd love that. Next time we hang out, you'll be the Swanson Grant recipient."

Mari rolled her eyes. "Don't hold your breath." But when the shuttle doors shut behind her, she smiled. Had she just offered to get lunch with a guy, like it was no big deal? As the bus traveled down the hill, Mari watched the sun sparkle on the Pacific and let hope balloon in her chest. She had a chance of winning that grant money and making something of herself. And she looked forward to seeing Jason again.

THE OCEAN BREEZE cooled Mari's skin, ruffling the hem of her yellow sundress. Tonight was one of those warm summer nights in which magic seemed to permeate the air. Was it because she was developing a crush on someone? She smiled to herself. It'd been a long time since she'd had this feeling. The neon lights of the boardwalk rides illuminated the twilight, and shrieks of delight carried from the Giant Dipper roller coaster.

A young couple approached her booth, arm in tattooed arm. The girl wore a swipe of red lipstick, her hair done up in a 1940s style popular with rockabillies.

"I like your dress," Mari said.

"Thanks," she answered, holding out the hem of her blue, polka-dot frock. "I got it at the vintage shop over on Pacific Avenue."

"We'd like to buy some raffle tickets," the guy said, his hair close-cropped at the sides and slick with pomade. Aside from the tattoos, these two could be straight out of Mari's grandmother's era.

"Sure, they're ten dollars each. How many?"

"Let's get three."

As Mari ripped three raffle tickets from her wheel, the girl pointed at the Giant Dipper. "Do you know how old that thing is?"

"It opened on May 17, 1924, so it's eighty years old. It's the only wooden roller coaster on the West Coast that's still the centerpiece of an amusement park."

"This place is awesome," the guy said, handing Mari a twenty-dollar bill and a ten. "We grew up in Michigan, and we don't have anything like this back home. But we love living in Santa Cruz. We got married here, on the beach."

"At the gazebo?" Mari blurted.

The girl gave her a funny look. "It's kind of decrepit, I didn't think it would look great in photographs." She pointed in the opposite direction, toward the pier. "We got married there, at the Carousel Beach Inn."

"Oh," Mari said, hiding her disappointment. "That's a nice hotel."

Watching the couple walk away, she checked the time on her phone. Her mom was supposed to drop Lily off at seven, so they could get the funnel cake she'd promised. But first the raffle winners would be announced.

Mayor Harcourt took the stage, and Mari clapped half-heartedly. He smiled and waved at the crowd, his thick mustache and round belly lending him a friendly appearance, like the uncle who made everyone laugh at family parties.

He took the microphone in his hand. "Hello, Santa

Cruz locals and visitors! It's wonderful to see you all tonight."

The applause grew louder, and people gathered around the stage, some carrying tots on their shoulders who happily licked ice cream cones.

"There are a number of special events planned to help celebrate the hundredth summer of the Santa Cruz Beach Boardwalk. Don't miss the gymnasts from the Moscow Circus, who'll put on a free performance tomorrow night here at the beach bandstand."

He paused, looking at Mari. "And if you haven't already, please stop by the Santa Cruz Museum of Art & History booth, which is displaying artifacts from the Beach Boardwalk archives that are rarely seen outside the museum."

Mari felt her neck flush with so many pairs of eyes turned toward her, but she smiled and waved at the crowd of onlookers.

The mayor continued, "And at ten o'clock tonight, we'll be screening one of the most popular movies ever filmed at the boardwalk. *The Lost Boys*. Whoo, vampires! Spooky."

The crowd laughed, and Mari couldn't help herself from smiling. The mayor, with his goofy dad humor, was so different from his son, Travis.

"Before I announce the raffle winners," the mayor said, strolling across the stage, "I'd like to say how proud I am to call this city home. My father, Charles Harcourt, established roots here with the Oceano Golf Club, but he was also a man of the people, committed to helping our community. Like many, he made personal sacrifices for the betterment of his family. He sold the club and donated the proceeds to charity."

Mari scoffed. *Sacrifices? He didn't even serve in the war!* She looked longingly at the gazebo, a pale specter against the deep blue ocean. The rush of the waves drowned out the mayor's voice. In her mind, jazz music played and Abuelo spun Abuela around the dance floor, a white flower tucked behind her grandmother's ear.

Raffle numbers were being called out vaguely in the distance while Mari continued to watch her grandparents dancing. Her throat tightened.

"You must be the young woman in charge of the museum booth."

Mari's mouth fell open, startled to see the mayor standing in front of her. Lost in her daydream, she hadn't realized he'd finished speaking.

"Yes," she said, putting on a bright smile, though she hadn't forgiven him for the construction project he'd approved. "Mari Cruz. It's a pleasure to meet you."

He shook her hand heartily. "Mayor Harcourt, but you can call me Tom. I wanted to personally congratulate you on how many raffle tickets you've sold. I've heard it's a town record!"

"Thank you," Mari said. While his kindness seemed genuine, he was likely working in his own best interests as a politician. "I listened to your speech," she said, her heart beating faster, "about your father selling the Oceano and donating the proceeds to charity. What charity was that?"

"The American Friends Service Committee," Mayor Harcourt replied. "It's a U.S.-based Quaker aid society, which was instrumental in providing relief services in Germany and later throughout Europe during World War Two."

Mari's jaw fell open. "The one that helped evacuate Jewish children from Europe and bring them to America?"

"That's right." His eyes twinkled with pride.

Mari bit the inside of her cheek. Perhaps she had the wrong idea about Charles?

"Mom!" Lily skipped toward Mari, Paulina trailing behind her. "Are you finished yet? I want funnel cake! Can we go on the rides?"

Mari wrapped an arm around her daughter's shoulder, holding her tight. "In a minute, sweetheart. Go back to Abuela."

"Well, hello there," Mayor Harcourt said, bending down to eye level with Lily. "What's your name?"

"Lily," she said, sticking out her chest. "I'm four. I go to preschool and my favorite animal is a horse. What's your favorite animal?"

"Lily, that's enough," Mari said. "Give the mayor some space."

He studied her daughter. Slowly his smile faded.

"Ma," Mari said, turning to her mother. "Can you take Lily over to the funnel cake stand? I'll meet you there in a minute."

Paulina guided Lily by the shoulders, her eyes meeting Mari's with a look of concern. "Of course, *mija*."

"Bye!" Lily shouted at the mayor. "It was nice to meet you!"

"You too," he said, recovering his genial smile. "My favorite animal is a tiger."

"Cool!" Lily called as she skipped away.

Mari watched Mayor Harcourt as his eyes followed her daughter. Her stomach knotted as she saw the speculative look on his face. She hoped his confusion would pass, washing away like footprints in the sand.

CHAPTER 13

Violet Harcourt

1940

As I followed Roxy down Hollywood Boulevard, I stopped to stare at Grauman's Chinese Theatre. The stunning Oriental architecture was so different from anything I'd seen in Santa Cruz. Bleachers had been set up around the entrance and had already begun to fill with people, though it was only ten in the morning. Now that I noticed, cars were parked for blocks, and tourists lined the street.

"Is there a movie premiere tonight?"

Roxy nodded, pointing to a woman with a picnic basket. "Sure is. You see her? That's how you come prepared. And if you're really smart, you bring blankets and pillows for when it gets chilly after the sun goes down."

"Have you been to one?"

"A premiere? Of course."

"Oh, I would die! Can you tell me about it?"

Roxy laughed, and then paused to light a cigarette. "For *The Wizard of Oz* there were people standing on rooftops, craning their necks for a glimpse of the stars. Then Judy Garland arrived, stepping out of a limo in a fabulous gown. There were fresh flowers everywhere, so the air smelled like roses. The radio announcers called out celebrity names, and the paparazzi captured it all with exploding flashbulbs."

I closed my eyes, lost in Roxy's description. Then I opened them, determined to experience a movie premiere too. "How magnificent it sounds."

"Oh rats," Roxy said, stubbing out her cigarette. "That's our streetcar."

I followed her as we boarded the yellow bus, then dropped a nickel into the turnstile and found a vacant seat. My heart dipped into my stomach as I thought about Charles. *Was he searching for me? Was he heartbroken?*

I also wondered if Evie had heard that I'd departed for Hollywood. I'd lied to her, and I felt wretched about it. I ought to have told her of my plans to divorce Charles, but it had felt too dangerous to confide in my friend. Sending a letter with my return address at the Tropicana would be too risky. Yet I longed to write to Evie, to tell her of my adventures in Hollywood. And had Ricky received my postcard by now?

I'd accepted Roxy's offer, telling Harry I'd made a friend at the audition, and that we'd be rooming together. Harry wished me the best of luck, no questions asked. My palms began to sweat as I pictured my husband's face, contorted with rage when he woke to an empty bed. But my heart ached. *Did he miss me? Could he change?*

I shivered, dispelling the thought. What was done was done. I would find a lawyer this week. I would file the divorce papers as soon as possible.

Roxy pulled the chain, and the streetcar stopped on Sunset Boulevard. The California sunshine drenched the sidewalks as if they were made of gold. I pushed Charles to the back of my mind. By golly, this was Beverly Hills!

"Oh my word," I said, glimpsing what looked like a pink palace across acres of lush grounds. "Is that where we're going?"

Roxy winked. "The Beverly Hills Hotel and Bungalows. It's where the crème de la crème of society meet."

My heels clicked against the pavement as I followed Roxy down the palm-lined footpath, trying to keep my mouth from gaping. The scent of exotic flowers filled the air. They burst from the bushes in blooms of pink and yellow. I recognized hibiscus and birds of paradise. How lovely.

When we stepped inside the hotel, I longed to twirl in circles beneath the crystal chandelier like a dancer in a film. The pink-and-mint-striped décor was opulent, yet beautifully tasteful. Watching women in dark sunglasses and stylish dresses, I wondered if they were heiresses, or perhaps starlets. I wanted to pinch myself, because it felt so much like a dream. I'd been to beautiful hotels before, but always with Charles, which meant I'd been walking on eggshells, terrified of making the wrong move. Now I was finally free to be myself.

"This way," Roxy said, swaying her hips as we walked toward the pool and cabanas. "We're meeting a friend of mine."

The rectangular pool shone beneath the perfect blue sky, and the sun warmed the terra-cotta rooftop. Last night, I'd discovered Roxy's room to be cramped, dingy and smoke filled. She'd pushed her dresses to the side of the wardrobe to make room for my things, but the gesture did little to make up for the lack of space. The Tropicana with its faded carpet and battered blinds looked like a mouse hole compared to this grand hotel.

"Who's your friend?" I asked, trying not to stare at the tanned women wearing two-piece swimsuits and pearls. *Was that Greta Garbo?*

"He's a screenwriter," Roxy said, adjusting the white scarf tied jauntily around her neck. It perfectly complemented her curve-hugging pencil skirt. She'd let me borrow a blue sundress, which brought out the deep blue of my eyes. I'd lamented that my trunk had been stolen at a gas station, to explain why I had hardly any clothing.

Roxy led me toward the pink-and-white curtains of a poolside cabana. "Benny Bronstein. He works for one of the Big Five studios and makes lotsa dough."

"Which studio?"

"MGM or RKO," Roxy said, lighting a cigarette. "I can't recall. You can ask him yourself." She grinned. "Here we are."

I peeked inside the cabana and gawped at the interior, the walls painted with palm fronds, and the pink couches lining the walls probably worth a fortune. A round mirror hung on the wall, adding a bit of Deco glamour to the white wicker furniture. Even the cabana was nicer than our motel room at the Tropicana.

A boyish man stood up from the couch, dressed in crisp white shorts and a polo shirt. His deep tan highlighted his blue eyes, and his thick curly hair looked as if it wished to defy the pomade he'd used to tame it.

"Roxy," he said, kissing her on the cheek. "You made it." He turned his gaze to me, his smile bright and inviting. "And who is this gorgeous thing?"

My cheeks flushed.

"Violet," I said, extending my hand. "Pleasure to—oh!" Without warning he pulled me in for a kiss on the cheek, as if we were already familiar with one another.

He laughed. "Don't be shy, doll! We're all friends here. Sit down. What can I get ya to drink? They make a killer mint julep here."

"I'll have a Pink Lady," Roxy said.

"And you?" Benny asked, smiling at me.

"I'll have what she's having."

Sitting on the plush couch next to Roxy, I drank in the scene as a Negro waiter in a smart blue uniform took our orders. While Benny and Roxy treated him like hired help, I smiled with genuine gratitude.

I'd been served at the Oceano many times, and I aimed to treat each employee as I would a friend, no matter his or her background. Charles didn't like the amiable relationships I had with the cooks and waiters, many of whom were Mexican. Oftentimes, I wandered into the kitchen to return a glass or to drop the used napkins in the laundry. He found it horribly improper and had reprimanded me with the back of his hand. Often, he accused me of flirting with the staff, which was never the case.

"Violet, Benny asked you a question."

"Oh," I said. "I apologize. I don't know where my head is today. What did you ask?"

He smiled. "Roxy tells me you're new in town. Where are you from?"

"Santa Cruz."

"So you're a *real* California girl."

"She was a beauty queen," Roxy said. "Now she wants to be in the movies."

I smiled at Benny. "Roxy tells me you're a screenwriter for one of the big studios. That sounds awfully exciting."

Benny laughed, clapping Roxy on the back. "I'm afraid she's misled you. I work for one of the little three, not the Big Five. I write for Universal Pictures."

"Not RKO?" Roxy asked, pouting at him. "Say, what kinda films does Universal produce?"

"Horror," Benny said, lighting a cigarette for himself, and then lighting one for Roxy. "*Frankenstein, Dracula*. You smoke?"

I shook my head.

He smiled at me, putting his lighter away. "It's not my cup of tea, but it's a starting point. Every studio has its genre. MGM does the lavish and star-studded films like *Gone with the Wind*. Warner Brothers has their gangster films like *Little Caesar*, and Fox does historical adventure—*Sherlock Holmes* and all that jazz."

A cool breeze ruffled the hem of my dress, and the waiter arrived with our drinks. I took a sip of my Pink Lady, the grenadine tart and delicious, and the gin packing a punch. The sun sparkled on the surface of the swimming pool, and I let the alcohol pleasantly soften the edges of my surroundings.

Benny leaned toward me conspiratorially. "Roxy's a good friend of mine, and that's why I'll give you two gals the scoop. John Huston has a new script, and his movie is supposed to be the next big thing. The casting call is this Saturday. It's called *The Maltese Falcon*. A noir detective film."

"After Dashiell Hammett's novel?"

"You've read it?"

I nodded. "I enjoy all types of fiction."

"Beauty and brains," Benny said, blowing smoke from his cigarette. "Have a drink with me tonight at Don the Beachcomber and I'll invite you to a shindig at Ernst Lubitsch's hacienda tomorrow night. He's a respected director at MGM. I can introduce you."

My stomach knotted. I wore no wedding ring. What if I'd given Benny the wrong impression? Yet I couldn't think of a reason to refuse his invitation.

"Oh well, tonight I—"

"She'll join you," Roxy said, slurping the remainder of

her Pink Lady through a straw. "And I'll take another one of these. Say, what a gorgeous day it is!"

I tried to ignore the feel of Benny's eyes on my bare legs as Roxy ordered me another Pink Lady. This could be my big break. Considering the grand hotel he lived in and the people he knew, Benny Bronstein was well connected. Perhaps he already had a gal, and this was simply a friendly gesture? I had to take the chance.

STEPPING OUT OF the taxicab onto Hollywood Boulevard, I looked up at the mysterious restaurant shrouded by palm fronds. A wooden sign hanging above the door clearly marked the building as Don the Beachcomber.

Setting foot inside, I felt the humid warmth that filled the room. I studied the thatched ceiling, and the glass fishing floats in nets draped from the rafters. Everything was made of wicker and wood, the entire place like something out of the South Pacific. Laughter traveled across the tables as men and women sipped drinks together.

I spotted Benny at a corner table. He smiled and waved me over. My shoulders relaxed as I took in the casual atmosphere of the restaurant. It was a bit too raucous to be romantic. This was a business meeting, nothing more.

"You made it," Benny said, standing up to kiss me on the cheek.

I tried not to flinch. Charles always admonished me for speaking to other men. He'd demanded I quit working as a waitress at Mary's Chicken Shack because he couldn't stand the thought of me talking to male customers.

"Thank you," I said, as Benny pulled out a chair for me.

"What can I get you?" he asked, handing me a drinks menu of tropical concoctions with bizarre names.

"I'm not sure," I answered, looking it over. "What's good here?"

"The Zombie. But watch out, it packs a punch."

Benny smiled, his arms tanned beneath his tropical shirt. He couldn't be a few years older than twenty. Yet he appeared so self-assured, like he had the confidence of a much older man. "Tell me about yourself. You got a fella at home?"

My mouth felt dry as cotton. "Oh, there's not much to tell. No, I don't have a beau at home." The lie churned my stomach as I pictured Charles.

"Good," Benny said, winking.

The waiter arrived with our drinks, and I couldn't help pulling a face as I took a sip. "My goodness!"

Benny laughed. "Told you it was strong." He took a sip, and then paused. "Have you always wanted to be an actress?"

I nodded. "I starred in a few stage productions in Santa Cruz. I love theater. In high school I couldn't get enough of it."

"If you want to see good theater, there's the Hollywood Playhouse. It's mostly older vaudeville stars, but for some who work there, it gives them a career boost."

Once again, the queasy feeling began to agitate me. Perhaps this drink was too strong. Taking a deep breath, I tried to dispel the nausea. "I saw so many theaters downtown, I wouldn't know where to start."

Benny smiled. "The Iris and Vogue theaters are the favorites for studio previews. There's also the Roxy. I'm sure you've seen Grauman's—that's for first-run showings, where you'll find the stars. Then you've got the Tele-View Theater. You can watch newsreels there. An hour of current news is twenty-five cents. It used to be called the Hitching Post and show Saturday matinee westerns."

His face grew serious. "What do you think of the war in Europe?"

"Oh, I—"

Charles berated me, told me I knew nothing of politics. But Benny waited for my answer.

"To be honest, I'm frightened. I feel there's a very dark cloud on the horizon and it's coming toward us. I fret for the people of England, constantly under siege by bombs." A lump rose in my throat.

Benny reached out his hand and covered mine. I sharply drew in my breath.

"It *is* frightening. You're absolutely right. There's a storm gathering in Europe and it's going to have a direct effect on Hollywood. Some of our best filmmakers are concerned that soon we'll be making nothing but propaganda films."

"Do you think America will join the war?" I asked, slowly pulling my hand away. My eyes darted about the restaurant, fearful that someone may have noticed us touching. But everyone appeared engrossed in conversation.

Benny nodded gravely. "I do. And if it happens, our best

actors and Hollywood stars will likely join the war effort. And what then? The talent pool will be depleted."

I shook my head. "The movie palaces are such a needed escape for the American people. If we don't have laughter, then what do we have?"

Benny smiled at me. "You're a smart cookie. You know that? Humor is absolutely essential when fighting a dictatorship. Look at the Charlie Chaplin film lampooning the Third Reich. Have you seen it?"

"I haven't," I said, slowly taking another sip of my drink. "Is it funny?"

"You haven't seen *The Great Dictator*? It's a hoot!" His blue eyes fixed on mine. "If it shows again, I'll bring you along. Roxy can come too. Well, she may talk through the whole thing. But I'd like to hear what you think of it."

I giggled. Talking with Benny felt nice, as though he were truly listening to me. How many times had I cautiously brought up a topic of concern with Charles, only for him to flip it around so that I became the problem? Whenever I tried to assert my opinion, Charles told me I was ridiculous and overreacting. Or he'd simply leave the house, like the morning of the bacon grease incident.

Benny looked at me. "It's a tragedy what's happening in Europe. But it's for our gain in Hollywood. Do you know how many German artists and intellectuals have immigrated here since the outbreak of the war? The Nazis have driven out the best talent. Ernst Lubitsch, Hedy Lamarr, Salka Viertel, Billy Wilder—I could go on and on."

I didn't recognize all the names, but I smiled. "Hedy Lamarr is so beautiful. There's not another face in the world like hers."

Benny winked at me. "Yours ain't bad either. I think Ernst Lubitsch will take a shine to you. And you'll like him. Hell, he got Garbo to smile."

I chuckled. *Ninotchka* had been promoted with the tagline "Garbo laughs!", commenting on the departure from Greta Garbo's serious roles. I'd found the film quite funny, and enjoyed its subtle criticism of the Soviet Union.

My stomach fluttered as I imagined shaking hands with the famous and sophisticated Hollywood director. From what I'd heard, films that received the "Lubitsch touch" made them all the more prestigious. But my butterflies scattered when an image of Charles popped unbidden into my mind.

"Say." I carefully met Benny's eyes. "Do you have any lawyer friends? I have a matter I'd like to discuss in private."

Benny raised an eyebrow. "Well, that sounds rather intriguing. You're not in some kind of trouble, are you?"

I put on my pageant smile. "Not at all. I've received an inheritance from my late grandmother, but my cousin feels she's entitled to a larger share than I am."

Benny laughed. It shocked me how easily lies came to me now—as if a little creativity could erase my past entirely.

"I know some lawyers," he said. "And I'm happy to help out a gal in need. Roxy tells me you're working as a cigarette girl with her at the Tropicana. Come with me to Ernst

Lubitsch's party tomorrow night. Between your charisma and your late grandmother's dough, I have a feeling you won't be selling cigarettes for much longer."

I smiled. "I hope so. Will Roxy be joining us?"

Benny shook his head. "I can only bring one date. I'm a lowly screenwriter. It wouldn't do to arrive with too many people."

"I see," I replied, though my stomach knotted at the word "date." "It's awfully kind of you to invite me, but won't Roxy be put out?"

Benny's eyes glinted. "Roxy's had plenty of chances in this town. You're fresh off the bus. Seize your moment. You can't be afraid of stepping on toes."

"I suppose you're right," I said, my nerves abating slightly with another sip of my drink. "Thank you. Truly."

Benny brought my hand to his lips and kissed it. "The pleasure is all mine."

A jolt of fear worked its way down my spine in a shiver. My eyes traveled from Benny's mouth to the man in the fedora at the next table over. Had he been watching us? The man returned to his drink, appearing disinterested. But if he were a private investigator sent by Charles, it would be his job to appear normal.

"I'd better be going," I said. "It's getting late."

"Of course," Benny said. "I'll call you a cab."

As he stood up and strolled toward the bar, I glanced at the man in the fedora, only to find his table empty. I took a deep breath in and let it out. Charles couldn't find me here. I hadn't told Harry the name of the motel where

I was staying. But suddenly the city of stars felt small—claustrophobic.

Benny returned and extended his arm to me. He grinned when I took it. "Bring a bathing suit for tomorrow night's soiree and an evening dress. Lubitsch's pool parties are unlike anything you've ever seen."

"Indeed," I said, the warmth of excitement pushing away the last shivery remnants of fear. "I can't wait to see what's in store."

CHAPTER 14

Marisol Cruz

2007

Mari opened the kitchen windows to let in the summer breeze. Sinking onto a high-backed chair, she listened to her father reading to Lily in the living room. Lily giggled. She loved it when her *abuelo* did funny voices for their bedtime stories.

"*Mija,*" Paulina said, taking a seat next to Mari. "Is everything all right? You seem off tonight. You acted strange when the mayor came to speak with you."

Mari's jaw tightened. "Did I? I guess I'm still upset about the construction plans to knock down the gazebo."

Paulina stared at Mari, the crease between her brows evidence that she wasn't satisfied. "Are you sure? Because I'm here if you want to talk."

". . . And the big bear, he's also a tickle monster!"

Lily shrieked in delight. Mari's father had to be tired after a long day at work, but around Lily, he never showed his fatigue. Lily was lucky to have him as an *abuelo*. He was an amazing dad and grandfather. But he was getting older. And it broke Mari's heart that Lily would never have a father—one who loved her, was there for her first smile, first steps and first day of school.

A tear slipped down Mari's cheek. "It's hard, Ma. She's getting older, and she's asking questions. I don't have answers for her. I'm still so angry that her father chose not to be a part of her life."

Paulina gently rubbed Mari's back. "I know it's hard. But we're not going anywhere. Do you know how stubborn your dad is? He's going to live to be at least ninety years old. Look at him."

They glanced into the living room, where Lily was now riding on her *abuelo*'s back, while he pretended to be a bear.

Mari laughed, wiping the tear from her cheek. Her final year of college, she'd had so many plans: to move to the Bay Area, to get her own apartment. She'd already applied for the graduate program in history at Cal. She imagined visiting San Francisco museums on the weekend, shopping with friends, going to concerts. She'd even found a room on Craigslist, sunny with hardwood floors, near the Berkeley campus and the Greek Theater, where she'd listen to her favorite bands beneath the stars.

She hadn't intended to move back in with her parents.

Her acceptance letter from UC Berkeley had arrived a week after she'd found out she was pregnant. She'd cried, looking at the letterhead, thinking of the apartment she'd never move into. Then her beloved grandfather died, and her parents inherited his house. Life had come full circle, and with Ricardo's death, the gift of this beach cottage brought them all together. Being a single mom was hard, but Mari couldn't imagine doing it without her family.

"Come here," Paulina said. "Give me a hug."

Mari closed her eyes, feeling like a child again in the comfort of her mother's embrace—not the mom who needed to take care of Lily.

"Thanks, Ma," she whispered. "We better go in there before Dad gets Lily so riled up she won't sleep. It's time for her bath."

WIPING A TABLE in a circular motion, Mari lost herself in the repetition. She tried not to think about her grant application, which she'd submitted that morning. Hope was a dangerous thing. If she allowed herself to hope, she'd set herself up for disappointment when things didn't go as planned. What if the summer came to an end, her job at the boardwalk led nowhere, and she worked at the Jupiter Café until she was fifty years old? Hell, she could become the new Wanda, cat's-eye glasses and all.

Sighing, she threw the dirty dishcloth into her apron pocket and walked toward the heat of the kitchen. Tacky plastic bracelets jingled against her arms. She'd even worn a pair of hideous clip-on earrings to appease Wanda, and put on a swipe of pink lipstick. If Wanda wanted tacky, she wasn't going to fight her today.

Covering her mouth, Mari yawned. She hadn't been able to sleep last night, and her thoughts had drifted to Violet. Why had she committed suicide? Mari wondered if Violet had felt isolated. She didn't have any proof that Charles was a bad husband, but his quote from their wedding announcement stuck in her mind. *Violet is my most prized possession.* She'd likely been very depressed. Maybe she felt trapped.

Throwing the dirty towel into the laundry hamper in back of the kitchen, Mari walked toward the restroom to wash her hands. She was nearing the end of her shift and looking forward to a quiet night at home. Her cell phone vibrated in her apron pocket. Glancing around the back room, Mari didn't see Wanda, so she flipped it open.

"Hey, Mari?"

At first, she didn't recognize the male voice.

"It's Jason. Did I catch you at a bad time?"

"No, I'm just about to end my shift at work. What's up?"

"I won a raffle prize."

Mari smiled. "That's great! You *did* buy a hundred dollars' worth of tickets, so your odds were pretty good. What did you win?"

"Dinner for two at Trabocco."

The butterflies in Mari's stomach refused to settle. Shutting the restroom door behind her, she leaned against the stall door away from prying eyes. Hopefully Wanda couldn't hear her through the wall.

"Oh, um, nice."

"Yeah, I've heard it's really good. Hopefully you'll join me?"

Mari wondered if he could hear the smile in her voice. "I'd like that."

"Wonderful. Any chance you're free tonight? The weather's great, we could sit outside, and it's Friday."

Mari bit her lip, thinking about what she'd planned to do: hang out with Lily and then curl up in bed with a good book. But something about Jason's enthusiasm made her change her mind.

"I'll check with my parents to see if they can babysit. Let me call you right back."

WHEN MARI STEPPED into the kitchen wearing a yellow lace sundress and wedge-heeled espadrilles, Lily's whole face lit up.

"Mama. You look so pretty!"

Mari smiled. "You think so?"

She'd taken the time to curl her hair, and to put on some mascara and lipstick.

"Like a princess!" Lily said. "Where are you going?"

Mari looked at her mother, and Paulina smiled approvingly.

"I'm meeting a friend."

"A *boyfriend?*"

"A friend who is a boy."

Lily giggled. "Mama has a boyfriend!"

Mari hoped her daughter didn't notice the blush in her

cheeks as she bent down to hug her goodbye. "Have fun with Abuela. I love you."

Lily smelled like apple shampoo and her sweet, soft skin. "Love you too, Mama."

"Thanks, Ma," Mari said. "I won't stay out too late."

Paulina winked. "You stay out as late as you want to."

Mari smoothed her dress, feeling an unexpected jolt of nerves. When was the last time she'd been on a date? She tried to dispel them, waving goodbye to her family as she stepped out the door. It was just Jason. They were friends. People her age got together for dinner and drinks on a Friday night all the time—this was normal.

Walking through the neighborhood from Beach Hill, Mari listened to the calming ocean waves and watched the surfers bobbing on their boards in the fading sunlight. Seagulls cawed overhead, and the smell of sea brine and wildflowers carried on the summer breeze. Jason was right, something about the unusually warm weather made this summer night feel magical, like anything was possible. Mari hadn't felt the excitement of possibility in a long time.

When she stepped through the threshold of Trabocco, the host ushered her through the restaurant and into the courtyard in back. Brick walls covered in ivy enclosed the intimate space and lanterns strung overhead winked like fireflies.

"Here you are," the waiter said, pointing to a table in back.

Jason stood, and all the butterflies in Mari's stomach took flight like the monarchs at Natural Bridges. He'd changed out of his usual jeans and a hooded sweatshirt, looking smart in a short-sleeved button-down checkered shirt and a pair of gray slacks. He smiled when he met her eyes, his own eyes twinkling. She felt something then—the strangest thing. A feeling of calm came over her, almost relief to see him.

"Hey," he said, wrapping her in a hug. "You made it."

She breathed in the scent of his cologne, sweet and spicy—like sandalwood and bergamot.

"I did," she replied. "Not too far of a walk from my house."

"You walked over in those?" Jason asked, looking at her espadrilles.

Mari laughed. "They're comfortable. You'd be surprised."

Jason smiled. "You look really beautiful."

Mari brushed a wayward strand of hair from her face. "Thanks. You actually clean up very nicely yourself."

"Well, I almost wore my strappy sandals too, but then we'd be matching, so I decided against it."

Mari rolled her eyes. "Ha ha."

"So," Jason said, his hair shining under the lights. Had he put product in it? His thick waves looked especially good. "I checked out Yelp, and the pasta Bolognese is supposed to be great. You're not vegetarian, are you?"

"Are you kidding?" Mari shook her head. "I'm all for the humane treatment of animals and sustainable farming, but I think my *abuela* would have cried if I told her I wasn't going to eat her homemade *carne asada*."

Jason smiled. "Did you spend a lot of time with your grandparents growing up?"

Mari nodded. "Before we moved into my grandfather's house, my parents and I lived in an apartment near Seabright Beach. We hung out with my grandparents every weekend, cooking together or going for rides on the boardwalk."

"Do you have any siblings?"

Mari shook her head. "No. I'm an only child. Most people assume Mexican families are huge, but my mom and dad had me kind of young, and then they decided one kid was enough for them."

Jason smiled. "Hey, I'm an only child too! People always think we're self-centered weirdos."

"*Right*?" Mari laughed. "We don't know how to share and have no social skills."

"I have a confession to make," Jason said in a whisper. "I used to play a game with the cars passing by. I would freeze whenever one went down my street, and then start moving again when it passed. I literally had no one to play with sometimes. And honestly, I'm an IT programmer; my social skills are questionable."

"I don't know," Mari said, warming to him. "I'd say you turned out all right."

The waiter returned to take their orders, and Jason chose a bottle of Shiraz. The wine was delicious, fruity and light. Mari felt herself laughing more with every sip, feeling lighter than she had in years.

"Okay," she said, grinning. "My turn for a confession. I used to pretend that I could talk to animals. Growing up, I had a cat named Sylvester, and I swore to my mom that we could communicate. I'd tell her that he wanted a cookie, trying to get an extra one for myself. So yeah, I guess I was kind of lonely too."

Jason laughed. "Here," he said, offering her his plate of spaghetti Bolognese. "You have to try some of this."

Mari scooped a spoonful onto her plate and then pushed her pesto gnocchi toward him. "Nope. I made the better choice. *This* is delicious."

"Look at us sharing," Jason said. "We're not lost causes after all."

"Family style," Mari said. She felt her neck warm and took a gulp of wine. It had already gone straight to her head.

But Jason grinned back at her. "Tell me something else I don't know."

"Well," Mari said, taking another sip of wine. "Working at the Santa Cruz museum booth, I came across an article about a beauty queen who committed suicide. She was Miss California in 1940. Then she tried to become a Hollywood actress, but two months later, she returned to Santa Cruz and jumped off a cliff."

"This took a dark turn."

Mari laughed. "I'm sorry. You want to hear more about Sylvester?"

"I'm kidding. Tell me more about the beauty queen."

"Her name was Violet Harcourt, and she was the first wife of Mayor Harcourt's father, Charles Harcourt. I don't know why, but I can't stop thinking about her."

"The mayor's father's first wife? That's interesting. Why do you think she killed herself?"

Mari sipped her wine. "I don't know. It doesn't make sense. She was this beautiful young girl, with all the potential in the world. She goes to Hollywood to make it as an actress, but gives up really quickly. It's so sad. And get this—she *knew* my grandfather. But he never once mentioned her."

"Wait," Jason said, leaning forward. "Back up a minute. She knew your grandfather?"

"I found a picture of them together in this trunk in the attic. She was a waitress when he was a stunt diver at the boardwalk."

"He was a stunt diver?"

"I thought I told you that. He and his diving partner had a dangerous routine where they would zip line over the beach, my *abuelo* dangling from the trapeze, and then drop into the ocean. It was really popular."

Jason smiled. "You're pretty amazing, you know that?"

Mari shook her head. "Why?"

"You have such a thirst for knowledge, for life, a passion about history—for bygone beauty queens. You come from this super-interesting family. I'm just a boring guy from the Midwest."

"I don't think you're boring," Mari said. "I think you're pretty cool."

"Sorry to interrupt," Jason said, taking a sip of his wine. "Tell me more about Violet."

And so she did, surprised by how naturally conversation flowed, as if she and Jason had already known each other for years. He didn't think she was crazy for believing the postcard from "V" was from Violet, and rubbed his jaw thoughtfully when she mentioned that Charles sounded creepy and possessive.

With her belly full of delicious food, and her surroundings pleasantly hazy from half a bottle of wine, Mari looped her arm through Jason's as they left the restaurant. Strolling down Pacific Avenue, she realized she didn't want the night to end.

"I had a really nice time," she said, as they neared the bus terminal. "I figure you need to catch one of these back up to campus. You live in faculty housing, right?"

"I can walk you home," Jason said with a smile. "I'm in no rush, and besides, it wouldn't be very gentlemanly of me to let you walk back alone. Or would you like me to get you a cab?"

"It's a nice night," Mari said, breathing in the warm summer breeze, fragrant with jasmine and ocean brine. "Let's walk."

As they drew closer to the boardwalk, the lull of the waves rushing in and out accompanied their silence. The gazebo stood alone beneath the moonlight and Mari's heart ached. Perhaps it was an only child thing, but sometimes she attributed feelings to objects. As a child, she always rescued her stuffed animals that had fallen out of bed so they wouldn't be alone on the floor. The gazebo appeared lonely tonight.

"Hey, follow me," Jason said, tugging her hand as he began to cross the sand.

"What? Where are we going?"

"This way," he said, smiling.

Mari followed him down the beach, and then realized where he was taking her. He led her up the creaky steps onto the gazebo's weathered porch, where they stood together underneath the dome. The crashing waves sounded in her ears.

"You said your grandparents danced here," Jason said softly, taking her hand in his. "Will you dance with me?"

Mari's heart fluttered. "There's no music."

"Sure there is," Jason said. He began to hum the tune to "The Girl from Ipanema" and Mari laughed as he spun her around. She closed her eyes and draped her arms around his neck, imagining fairy lights, and the click of heels against polished floorboards.

Her giggles faded when she found her mouth a hair's breadth from Jason's, their faces turned toward each other as their movement slowed. His arms encircled her waist and ever so slowly, he inched his face toward hers. Mari closed the distance, tingling at the kiss she'd been anticipating all night. Jason gently ran his fingers across her hips, and behind her closed eyelids she saw bursts of color.

When they pulled apart, they were smiling at each other.

"Thank you," Mari whispered.

"For kissing you?"

"For bringing me here. So I can have this memory . . ."

Her voice turned bitter. "Before Travis Harcourt tears this place down."

"You have a lot of animosity toward him."

Mari's throat tightened. The moment they shared had been wonderful. And she didn't want to ruin it. But her words tumbled out like water from a dam.

"He's Lily's father."

With the release of her secret, tears streamed down her cheeks along with years of built-up resentment. How could he want nothing to do with his perfect daughter? Lily, gorgeous Lily, she deserved so much more. Jason pulled her close, stroking her hair as she cried. But the night had already lost its magic.

CHAPTER 15

Violet Harcourt

1940

Through a canopy of trees, a beautiful hacienda came into view, with white stucco walls covered in bougainvillea and a terra-cotta roof. The steps leading to the entrance were lined with lanterns, and the scent of jasmine filled the air.

Though we hadn't driven far to reach Ernst Lubitsch's home in the Hollywood Hills, I felt as though I had entered another world. Notes of jazz carried on the breeze. My shawl slipped, revealing a bare shoulder. Roxy had lent me a lovely floor-length gold evening gown, which exposed my entire back, hugging my curves and rounding my derriere. It was rather daring for my tastes, but tonight was my chance to catch the eye of the renowned director. I needed to make an impression.

"What do you think?" Benny asked, leading me into the garden.

A rectangular swimming pool shimmered beneath the full moon, surrounded by colorful Mediterranean-style tiles in the center of a lush lawn. Tables laden with appetizers held purple candles flickering in jars, and urns bursting with flowers lined the garden path. Fruit trees surrounded the property, lending it secrecy.

"Oh, it's marvelous."

A jazz band performed in front of the French doors leading to the kitchen, the sweaty players strumming the base and blowing the trumpet with wild energy. With glasses of champagne in hand, glamorous women in evening gowns and fur stoles laughed beneath the stars on the patio. Men in suits puffed on cigarettes, their laughter erupting in staccato bursts. Everyone appeared loose and free, drinking and dancing.

"It's a private party for film folk and press writers," Benny whispered, leaning in close. "Shall I get you a drink?"

"Yes, please," I said, though once again, my stomach felt queasy. Perhaps my unsettled business with Charles had begun to manifest itself in physical symptoms. I took a deep breath in through my nose and let it out. I would find a lawyer this week and mail Charles the divorce papers. Once that was over and done with, I would be free to enjoy my new life. Thinking of Charles brought on a wave of sadness. In spite of everything, I missed him. He wasn't a monster all the time—he was my husband.

"Oh! Excuse me."

I backed away as I happened upon a couple necking in the shrubbery. The girl giggled, the thin straps of her gown hanging down below her elbows, and a pale breast fully exposed. I darted toward the appetizers, eager to avoid interrupting another amorous encounter. The party appeared to be in full swing, but I raised a hand to my mouth to cover my yawn. It was quite late—nearly midnight. Benny had insisted midnight parties were very *du jour*—midnight swimming, midnight Ping-Pong.

I looked around the property at the tall hedges and cyprus trees, drinking in the scent of the fragrant vines that climbed the walls of the hacienda. Strings of Japanese lanterns illuminated the garden, making me feel like a player in *A Midsummer Night's Dream*. The warm air felt tinged with magic.

Benny returned with two glasses of champagne. "Cheers," he said, touching his glass to mine. "Shall we seek out Herr Lubitsch?"

The champagne bubbles tickled my throat. "Yes," I said, smiling at Benny. "Let's find him."

We passed a group of people playing croquet on the lawn, and my kitten heels sank into the soft grass. An older woman approached, her wavy hair cropped close and a cross expression on her face.

"Benny Bronstein," she said, her English heavily accented. "I didn't expect to see you here." She looked at me with a calculating gaze. "And who is this?"

"Violet Sweeting," I said, extending my hand.

"Salka Viertel," she replied, shaking it firmly.

Benny lit a cigarette. "Salka's an incredible scriptwriter. She's also a close friend of Greta Garbo's. She cowrote the script for *Queen Christina*."

"It's a pleasure to meet you," I said, my stomach fluttering. She knew Greta Garbo!

"Benny B!"

Benny jerked his head to attention as a man in suspenders and a fedora threw an arm around his shoulder. "Come here. I want ya to meet somebody."

"I'll just be a moment," he said, winking.

Once he'd left, Salka Viertel locked me in her unflinching gaze. "What's your story? You want to be an actress?"

"Yes," I said. "I suppose that's what every woman in this town wants."

She didn't smile. "I was like you once—a young stage actress in Berlin and Vienna. Now I have a salon for German and Austrian émigrés at my bungalow in Santa Monica." She frowned. "Here in Hollywood, there's a place for us."

"How lovely," I said, feeling foolish at the frivolousness of my acting dreams in light of the war in Europe.

Her gaze intensified. "You don't need a man's help to become an actress. Benny Bronstein is not the *mensch* that he seems."

I opened my mouth to reply, but Benny returned, draping an arm casually around my shoulder. "Sorry, doll. I had to catch up with an old pal. Shall we go inside?"

Salka's eyes held a warning.

"Sure," I replied, and then smiled at Salka. "It was nice meeting you."

Benny steered me toward the French doors, and the music grew louder. "I hope she wasn't too much of a sourpuss. Old European Jews . . . they kvetch a lot."

"She was kind," I responded, annoyed at Benny's misconception. My stomach knotted, wondering what Salka meant about Benny not being a mensch.

In the large and airy kitchen, women and men danced to the music, their sweaty bodies jostling up against one another. I admired the cut of a gorgeous green silk evening gown as it swished back and forth. Diamond earrings and necklaces sparkled in the light, and I thought of my jewelry box at home in Santa Cruz, filled with baubles. All of my jewels were a show of Charles's wealth and power. It was silly to miss them.

"Look, there's Ernst Lubitsch," Benny said, leaning toward me.

I craned my neck to see an older dark-haired man with strong features. He stood in a dining room off the kitchen, speaking with two others. His dark eyes met mine, and then his brow furrowed as he noticed Benny. A cold feeling passed over me.

"I may have imagined it," I said. "But he didn't seem pleased to see us."

Benny laughed. "He's a serious guy, a member of the Hollywood Chess Club. He plays with Josef von Sternberg. They used to be enemies at Paramount, but now that Lubitsch is at MGM, they're friends. That's just how he is."

I frowned, not sure that was what I'd seen.

"Here," he said. "Have another glass of champagne."

"All right." I accepted the glass, though I'd hardly finished the first. Pressing my lips together, I watched the powerful director slip away. I'd come here for one reason only—an introduction, like Benny promised.

"Did you meet Ernst Lubitsch at the chess club?"

Benny shook his head. "I got to know Lubitsch at the Tele-View Theater. Remember the one I told you about? In April, when the westward blitzkrieg through Europe started, he and the other Europeans living here in Hollywood would go every week for an hour of current news."

"Oh," I said, sipping my champagne. "Did you strike up a conversation there?"

"We did. And sometimes we eat lunch at the Brown Derby. He's a regular." Benny's eyes darted to a woman standing in the corner smoking a cigarette. "So is Louella Parsons over there. She's the biggest gossip in town, always perched at her booth in the Brown Derby, eager to criticize someone's table manners."

I recognized the same busty, dark-haired woman I'd seen at the Brown Derby. She pursed her crimson lips at me, her eyes calculating. Benny placed his hand on the small of my back. I nearly flinched at the contact, his warm hand against my bare skin. The room felt too hot and crowded.

"Why don't we step outside for a moment? Get some air?"

"Sure," I said, allowing Benny to lead me outside. I

looked back over my shoulder, hoping I'd get a second chance to acquaint myself with Mr. Lubitsch.

Benny led me through the garden, around the side of the house to a secluded area surrounded by orange trees. The soft gurgle of a fountain sounded in the distance, and the noise of the party faded to a pleasant hum.

I smiled, "This is much bett–"

Benny grabbed a lock of my hair and pressed his lips against mine. His tongue forced its way into my mouth, and he tasted of champagne and cigarettes. I pushed against him, feeling vomit rise in my throat.

"Get off me!"

He bit his lip, a wild look in his eyes. "Oh you want to play coy? Show me what's under that dress."

He tugged down the thin straps, pawing at my breasts. Tears pricked my eyes as I swatted his hand away. "Stop! Don't touch me!"

When he didn't listen, I pulled back my hand and slapped him hard across the jaw. The look in his eyes changed and my blood ran cold. It was the same glassy-eyed look Charles would give me before a beating.

But Benny didn't strike me. Instead he gripped my wrists.

"What'sa matter with you? I bought you drinks at Don the Beachcomber. I brought you here. Show a little gratitude."

He grabbed me again, taking a fistful of my hair and pressing his mouth against mine. I fought him, scratching at his skin with my nails, but he tugged the thin straps of Roxy's gown until one broke loose.

I bit his lip, hard.

Benny pulled back, touching his bleeding lip with one finger. "You little cocktease. You want me to hurt you? Roxy didn't tell me you'd put up a fight."

He unbuttoned his pants, his eyes wild. "I did my part, now you do yours. That's the deal."

"What? There's no *deal*. Take me home."

Benny laughed, but his eyes didn't smile. "You think you're going to make it as an actress? You ain't got no talent. But you do have a nice pair of tits. Give me what I want and I'll give you an introduction to a director."

Tears streamed down my cheeks as I pulled up the broken strap of Roxy's gown. The hem had been trampled in the dirt. Wiping my eyes, I struggled to back away from Benny, then tripped and fell to the ground.

"I don't know what Roxy told you, but I'm not that kind of girl. Neither is she."

"Oh yeah? Why do you think they call her the Mouth?"

I wanted to respond—she'd told me it was because she talked too much, but then with a sinking feeling, I wondered if I knew Roxy at all. Did she sleep with men for favors? Had she slept with Benny?

He chuckled. "Because she knows how to use it. And you're going to do the same. Get on your knees."

"Hey! What is happening back here?"

Ernst Lubitsch appeared with two burly men in suits. His dark eyes widened as he spotted me, and then narrowed when he turned to Benny.

"Out! What did I tell you the last time? You are not welcome here."

"Hey now," Benny said, raising his arms as the two men grabbed him by the collar of his jacket. "We were only having a little fun, weren't we, doll?" He looked at me.

I cringed with shame, covering my exposed breast. "No," I whispered. "Please, can you call me a cab home?"

Ernst Lubitsch looked at me with pity. I couldn't bear to make eye contact. I could never introduce myself to him *now*. What if word got out about this?

With a warm hand, the director helped me to my feet, and then pointed toward a door at the side of the house. "In there, you will find a bathroom. Clean yourself up, and I will have someone call you a cab. But then I'm afraid I must ask you to leave."

"Of course," I said, my cheeks burning. "Thank you."

"Violet," Benny called as the men hauled him in the other direction. "Violet! I'm not leaving without you."

Ignoring him, I hobbled down the footpath, the heel of my shoe broken. Wiping the tears from my cheeks, I felt disgusted with myself for attending this soiree with Benny. Did he even know Ernst Lubitsch? Or was he a habitual party crasher?

I pulled open the door to the side of the house and slipped off my heels; the cool tiles felt nice against my feet. Turning a corner, I found a bathroom. When I glimpsed my face in the mirror, I gasped. *Oh, what an absolute disaster!*

Fresh tears streamed from my eyes as I turned on the tap to wash my face. Mascara ringed my eyes, and my lipstick was smeared clownishly around my mouth.

Scrubbing my hands and face vigorously, I tried to remove the stain of Benny Bronstein. How had I been so foolish? I had trusted Roxy—had thought she was my friend. But I had no friends in this town.

Using a washcloth and a bit of lotion from a drawer, I removed my makeup, and then cleaned the scratches on my arms and face. With shaking fingers, I managed to tie the broken spaghetti strap of Roxy's gown back together. I braced myself on the sink, nausea rolling through me like a tidal wave.

Vomit spewed forth unbidden, and I let out a sob. The taste of bile burned my tongue, along with the sickeningly sweet remnants of champagne. Suddenly, I brought a trembling hand to my mouth. I hadn't used the Kotex in my purse. My period was due to start the week that I left Santa Cruz. But it never arrived.

It was now three weeks late.

CHAPTER 16

Marisol Cruz

2007

Mari opened the front door, slipping off one wedge heel and then the other. The house was quiet, except for the hum of the television in the living room. She wiped underneath her eyes to dry the last remnants of her tears.

Jason had been wonderful, assuring her that it was okay to cry, and then walking her the rest of the way home. But her emotional outburst had been mortifying, mostly because it was so unexpected. Mari wasn't someone who cried in public. Travis making plans to destroy the gazebo had reopened an old wound.

"*Mija,*" Paulina said, rounding the corner with a dish towel in hand. "How did it go tonight?"

Seeing her mother's concerned face, Mari burst into

fresh tears, and rushed into her outstretched arms. "I ruined everything."

"Shhh," Paulina said, stroking her daughter's hair. "Come into the kitchen. I'll make you some hot chocolate the way Abuela used to."

Mari nodded. She loved her grandmother's traditional Mexican hot chocolate with vanilla, cinnamon and cayenne pepper. "Is Lily asleep?"

Paulina turned on the gas to heat a pan of milk. "She went to bed about an hour ago. Now tell me, what happened?"

Once Mari had a warm mug of hot chocolate in her hands, she took a deep breath in and let it out. "The date started off great. We had a nice dinner at the Italian restaurant, and then Jason offered to walk me home. But instead he took me to the gazebo so that we could dance, just like Abuelo and Abuela did."

Paulina smiled, sipping from her mug. "Sounds romantic."

"It was. But then . . ."

"What?"

"Ugh, it's so embarrassing. I thought about Lily's father, and I got angry, and then I got really sad and started crying."

Paulina reached for Mari's hand. "I'm sorry, *mi amor*."

Mari remembered the June day four years ago, the spring quarter of her final year. It was final-exam time, and Mari had been so stressed about maintaining her 4.0 grade point average, and worrying whether she'd get accepted into Berkeley's graduate program, that she'd been focused solely on schoolwork. But she couldn't help noticing how cute Travis was every time he showed up late for lecture, his skin tanned and hair disheveled from water polo practice. Sometimes she caught him staring at her from across the room.

The night of her last final, there was nothing left to do except celebrate. Normally she didn't go to house parties, but the weather was warm and she got swept up in the excitement. It was okay to let loose for one night. Mari and her friends had gone to a house on West Cliff Drive, overlooking the ocean. Whoever rented it had rich parents, because it was nicer than any student house she'd ever been to. There were sweeping views of the Pacific Ocean from the balcony, where a keg sat in a bucket of ice.

She'd been pouring beer into a plastic red cup, when Travis had sidled up next to her. "Hey! You're in my history seminar, right?"

"Yeah," she'd said, her heart beating a little faster. "How did you do on the final? It was kind of tough, wasn't it?"

He shrugged. "I'm sure I passed, I'm not worried. Come do a tequila shot with me inside. We've got to celebrate!"

"Okay," she said, tingling as he threw his arm around her shoulder. Her secret crush was acting like they were old friends.

"This place is gorgeous," Mari said, looking around the state-of-the-art kitchen with chrome appliances and granite countertops. "Do you know who lives here?"

Travis smiled. "I live here. My dad bought it for me and the water polo team."

"He *bought* it?"

Travis chuckled, his green eyes and white teeth bright against his summery tan. "We've been here four years. All my teammates pay rent, so it's a good real estate investment. He'll sell it once we leave."

Mari frowned as he poured her a shot. "I guess you have a point. But still, a house like this doesn't come cheap."

Travis pushed the tequila shot toward her. "Lime?"

"Yes, please," she said. "I can't do tequila straight."

He gave her a slice, and passed her the salt. "You don't know who my dad is, do you?"

She licked her palm and sprinkled some salt on it. "Should I?"

Travis chuckled. "Never mind. Bottoms up."

She winced at the burn of the tequila going down her throat, and quickly bit into the lime wedge. Once the gross taste was gone, she felt pleasantly warm and relaxed.

They took a few more tequila shots, and then someone turned down the lights and turned up the music. She and Travis started grinding against each other on the dance floor. For a white guy, he had serious moves. She told him this, and he laughed. He was cocky, just shy of being obnoxious, but she liked it. In between drinks he told her about his plans to backpack through Europe with his friends that summer, and his internship at a tech company in Silicon Valley that he'd be starting in the fall.

"To the future!" she'd cried, laughing as he wrapped

his arms around her waist. She was *drunk*. And then they were making out in the middle of the dance floor. "Come to my room," Travis whispered against her hair. "It has a killer view of the ocean."

"Okay," she said and giggled, aware of what might happen. It was kind of thrilling, the thought of a one-night stand. She'd never had one before. The last guy she'd dated had been the opposite of Travis: dorky and quiet Marcus, who always asked her if it was okay to touch her breasts. She liked Travis's take-charge attitude.

The sex itself was somewhat of a blur, though she remembered him whispering, "You're so hot," over and over again, and feeling a surge of pride at the compliment. His room *did* have an amazing view of the ocean, and his king-size bed with soft, clean sheets was nicer than anything she expected a guy her age to sleep in.

It wasn't until she excused herself to the en suite bathroom to pee that panic set in. She saw a condom floating in the bowl. *How on earth had it gotten there?* But in her tequila haze and embarrassment, she'd quickly flushed the toilet.

When the next day arrived, along with a blinding hangover, Mari wasn't sure she'd seen the condom after all. Perhaps she'd imagined it? Or maybe it had belonged to Travis, and he'd thrown it in there from a separate hookup?

Four weeks later, she got her answer when a digital pregnancy test clearly read "pregnant." She crumpled in a heap on the bathroom floor, berating herself for her stupidity. She hadn't talked to Travis since that night, and he was probably in the Swiss Alps at the moment on his grand European adventure.

But she had his email address, and hadn't he said he was starting an internship in Silicon Valley in the fall? That wasn't too far away from Santa Cruz. The timing couldn't have been worse, but like Abuela used to say, sometimes God worked in mysterious ways. Travis needed to know he was going to be a dad.

Her heart was pounding when she finally got ahold of him by phone.

"Hey," he said, the friendliness he'd shown that night of the party replaced by suspicion. "What is it? You said it was really important."

Mari fidgeted with her necklace. There was no easy way to impart the news. "I'm pregnant. The baby is yours. I'm a few months along now, and I'm going to keep it."

Silence.

"Travis?"

"I'm sorry—you're going to *keep* it?"

"Yeah," she said, placing a hand protectively over her stomach. "Look, I know it's a shock. And I'm not asking you to marry me, or anything crazy like that. But you're going to be a dad, and I want you to be a part of this baby's life."

"No way," Travis said, his voice taking on a hard edge. "Are you crazy? Fuck—I'm in France right now. I'm twenty-two. You're not going to ruin my life. How do you even know it's mine?"

Mari's throat tightened. "Because you're the *only* person I've slept with this year. Travis, please. I think if—"

"Get an abortion and I'll pay for it."

"No," Mari said, the burn of anger creeping up her skin. "That's not my plan. Look, we can work something out. Maybe you see the baby only on weekends. I know it's a lot to take in but I really think—"

But he'd already hung up the phone. She waited for him to process the shock. She'd reach out again when he came home from Europe. Except her emails went unanswered. A couple of times she worked up the courage to go to the house on West Cliff Drive, taking a deep breath as she rang the doorbell. But no one ever answered.

When Lily came into the world, red-faced and screaming, Mari cried tears of joy at the miracle of her perfect baby girl. This time Travis would come around. She sent him pictures of Lily swaddled in her little blanket from the hospital, covered in tiny footprints. She had a shock of dark hair, Travis's straight nose and full lips.

Her name is Liliana Elena Cruz, Mari wrote. *She's 8 pounds, 2 ounces and perfectly healthy. She would love to meet you.*

By this time she'd Googled Travis, and seen that his dad was a popular city council member running for mayor of Santa Cruz. In his smiling photos, Tom Harcourt seemed like the type of man who would love to be a grandpa.

Every month for the first year of Lily's life, Mari emailed Travis photos, along with updates. *She learned to sit up on her own today. She has your green eyes. She likes to babble and say "baba." Please meet her? Travis, she's your daughter. You'll love her. I know it's scary, but it's not too late to be a part of her life.*

But after an entire year of unanswered emails, Mari stopped sending them. The soft part of her heart that believed in hope and happy endings hardened. Travis had seen pictures of his beautiful daughter. He knew Mari wasn't asking him for money, only for a father's love—and he'd chosen to turn his back on them both.

Staring into her empty mug, hot tears slid down Mari's cheeks.

"I haven't seen him or spoken to him in four years. And now he's back."

Paulina rubbed Mari's shoulder. "I know it's hard."

Mari's jaw tightened. "And he talks about the value of family like he knows something about it. I want to punch him in the face."

Paulina sighed. "I understand that you're angry, but punching him isn't going to solve anything. It will only make you look crazy."

Mari laughed. "I'm not really going to punch him."

Paulina smiled. "You sure? I wouldn't be surprised if you could throw a mean right hook." Her face grew serious. "Do you think Mayor Harcourt knows about Lily?"

"I doubt it."

Paulina blew out a puff of air. "I would want to know if I had another grandchild. Life is too short, *sabes*? Maybe you should tell him."

Mari's stomach knotted. She gripped her empty mug, thinking about the mayor's confused expression when he'd seen Lily at the boardwalk. Was it her responsibility to tell him? Or would it only make more of a mess of things?

"I'm tired," Mari said. Her body felt heavy, and it was all too much to think about for one night. "Thanks for the hot chocolate. I'm going to sleep."

Paulina stood, walked over and kissed Mari on the forehead. *"Duerme bien."*

But that night Mari didn't sleep well. She dreamed of Travis, the mayor and Jason, their faces blending together in a grotesque mask.

"DID I CATCH you at a bad time?"

Mari rubbed her forehead as she held her phone against her cheek. "No. But I wasn't expecting to hear from you."

"Don't worry," Jason said, a smile in his voice. "I make all my dates cry."

Mari laughed. "So that's, like, your thing?"

"Totally." He paused. "Seriously, though, thank you for sharing your past with me. I'm sorry if I brought up old feelings by taking you to the gazebo."

"There are no old *feelings,*" Mari blurted, eager to clear the air. "It was a one-night stand. I didn't date the guy."

"Well, that's good," Jason said. "From what you've told me, he's gone from semi-douchebag to a douchebag of the highest degree."

"You're telling me." Once again she felt that strange feeling—relief.

"The same thing happened to my older sister, you know. Some guys don't recognize a gem when they see one."

Mari remembered that Jason had told her his sister was a single mom. "How old was your sister when she got pregnant?"

"She was twenty-seven. She'd been dating this guy for two years and thought for sure they'd get engaged. But as soon as she told him, he split. She was devastated."

"That's awful," Mari said, feeling grateful she'd had no such delusions about a future with Travis. She wished he'd wanted to be a father to Lily, but she didn't miss *him*.

"It was. Thankfully my parents and I were there to take care of her during her pregnancy, to remind her how awesome she is."

"You're pretty good at that," Mari said.

"I have a secret," Jason said. "I learned that ice cream cures nearly everything. Would you like to come with me to Marini's this week?"

"I'd love that," Mari said.

"Nice. How about Wednesday night?"

"It's a date," Mari said, imagining for a brief moment bringing Lily along. No way—it was too soon. But she could picture the three of them sharing a sundae.

"Cool," Jason said. "Have a great day. I'll text you soon."

"Bye," Mari said. "You too."

As she hung up the phone, it struck her that she felt like she'd just talked with an old friend. She didn't feel wild butterflies, but she felt something better—trust.

Mari glanced at the clock. She had an hour before her shift started at Jupiter Café. She heard her dad singing in the kitchen and smelled frying eggs. She loved mornings hanging out with her family before heading over to the diner.

Opening her laptop, she quickly logged into her email account. Her heart seized when she saw the bold subject: Re: Swanson Grant Application.

For a minute, she stared at the email in her inbox, too nervous to open it. But Mari wanted to do it now, while she was alone. The sting of the rejection would hurt, but at least she'd have time to recover in the privacy of her bedroom. She wouldn't even have to tell anyone. She'd go about her workday with a lump of disappointment—then get on with her life. It had been silly to hope she could win.

Taking a deep breath, Mari opened the email.

Dear Ms. Cruz,

Congratulations! We are honored to award you the 2007 Swanson Grant for your proposal, "A Place Beneath the Stars: Cultivating Community Among Santa Cruz's Mexican Immigrants." Your first check for $600 will be sent upon completion of your progress report. The next $600 will be mailed two months later, at the finalization of your project. We very much look forward to hearing from you.

Best regards,
Dr. Mina Ragolevitch,
Swanson Foundation

Mari shot upward like the house was on fire.

"Ma! Oh my God."

Three pairs of feet thumped down the hallway. Paulina rounded the corner, Lily in tow. Suddenly Mari's dad, Ernesto, burst in behind them, wearing her mother's apron. "*Mija,* are you okay? Why are you yelling?"

Lily looked up with wide green eyes. "Mama?"

Mari laughed, placing a hand over her pounding heart. "I'm sorry. I didn't mean to scare you. I have good news!"

She brought her trembling hands to her lips. "I won a grant. I applied to create a diorama of the gazebo, so it can go on display at the Centennial Celebration and people can understand its importance. They've awarded me twelve hundred dollars."

Paulina's eyes widened. "What?"

"Come here," Mari said, wrapping all three of them in a bear hug. "I love you guys. I can't believe this!"

"A bazillion dollars!" Lily cried, hugging Mari's legs.

Mari smiled. "Not quite, honey."

Ernesto kissed his daughter's cheek. "Marisol, I'm so proud."

"*Yo también,*" Paulina said, her eyes shining.

"Me three!" Lily chimed in.

As she hugged her family close, Mari felt like her *abuelo* was there with them. She could see him smiling, his brown eyes crinkling at the corners. Had he been guiding her this entire time?

A tear slipped down Paulina's cheek. "I think Abuelo is proud too."

Ernesto smiled. "My pops? I know he is."

CHAPTER 17

Violet Harcourt

1940

My eyes darted to Roxy across the dim and noisy dance floor of Tropical Gardens Nightclub. She bent over to hand a gentleman a packet of cigarettes, her cleavage spilling out of her tight satin uniform.

I gritted my teeth as I picked up an empty glass. After my disastrous evening with Benny last night, I'd come home to find the motel room empty. Though I'd been relieved to have the room to myself, I wondered now where Roxy had spent the night. When I left the motel this afternoon to get lunch, she still hadn't returned. Could it be true that men paid her for her company?

"Hey, beautiful! Over here."

I turned to see an older, overweight Italian man in a booth, beckoning to me with thick fingers. My heart thumped. I didn't want to be here, serving this man. But I had no money, and nowhere else to go. The cash tips were my only income.

Putting on a weary smile, I approached his table. "Good evening, sir. What can I get you?"

"I'll take a slice of you," he said, his eyes traveling up my legs and resting on my bottom. Every instinct told me to run. I wanted to place a hand protectively over my belly. This was no place for someone in my condition.

"You're a gas," I said, forcing a smile. "Would you like to buy a pack of Marlboros or Chesterfields?"

"Neither," the man said, reaching his outstretched fingers toward my exposed thigh. His gold rings glinted in the light. "Like I said, I want a piece of *you*."

"I'm not for sale!" I spat. Then I turned on my heel and marched toward the back room. A wave of nausea rolled through me, and I took a deep breath in through my nose. Pushing back the curtain to the dressing room, I braced myself against the mirrored wall. *Heaven help me. How had I gotten myself in such a predicament?*

It all made sense—my heightened sensitivity to smell, my sore breasts, the ever-present feeling of sickness. My lip trembled. But I *couldn't* be pregnant. Because if I were, then what? My dreams of becoming an actress would come crashing down around me. And I was so very, frighteningly alone.

Roxy pushed the curtain aside. "What has gotten into you? Do you want to get canned? I'll tell Tommy that you're having an off day, but—"

"Why didn't you warn me about Benny?" Anger rushed through me. "Do you know what he tried to do to me?"

She pursed her red lips. Standing close to her, I could see the tiny wrinkles around her eyes and the parentheses framing her mouth. She looked tired and worn.

"You needed a meal ticket. Benny Bronstein is young and easy on the eyes. I could have set you up with someone much worse."

I scoffed. "A meal ticket? How dare you assume I would want anything of the sort! I am perfectly capable of earning my own money."

Roxy's gaze hardened. "Are you? Because you only have one dress and I'm tired of you borrowing my clothes. You ain't got two pennies to rub together."

"I told you, I left my bag in—"

"Oh, stop with the baloney!" Roxy yelled. "You're hiding something and don't think I don't know it. What are you, a runaway? Papa didn't love you?"

"Don't talk about my family or I'll—"

I balled my hands into fists. My heart ached for my mother and father, for Evie, for Charles. Why had I left behind my life in Santa Cruz? The people who loved me? I'd made a horrible mistake in coming here.

"Or what?" Roxy said, taking a step closer.

I tensed in readiness.

"Hey, what'sa commotion in here?" Tommy stepped out of his office, his black hair shiny with pomade. "This isn't a goddamn zoo. The two of you are screeching like animals."

Roxy cocked her hip. "Violet here gave lip to one of our best customers. Salvatore tried to order a pack of cigarettes, and she stormed off without so much as a smile."

Tommy turned to me, his thick eyebrows drawn together like two caterpillars. "You was rude to Sal?"

I thought of the fat man with the thick fingers covered in gold rings. "He told me he wanted a slice of me. I told him I wasn't for sale."

Tommy's dark eyes flashed with anger. "In my club, show a little respect. That's Salvatore Corlatone. Do you even know who he is? When Sal asks for something, you smile, and then you give him what he wants. *Capisce*?"

My lip trembled. "I don't care if he's the head of the mob. I'm not serving him."

"Then you're finished," Tommy said, curling his lip. "Take off that uniform and get outta my club."

"Gladly," I said, tears stinging my eyes.

Once Tommy left the room, I tugged at the zipper of my tight one-piece. I turned away from Roxy, shimmying out of the black strapless number. I'd only missed one period, which meant I couldn't be more than six or seven weeks along. Still too early to show, though I felt bloated bigger than a blimp.

"You're making a mistake," Roxy said, the fire gone from her voice. "I was only trying to look out for you. Now what are you gonna do?"

"I'll figure it out," I hissed, throwing the uniform on a clothes hanger.

"Suit yourself," she said. "I've gotta get back out there." She pushed the velvet curtain aside and made her way toward the crowded floor of the club.

I blinked rapidly to keep the tears at bay. Had Roxy really thought I would sleep with strange men for a foot in the door? Placing a hand protectively over my belly, I shut my eyes. My baby likely wasn't any bigger than an olive, but already I felt a mother's love. And I was frightened for both of us.

WALKING THROUGH THE gateway of Paramount Pictures, I took a deep breath for luck. I'd hardly slept a wink the night before, tossing and turning in the dark motel room. Roxy and I hadn't spoken since our fight, and I didn't know if I could forgive her for the way she'd treated me.

I had a feeling she would find another roommate, and I would be out of a job and a place to stay. Her words rang in my ears: *You ain't got two pennies to rub together.* A woman in sunglasses and a white head scarf rode past me in a mint-green golf cart. I craned my neck, trying to figure out who she was.

My shoulders tensed. I longed to be an actress transported from set to studio, dancing to the tune of whimsical musicals, or crying tears on command. The tears that threatened to come now were those of desperation. I had a few months, perhaps three or four, before I would no longer be able to conceal my growing belly. I had to land a part—*immediately*—or my dream would vanish before my eyes.

Standing with the other girls in the waiting area, I looked around for a friendly face. Everyone buried their noses in their scripts, and a few gals shot me suspicious looks. I'd curled my hair and put on an extra swipe of blush, but I felt less fresh-faced than some of the gals I saw in line, who couldn't be more than teenagers. In no time I would be old news—my chance to become the next ingénue would pass.

I placed a hand protectively over my belly, and then remembered I oughtn't do that in public. I dropped it to my side. Taking a deep breath, I let it out in a shudder. I *had* to nail this reading. I had to.

"Violet! Is that you?"

I spun on my heel to see Harry Goodman strolling toward me. At the sight of his familiar jolly face, the tension between my shoulders eased. I wanted to embrace him.

"Oh Harry, what are you doing here?"

"I'm here for an audition. My agent sent me. How've you been?"

"Wonderful," I lied, wondering if he could see the sadness in my eyes. "How about you?"

"Couldn't be better," he said, reaching into his shirt pocket. "I got a telegram for you at the Pink Flamingo. It must've arrived before you gave your husband your new address. I've been carrying it around in case I ran into you."

My heart dropped into my stomach. "Charles sent me a telegram?"

"Sure did," Harry said, handing me the folded pink slip of paper. "He misses you." He looked sheepish. "Sorry, couldn't stop myself from peeking."

With trembling fingers, I opened the message.

Santa Cruz, CA August 15 1940

Violet I miss you dearly. Everything will be different. I promise. I love you. Please allow me to take you home. I can be there tomorrow if you ask me to.

My eyes welled with tears. I thought of my beach bungalow overlooking the Pacific Ocean, the path bursting with wildflowers, poppies and purple ice plant. I thought of Evie, wrapping me in a hug, congratulating me on becoming a mother, and telling me everything would be all right. Perhaps this baby would change things—perhaps this baby was what Charles and I needed to become a loving husband and wife again.

"You miss him," Harry said.

I nodded, my lip trembling. "A great deal."

Harry placed a comforting arm on my shoulder. "There's no shame in returning home, Violet."

I nodded, feeling as though I were in a dream. Looking around at the studio hands, golf carts and strangers with scripts, it was as if I didn't belong here at all. Like Alice, I had tumbled down a rabbit hole to find myself in unfamiliar surroundings.

"Everyone here to read for John Huston's film, follow me to soundstage five."

I startled, turning to see the man who'd announced the casting call.

"Good luck," Harry said, giving me an apologetic smile. "I'm in room 305 at the Pink Flamingo. If you need me, you know where to find me."

"Thank you," I replied. "I will."

"Oh," Harry called after me. "Where are you staying? You forgot to mention it."

"Did I?" Watching the other girls queue up for the audition, no lie came to mind in time, and Harry waited for an answer.

"At the Tropicana," I said, turning to follow the girls to the soundstage.

"At the other end of Hollywood Boulevard?"

"That's the one."

As I walked a few paces behind the gaggle of women across the Paramount lot, I clutched the telegram from Charles with both hands.

I miss you dearly.

I love you.

Everything will be different.

His words touched my heart as only a husband's could. Suddenly his absence ached like an open wound.

I longed for his reassuring embrace, his warm brown eyes, and the familiar scent of his cologne. He could take me home. He'd seen my note requesting a divorce, but he'd forgiven me.

And my child, my little olive—already I'd come to think of her as a little girl. She needed a father. We could be a family again.

CHAPTER 18

Marisol Cruz

2007

"You know," Jason said, looking around at the giggling kids in Marini's soda fountain. "Santa Cruz is the perfect place to raise a family."

Mari smiled, watching the little girls put quarters in the gumball machine. She'd come to this ice cream shop with her *abuelo* and *abuela* during her childhood, and loved that the family business was still thriving. The mint chip ice cream still tasted exactly the same, the best she'd ever had.

"It really is. I feel so fortunate to have grown up here, and to be able to raise Lily here. There's no more beautiful place in the world."

Jason's brown eyes twinkled. "I really like you," he said, twirling the stem of his maraschino cherry. "I hope you don't think I'm too old-fashioned, but honestly, I'm almost thirty, and I'm ready to settle down."

Mari's heart skipped a beat. "Jason, I really like you too, but we've only been on one date . . ."

He laughed, looking adorable as he grinned at her. "Don't worry, I'm not popping the question. Though I could get down on one knee right now to embarrass you."

"Please don't."

"Then listen. What I want to say is, I'm totally over game playing. I want someone I can be honest with. And I feel like I can be honest with you. I don't want to date anyone else. And I'm hoping that you don't either . . ."

"Oh, so you don't know about my other boyfriend, Tyrell?"

"Shut up."

Mari smiled. "You're cool and all, but Tyrell lets me ride his motorcycle. He's got this bad-boy thing going on, and it's really sexy."

Before she could continue, he'd placed his lips on hers. The kiss was soft, yet passionate. Mari closed her eyes and the soda fountain faded away. Jason smelled like the forest, like summer. She could kiss him over and over again.

"I could get used to that."

"Good," Jason said. "Because I'm not going anywhere."

Mari took his hand in hers. "There's something I want to tell you too."

Jason raised an eyebrow. "Tell me."

"I won the Swanson Grant."

Jason's mouth dropped open, then he broke out into a huge smile. "Are you kidding me? Mari, congratulations!"

He wrapped her in a bear hug, and then stood up, addressing the room full of children. "Everyone! You're looking at the next Swanson Grant recipient right here. This is one *very* smart lady. Let's give her a round of applause."

Mari wanted to cover her face and she tugged at Jason's hand, but the little girls smiled at her with missing teeth and clapped excitedly.

"Oh my God," she whispered. "You're the worst."

Jason sat down. "I'm sorry if I'm embarrassing, but I'm proud of you. This is exciting! See, I told you that you could do it. What happens next?"

"I got the idea to create a diorama of the gazebo—well, have artists create it, because I don't have an artistic bone in my body. I want to record Santa Cruz senior citizens talking about their memories of the gazebo, and play the audio recording. It'll be set up at the museum booth like an art installation."

"That sounds cool," Jason said, smiling.

"Thanks. If I can get the project finished in the next month or so, I'll have time for it to be on display at the Centennial Celebration through August. This should help gain public interest in the gazebo and show its historic significance."

Jason frowned. "I don't mean to be a downer, but what if it gets demolished before you're able to put the art installation on display?"

Mari tapped her bottom lip. "I have to officially oppose the condo development to stall them. I'm going to distribute flyers to the neighborhood, to everyone whose views would be obstructed by the tower. I'm going to rally as many people as I can to attend the next planning commission meeting. Can I count you in?"

"You bet. I'll offer my photocopying services courtesy of the UC Santa Cruz English department to help you save some money."

"Really? Thanks."

"Do you think you'll have a tough time getting people on board?"

Mari shook her head. "I think residents are ready to fight this. A tall glass building doesn't conform to the character of a neighborhood with single-story homes."

She sighed, her stomach sinking. "There's just one problem."

"What?"

"Travis Harcourt." His name felt hard in her mouth. "I haven't spoken to him since the summer of my college graduation. Unless you count the roughly one hundred unanswered emails I sent him with pictures of Lily."

Jason rubbed Mari's hand. "I'm so sorry. I can't imagine how that must've felt. You have to be missing a soul to turn your back on your kid like that."

"I'm going to have to confront him, talk with him face-to-face, and tell him that I'm opposing the development." She swallowed, but her mouth felt dry. It was not an encounter she wanted to have. In fact, she was dreading it.

"You can do this," Jason said, looking at her with such conviction that she felt a swell of confidence. "It won't be comfortable, but you can. I have faith in you."

"Thank you. It feels really nice to know someone has my back."

"Always," Jason said. "In fact, email me the flyer you want to distribute to the neighbors today. I'll photocopy as many as you want."

She raised an eyebrow. "Won't the English department staff get suspicious if you're abusing the copy machine?"

He shrugged. "I fix their computers. They let me do whatever I want."

"Touché."

"So, do you need to get going, or do you want to walk down Pacific Avenue with me? It's a gorgeous day out, and I'd love to spend it with this gorgeous lady."

Mari rolled her eyes. "If you stop being cheesy, I'd be happy to walk with you. I'll even ride the bus with you up to campus, because I want to do some more research at McHenry Library."

MARI SAT IN an overstuffed armchair, looking out the floor-to-ceiling windows at the forest of majestic redwood trees. Though she'd come to the library to research zoning requirements to see if Travis Harcourt's construction project was in violation of any city codes, Mari's mind had wandered. To be honest, the material on city zoning laws was bone-dry. A little procrastination wouldn't be horrible, would it?

Mari typed "Violet Harcourt" into her computer browser. It was a stretch, but if she could prove that Charles Harcourt had mishandled his business funds (or whatever it was he'd done that might've played a part in Violet's suicide), she could smear Travis's development campaign. The townspeople could see the mayor had taken office through inherited power, and that Travis was nothing more than a trust fund brat.

She seethed with anger toward Travis. It was stupid, but finding something incriminating about his grandfather would give her a bit of satisfaction.

Searching Violet's name, Mari came up with the one acting credit she'd seen on her previous search of Violet—a nonspeaking role in a John Huston film: "the vixen at the bar."

The role wasn't much, but it could have served as a stepping-stone to landing another part. Hadn't Katharine Hepburn had her first scenes cut from the films she shot, but she was encouraged to continue? Eventually she'd attracted the interest of an assistant director and shot a test scene that was shown to a producer. Mari remembered that tidbit from a film class she'd taken in college, to fill an arts credit requirement.

So why did Violet return to Santa Cruz?

Mari typed "Violet Harcourt, Hollywood Actress 1940" into her browser, and waited for the results to load. A few photos appeared: Violet's head shot; her California pageant photo, Violet wearing a retro one-piece swimsuit with a flared skirt. For a 1940s beauty queen she was slim—not quite the norm for an era when women were refreshingly curvy.

Scrolling through images of famous actresses of the

1940s, Mari saw Hedy Lamarr, Judy Garland, Lauren Bacall, Rita Hayworth and Ginger Rogers. They exuded timeless glamour, all red lips and sultry waves.

An image of an old Hollywood magazine caught her eye: *Screen Secrets*. The vintage copy of the magazine was for sale on Amazon, now forty dollars instead of twenty cents. Mari clicked on the link "Louella Parsons Blind Items."

Someone had posted it to a chat board. "Does anyone recognize the 1940s actress in this blind item?"

Under *"Best Answer"* someone had replied. "It could be anyone, really. Every Miss so-and-so thought they had a chance of making it in Hollywood even if they only ended up working as a cocktail waitress. But it looks like Violet Harcourt, who was Miss California in 1940, and then withdrew because she was married. Other Miss California winners from that time period are Evelyn Hastings, Edie Smith and Bettie Watson. Good luck.

Mari tapped her mouth as Violet's obituary came to mind.

Two months prior to her death, Harcourt, recently crowned Miss California, withdrew from the Miss America pageant, admitting her marital status rendered her ineligible to compete. Runner-up Evelyn Hastings took her place.

Not only would Evelyn be a good candidate for Mari's grant project, but also she might have been a friend of Violet's. Mari definitely had questions she wanted answered, like how Abuelo and Violet knew each other.

Opening another tab, Mari searched for "Evelyn Hastings, Santa Cruz." A result popped up from the white pages:

Evelyn L Hastings

Age 88

Lives in San Jose, CA

Used to live in Santa Cruz, CA

Related to Karen E. Smith, Ronald F. Hastings

Mari Googled "Karen E. Smith" and found a professional profile. Karen worked in nearby Capitola as a real estate agent. Finding Karen's professional website, Mari composed a quick email, explaining her grant project and asking Karen if she might make an introduction to Evelyn. Hopefully Evelyn was still in good health. Who better to record memories of the Beach Boardwalk than a former beauty queen?

Turning her attention back to her browser, Mari read the text from Louella Parson's gossip column.

> At a soiree at the home of a famous Hollywood director, known for giving his films a special "touch," a notorious lothario screenwriter and a former Miss California were necking in the garden. The pretty redhead was spotted at Don the Beachcomber with our young screenwriter a few nights previous. She donned a pair of diamond and sapphire swirl clip earrings, perhaps a gift from a wealthy suitor.
>
> With the lothario's advances thwarted, the famous director came to the rescue, pulling the aspiring actress from the grass, the hem of her gown trampled and scratches on her skin! He may appear

gentle but this foreign-born director is a knight in shining armor, giving the party-crashing screenwriter the boot. As for our damsel in distress? Her time in Hollywood is finished. No one recovers from that kind of mishap unscathed.

Mari brought her fingers to her lips. The date of the Hollywood gossip blind item was August 10, 1940. That fell within the timeline of when Violet was in Hollywood. She typed in another quick search, and then found the line she was looking for, describing Violet's bridal attire.

She wore custom diamond and sapphire swirl clip earrings as her "something blue."

The earrings matched the description. And Violet's obituary had described her as an auburn-haired beauty. She had to be the Miss California mentioned in this gossip column. Had Violet been sexually assaulted in the garden by a young screenwriter? What an awful introduction to Hollywood.

Ernst Lubitsch was a director from Germany, known for giving his films "the Lubitsch Touch." Mari typed "Lubitsch Hollywood Parties" to see if she could find anything. Sure enough, there were articles describing parties with midnight swimming, croquet and Ping-Pong, with elaborate floral displays and candles, along with images of the dark-haired director on set with various actresses.

It wasn't too much of a stretch to believe Violet had once been to his home. If Louella Parsons was convinced an encounter like that would ruin Violet's reputation, how intensely must Violet have felt the shame of what happened?

Maybe this negative experience convinced her to return to Charles. Mari shivered, thinking of the kind of man Charles Harcourt appeared to be. Possessive. Powerful. Louella Parsons painted a dark picture for Violet.

No one recovers from that kind of mishap unscathed.

CHAPTER 19

Violet Harcourt

1940

"You've got a call on the front desk phone."

Roxy glared at me with a face so sour, she could've swallowed a lemon. Since the Benny Bronstein incident, we'd hardly spoken. She'd left me alone in the motel room to work her shift at the Tropical Gardens, and while I had a few hours to myself, I lay in bed rereading Charles's telegram.

"Who is it?" I asked, my heart pounding.

"A second assistant director," she said, wrinkling her nose.

That explained the sour face. Hopping out of bed, I slipped on my sandals, tied my robe tightly around my midsection and scurried down to the hotel lobby.

The desk girl handed me the phone, and I brought it to my ear with a trembling hand. "This is Violet Sweeting."

"Miss Sweeting. This is Bill Chase. I'm the second assistant director at Paramount. I work under John Huston. I'm calling you in regard to your recent audition."

"Yes?" I replied, clutching the telephone cord.

"We liked what we saw. You've got a certain look about you. We'd like you to come back tomorrow to begin filming."

I brought my hand to my lips. "Did I get the part?"

"A speaking part? No. You'll be cast as an extra. But you can call yourself a supporting actor if you like."

"Oh," I said, my stomach sinking. "Is it paid?"

"Not as much as a speaking role, but you'll get free lunch on set and a steady paycheck for every day that you film."

"Well," I said, my smile returning. "That's marvelous. What time should I arrive?"

"Call time is at eight in the morning, sharp. Walk to soundstage eight on the Paramount lot. You'll see the trailers and buses."

"Thank you. I'll be there tomorrow."

I hung up the phone, squealing as I pushed the phone back toward the receptionist. She smiled at me.

"Got a part?"

"As an extra. It's not much, but it's a start."

"That's the spirit," she said, patting my arm. I wondered how many girls she'd seen over the course of her time working at this motel, hoping for their lucky break. I breathed a sigh of relief. Things were looking up.

I COUGHED, BREATHING in gasoline fumes as I sat in the back of the crowded bus. Shiny, luxury Airstream trailers had been parked around stage eight on the Paramount lot, but this old, battered Greyhound bus was reserved for extras.

My vision of the glamorous life of a film actor had dimmed when I was ushered away from the main stage and into this decrepit automobile. Occasionally members of the crew would come aboard to handpick extras for particular scenes. I waited, holding my breath, only to watch the stagehands choose another girl. It felt awful, much like being picked last in gym class. I'd never been the sporty type, and my teenage insecurities came rushing back to me all over again.

A freckled brunette sitting beside me opened up her knapsack, removing an apron, a knife and fork, a plate, a checkered cloth napkin and a bread roll. She caught me looking and smiled, her blue eyes twinkling.

"Everything but the kitchen sink, right?"

"You do have quite a lot in there."

She extended her hand. "Vera Stanley."

"Violet Sweeting," I replied, shaking it.

"The longer you work as an extra, the more you'll learn. For instance, if you're wearing period clothing, an apron is a must. You can't let crumbs dirty a medieval gown, or Wardrobe will have your head!"

I laughed. "Have you been in Hollywood a long time?"

"Two years," she said, spreading the napkin across her lap and slicing into the bread roll. "I was a stage actress in Rhode Island, but I wanted to come out west."

A ripple of nausea rose to my throat. I took a deep

breath, fighting the feeling. No one could suspect I was pregnant, or I'd be truly finished. The encounter with Benny Bronstein at Ernst Lubitsch's house had been mortifying enough, but he was only one director. Hopefully John Huston hadn't caught word of anything.

"How has it been?" I asked, looking at Vera's sweet face. She appeared to be an openhearted person. She hardly wore a stitch of makeup and didn't seem like the type to command attention, but she had a certain pale prettiness, like an English rose.

Vera shrugged. "Hard at times. I'd hoped to get a speaking role by now. But working as an extra is consistent. It pays the rent. And the food on set is quite good."

"Yet you brought your own?"

She tore off a piece of the bun. "We don't break for lunch until after noon. Trust me, you'll be starving by then."

"Thank you," I said, grateful for the soft bread. Chewing it helped to settle my stomach, the bland flavor inoffensive.

"Besides," she said. "Working as an extra isn't all bad. You can talk to a writer on set and perhaps get an audition out of it. You never know what's going to happen."

I cringed, thinking of Benny. *To hell with screenwriters.*

"Oh look," she said, setting down her bread. "A stagehand is back."

We straightened our posture as he climbed aboard the bus, his eyes scanning the sea of faces. He cleared his throat.

"Next up, we need a beautiful young woman. This is

a prime shot, the vixen at the bar. Ladies, here's your chance at the spotlight."

My heart began to pound as I silently prayed he would pick me. What if I were sitting too far back to be noticed?

He pointed at two girls in the front of the bus. "You, you . . ." Then his eyes locked on mine. "And you. Come this way."

Me!

Vera squeezed my hand. "Good luck. I hope your scene doesn't get cut. This could be big for you."

I smoothed my dress. "Is that common?"

"Unfortunately. Some of my best work didn't make it to film."

"I see."

"Don't mind me," she said, smiling. "I didn't mean to rain on your parade. Try to remain cautiously optimistic. That's the best advice I can give."

"Thank you," I said, standing and following the other two girls down the narrow bus aisle. "I will."

We disembarked, crossed the Paramount lot and passed the shiny Airstream trailers. Suddenly, I felt the urge to use the loo.

"Is there a lavatory inside?" I asked. The stagehand shot me a look. "The toilets inside are only for the actors. Extras use the porta pottys out back."

"Oh," I said, surprised. Perhaps it would be wise to get accustomed to feeling like a second-class citizen, or I might earn the reputation of being difficult.

I held it, following the other girls into a room in a large

hangar-like building. Racks and racks of clothing stood against the wall on wheeled carts. I felt giddy, glimpsing the assortment of gowns. The stagehand pointed to two women working the costume department. "Fay and Rita here will help you get dressed, then we'll call each one of you on set."

He disappeared, and we were told to disrobe. I eyed the other girls, envious of their creamy, unblemished skin and slim physiques. I felt acutely aware of my bloated belly. But my breasts swelled rather nicely, and would fill out any bodice.

One of the women, Rita, handed me a bloodred gown on a velvet hanger. It had a deep V-neck and cap sleeves. I shimmied into it, smiling when it zipped all the way up, a perfect fit. One of the other girls wore a green, strapless gown that gapped in the bosom. She tugged it upward. I noticed all three of us were redheads, about the same age.

"She looks like a scarecrow," Fay said to Rita, as if the girl weren't standing right in front of them. "The bust is a terrible fit. Take it off."

Rita nodded, unzipping the dress as if the girl were a set prop. The girl looked like she was going to cry. The poor dear! Next she tried on a floor-length blue velvet gown with a dramatic open back. But Fay shook her head dismissively. "She's not going to work."

I bit my lip as the redhead was dismissed, blinking back tears as she walked away.

The other gal managed to appease both costume department employees when she zipped into a black cocktail gown. She looked rather lovely in it, her hair parted to one side and auburn waves falling over her bare shoulders. I clenched my hands nervously. Would she land the part?

"This one could use a bit more makeup," Fay said. Then I realized she was talking about me. Rita nodded, her eyes meeting mine. "Do you have a compact with you? Put on another coat of lipstick and a bit more rouge."

I nodded. "I do."

Pulling my compact from my purse, I flipped open the little mirror. My dark blue eyes stared back at me, pools of sadness. I coated my lips again, the dark crimson striking against my pale skin. I didn't recognize myself—this haunted woman. I'd given up so much for the price of fame, and at what cost?

I shivered, placing my compact back in my purse. I didn't know what the future held . . . but this baby was coming, whether I was ready or not.

"Your turn," Rita said, pointing toward the set.

"Thank you," I said, gathering my courage.

When I stepped onto the soundstage, I couldn't believe the transformation. It had been decorated like a luxurious lounge, with a marble bar and dark wood-paneled walls. How magnificent that such a building could be created inside an aircraft hangar. I felt as though I were in a glamorous New York hotel.

"Stand here," a stagehand said to me. He ran back to his post, and then adjusted the light so it shone on my face. "Perfect, like that."

My heart fluttered as I saw Humphrey Bogart walk into the room. *My stars!* I hadn't known who'd been cast in the lead role, but now the cat was out of the bag. I'd seen him play the gangster in *Angels with Dirty Faces*. He was quite handsome.

"On your marks," the director called, rising from his chair. He was a gentleman in his mid-thirties with dark hair and hooded eyes. So that was John Huston? I didn't recognize the male actor with Humphrey Bogart, but both stood at the bar, drinks in hand. Swallowing, I wondered if any of them had paid me any mind.

"Here," a stagehand said, pushing a glass of gin toward me.

"You," John Huston said, addressing me.

I shot to attention. "Yes, sir?"

"Stare into that gin glass. Portray her sadness with your eyes. All right? We'll begin filming in three, two, one . . ."

Feeling the soft glow of the light overhead, I stared into my gin glass as Humphrey Bogart began to speak.

"What'sa guy gotta do to catch a break in this town?"

"Dunno," the other actor answered. "These are tough times."

"Everybody's gotta make a living." Bogart glanced over at me. "What's her story?"

I stared at the ice cubes in my glass. *What was my story?* I'd come here to chase my dreams, left my husband and my entire life behind. Now I was pregnant and alone. *So very alone.* I felt my eyes prick with tears.

"Who knows?" the actor said. "You ain't got time to

chase after dames. We're meeting Bobby at the docks in an hour. Bottoms up."

"Cut!"

I looked up, the faces of the film crew hardly visible in the darkened room. Stagehands adjusted lights and sound equipment. Humphrey Bogart stood at ease, chatting with his male costar.

"We've got it," John Huston announced. "Fantastic!"

"That's your cue to go," the stagehand whispered.

I looked around, waiting for some kind of recognition from somebody—anybody—but there was no one there to share my joy. Had I captured what the director was looking for in only one take?

After using the portable toilet, I returned to the Greyhound bus. A bell sounded on set, and soon everyone was queuing up for lunch. The smell of beef hit me, but instead of making me feel sick, my stomach rumbled with a craving for meat.

"How did you do?" Vera asked, coming up beside me.

"I think I did well. The director said we had the take."

"Violet, that's wonderful! And I heard today's meal is roast beef and mashed potatoes. Smells delicious, doesn't it?"

"It does," I said, picking up a plastic tray.

"You're going to want to borrow my apron," Vera said, giggling. "You're still wearing your gown from Wardrobe."

"Oh heavens, I am."

"Were the women in the costume department awful? Sometimes I feel like a prop, the way they talk about me like I'm not there."

I suppressed a smile. "One wasn't so bad. She told me to apply more makeup before shooting."

"She didn't pretend you were a coat hanger? Well, she sounds like a winner."

I laughed, the knot in my stomach loosening. Today had gone splendidly. And with a little luck, soon I would be watching myself on the silver screen.

THE SUNSET PAINTED the sky pink and orange as I walked down Hollywood Boulevard toward the Tropicana motel. It stood in silhouette against the darkening twilight, palm trees framing its blockish shape. Though Roxy and I hadn't been on the greatest terms lately, I felt excited to tell her about my day. Perhaps we could move past our spat and go out for drinks together.

I'd walked another ten paces when I recognized the shiny black Cadillac parked out front. I stopped dead in my tracks. *Charles.* My heart stopped beating, and then started again, pounding furiously. Time seemed to move in slow motion as he opened the driver's side door and stepped out of the car. His eyes met mine.

Electricity shot through me. He looked so handsome in his suit, his dark hair parted to the side. But his expression—I couldn't read it. He'd come for me, even though I hadn't asked him to yet. *How?* I recalled the other night, telling Harry the name of my motel. Charles must have gotten in touch with him.

With my lip trembling, I walked toward my husband, longing to feel his warm embrace. In his telegram, he'd told me he loved me. He'd apologized for his actions. He *could* change. My leaving for Hollywood had shown him what it would be like to lose me. And now that he knew that pain, he would treat me better. I could give him another chance and give our child a loving father.

A lump rose in my throat as I reached for my husband's hand. "Oh Charles, I received your telegram . . ."

Pulling me tightly against him, he kissed my forehead. I closed my eyes, drinking in the scent of his cologne. He opened the passenger door to his car and guided me toward it. My stomach clenched with a rush of nerves. What if he were to hurt me again? Something in my gut told me not to get in the car.

Yet I sat down in the passenger seat. Shutting the car door with a heavy thump, he walked around to the driver's side and opened his door. I breathed in the familiar scent of the leather, my stomach knotting uncomfortably.

He settled in the driver's seat, closing his door loudly.

"My darling," I said, my heart pounding. "I've missed you so much. I'm terribly sorry for how I left, but now that you're here, I suppose you want to talk."

I looked at my husband's somber profile. He sat in silence.

A cold feeling passed over me. "Charles?"

The slap came faster than I could block it, my cheek smarting.

Charles's eyes shone with rage.

"You thought you could leave me? That you could *divorce* me? And then you step out with another *man*?"

My heart dropped into my stomach. "Charles, please." These were not the loving words I had received in his telegram. "I can explain."

But in truth, I had no explanation for Benny Bronstein that would appease Charles. Heaven help me, he would be livid. How had he known?

Shoving his key in the ignition, Charles started the car, the engine rumbling to life. Panic set in as I tugged at the door handle.

"Unlock the door."

Whipping around, he gripped my arm so hard that I cried out in pain. His fingers dug into my flesh, in the spot where bruises of months past had faded. "You're coming home with me, you lying, cheating *whore*. If you hadn't embarrassed me, I wouldn't have to punish you. But mark my words, you will be punished."

"Let go," I whimpered, pulling my arm back.

Charles released his grip, returning his hand to the wheel. As he pulled away from the curb, I watched the Tropicana grow smaller in the distance, its palm trees fading in the rearview mirror. I thought of Roxy waiting inside, wanting to hear how my audition had gone. What would she do when I didn't return?

Nothing. She would find another roommate and wouldn't give me a second thought. Hollywood was cold like that. I should have confided in her about Charles. But I'd been too frightened to tell anyone the truth. No one knew the danger I was in.

"You've become gossip column fodder," Charles spat.

"Necking in the bushes with a goddamned *Jew*. How do you think it felt for me to read that? Do you realize what this could do to my reputation?"

My hands trembled. In the past, Charles had accused me of infidelity, and his suspicions had never been true. But now I had made him feel a fool. I swallowed, hard. My mouth felt dry as cotton. "Charles, we can't continue like this. You have a sickness. You frighten me. I intended to file for divorce, remember?"

"Divorce," he spat, pressing his foot down on the gas. I gripped the sides of my seat as I watched the speedometer needle climb higher and higher. "I abhor the notion. You *belong* to me. I thought I'd made that clear."

"You didn't tell anyone that I left you?"

"What I do is my business!" Charles shouted. "How would that appear to people, you leaving *me*?" He laughed, his knuckles whitening as he gripped the wheel. "After I discovered your spiteful note, it didn't take me long to find out you'd run away with that pathetic comedian. I walked into the dive of a restaurant where you used to work, and your sad little waitress friend told me all about your grand adventure."

Dot. She'd been there the night of the party. Thank God, Charles hadn't spoken to Ricky. With his abhorrence of Mexicans, he could put Ricky in much danger. Evie had counseled me to keep my distance from Ricky after marrying Charles, and she'd been wise to do so.

"What did Dot tell you?"

"That I was a wonderful husband for *allowing* you to

pursue your acting dreams. That used-up little piece of trash looked at me like I was a king."

"Please don't call her that. She's my friend."

"You don't have any friends," he said, revving the engine. The car jolted forward, nearly rear-ending the Oldsmobile in front of us.

I shut my eyes. "Slow down. You'll get us killed."

"You're lucky I haven't killed you already."

He said it with such conviction, a chill traveled from the crown of my head to my toes. I fought the urge to place a hand over my belly. If I told Charles that he was going to be a father, would his eyes soften, and would he slow down the car?

Dreaming this baby would change things between us was only that—a foolish dream. With his paranoia, I mightn't be able to convince Charles the child was his. I cringed, waves of hurt and humiliation washing over me. Charles became infuriated if I so much as talked to another man. And now he had proof another man had touched me.

A tear slipped down my cheek, my heart clenching for my little olive.

Charles's jealousy fueled his rage and cruelty. This time, he would kill us both.

CHAPTER 20

Marisol Cruz

2007

Turning down Younger Way, Mari's flip-flops slapped against the pavement, a stack of flyers tucked under her arm. True to his word, Jason had made one hundred copies and printed them on bright blue paper.

With the sun warming her shoulders, Mari smiled as she took in the stunning view of the Pacific Ocean from Beach Hill. This really was the most desirable neighborhood in Santa Cruz, and Abuelo had put down roots here. She had an easy downhill stroll to the ocean, the historic Santa Cruz wharf and the Beach Boardwalk.

In the distance, Mari saw surfers and boogie boarders enjoying the waves at Cowell's Beach, a much tamer spot than where the experts surfed at Steamer Lane, by the lighthouse. She hadn't taken up surfing, but she loved to ride her beach cruiser along West Cliff Drive with Lily in tow behind her.

So far, she'd had luck with every neighbor she'd spoken to about her petition. Almost everyone opposed the condominium development, agreeing that the character of the beach would be ruined, along with views of the ocean.

Stopping in front of a Craftsman-style bungalow with a brick porch, Mari pulled a flyer from her stack. She rang the doorbell and waited.

A woman in her sixties pulled the door open, her green eyes twinkling behind her glasses. She pushed her white-blond bob behind her ear.

"Can I help you?"

"Hi," Mari said, handing her a flyer. "I'm your neighbor. My name is Mari Cruz. I live over on Second Street. Have you heard about the recent luxury condominium development that's set to be built on the site of the historic gazebo?"

The woman opened the door wider. "Have I ever. The nerve of the mayor!"

Mari handed the woman a flyer. It had been Jason's idea to add "Join 2007 Swanson Grant recipient Mari Cruz in the fight against City Hall."

"My grandparents met at a dance at the historic gazebo, and it's a special place to me. They had their wedding reception there, which is why I'm so passionate about saving the structure."

The woman's face lit up. "Your family is from Santa Cruz? I'm third-generation. My name's Judy."

Mari shook her hand. "It's nice to meet you, Judy. Can I count on you to join me in signing this petition to fight the development?"

"Absolutely," Judy said. "Give me a pen."

MARI RETURNED HOME with aching legs, invigorated by her fight against Travis Harcourt. The first part of her checklist had been completed: getting neighbors to sign the petition. Sitting down at her desk, Mari opened her laptop, ready to set her grant process in motion. She'd reached out to the Latin American and Latino studies department on the UCSC campus, as well as the art department, looking for students willing to help with her diorama project. Hopefully they'd be passionate about it, and eager to add the opportunity for recognition offered by the Swanson Grant to their résumés.

Mari checked her inbox. She'd posted on a local neighborhood forum, asking if anyone had family who'd lived by the Beach Boardwalk in the 1940s, and if they would be willing to share their memories on film.

Though no one had responded yet, Mari smiled seeing an email from Karen E. Smith. Doing a little Internet research had paid off.

Dear Mari,

I read your email regarding the Swanson Grant. First of all, congratulations! Though my mother did not live in Santa Cruz year-round, she spent every summer there during the 1930s and 1940s, at a beach cottage our family owned at the time. She is 88 years old and currently resides in a nursing home in San Jose. You are correct in that she is the very same Evelyn Hastings who was nominated Miss California in the year 1940! She would love to have a visitor. In fact, recording her memories is something I have been meaning to do. Please reach out to me if you would like to arrange a time to meet. I'll be out of town next week, so the sooner, the better.

Sincerely,
Karen Smith

Mari clapped her hands together. She itched to ask Evelyn how well she knew Violet, and if she'd also known Abuelo. She composed another email to Karen, eager to set up a time to visit Evelyn Hastings at her nursing home.

After reading several artists' responses, and looking through their online portfolios, Mari decided which two she wanted to work with. Both were young Latinas, eager to create a meaningful piece of art for the community. Mari smiled. She'd done more today than she had in the past four years. And it felt *fantastic*. Meeting Jason had set off a chain of events: applying for the grant, talking to her neighbors, standing up to Travis, making new friends. She'd walled herself off for so long. Now that she'd started to let people in, it felt nice to be a part of the community.

"THIS WAY," a nursing home attendant in a pink uniform said, leading Mari down a carpeted hallway. Mari's mom had let her borrow the car for the drive over Highway 17 to San Jose. Swallowing, Mari tried to dispel her nerves. Evelyn didn't know her from Adam, and she might not take kindly to having a stranger show up.

The attendant stopped in front of the door at the end of the hall. She beamed. "Evelyn is such a peach. We all love her. Her health isn't great, but her mind is sound and she sure hasn't lost her sense of humor."

Pushing the door open, the attendant ushered Mari inside. "Here she is. I'll leave you two alone. Evelyn, you have a visitor."

Mari stepped inside, finding a wisp of a white-haired woman reclining in bed, veined hands with pink manicured nails settled across her lap. She turned toward Mari, her brows drawing together, her blue eyes struggling to place her.

"Good afternoon," Mari said, extending her hand. "My name is Marisol Cruz, and your daughter Karen said it was okay if I paid you a visit. Is that all right, Evelyn?"

Evelyn straightened, and then cocked her head toward a chair. "Karen sent you?"

"That's right. She responded to an email I sent her. I'm interviewing elderly people about their memories of the boardwalk."

"Do you live in Santa Cruz?"

"I do," Mari said, taking a seat next to the bed. "On Second Street. I live in the house my grandfather built. His name was Ricardo Cruz. He was a stunt diver at the Santa Cruz Beach Boardwalk in the 1940s."

Evelyn's eyes widened. "Ricky Cruz? He was a pal of my dear friend Violet. I didn't know him well, mind you, but I remember him. Is he still alive?"

Mari's throat tightened. Evelyn had known Abuelo, and that was a special thing. "No. He passed away a few years ago. But he had a very happy life. He was a wonderful man. He loved being a grandpa."

Evelyn's eyes glistened. "So many of my friends have passed away. It's very lonely to be the last one left. How kind of you to visit me . . . what did you say your name was? Maribel?"

"Marisol. But you can call me Mari."

She smiled. "You can call me Evie. My dear friend Violet used to call me that. Every summer I would stay at the bungalow my family owned, right across from the boardwalk. The Giant Dipper was so close, it would shake the walls!"

Mari smiled. "Do you mind if I record our conversation? I won't if you're not comfortable, but it's for my grant project."

Evelyn nodded. "Sure. I suppose that's all right."

"Thank you." Mari removed a tape recorder from her purse—a relic of the eighties, but decidedly less intrusive than a video camera. She pushed the button to begin recording. "How did you meet Violet?"

"We were teenagers when we met one summer. She asked to borrow my suntan lotion. We would ride our bicycles to visit each other. And we spent every weekend together at the Beach Boardwalk. Did your grandfather ever tell you about the bands that played? Oh, the dancing! Did I tell you that Violet was a beauty queen, and so was I? We did pageants together, you see."

Mari smiled. "Your daughter told me. Actually, I was hoping you could tell me a bit more about Violet. I read that she left for Hollywood to become an actress. I think she wrote my grandfather a postcard once she arrived in Los Angeles."

Evie's eyes narrowed. "Yes, she went to Hollywood before . . ." Her voice cracked with emotion when she spoke again. "She took off like a thief in the night."

Mari swallowed. Maybe it was better to leave the past alone, especially if it was upsetting this poor elderly woman.

"I'm so sorry," Mari said. "I read about Violet's death in the paper. We don't have to talk about her if it's too painful. But I was hoping you might give me more of an idea of who she was and what she was like."

Evie blinked back tears. "It's all right." She smiled. "Violet was a hoot. She was beautiful, a talented singer and dancer, determined to best me at everything. She dreamed of seeing her name in lights, on the marquee of a theater." Her eyes clouded. "After she married her husband, Charles, she changed. Became more withdrawn."

"How so?"

"Well." Evie clasped her hands. "She stopped riding her bicycle to visit me. I rarely saw her alone. Often we would have dinner with Charles and my husband, Frank. Charles was a charming and powerful man. He owned the Oceano Golf Club. Violet never wanted for anything . . . yet she seemed unhappy."

Mari scooted forward in her chair. "Was she happy when she entered the Miss California beauty pageant?"

"Oh yes," Evie said, smiling. "She was so very excited to win. But you see, we were both married at the time, and that was against the rules. Violet couldn't keep up the lie, so she withdrew and asked that I attend the Miss America pageant in her place. She told me she was keen to start a family with Charles. But then . . ."

"She left for Hollywood?"

"That's right. Without telling me! And we were quite close. Bosom buddies, you could say. It hurt when she left like that. Frank came home one evening, told me he'd spoken with Charles, and that Charles had given Violet his blessing to pursue her acting career. But it didn't add up. Charles had never been supportive of Violet acting. He was a possessive man."

"Did Charles try to control Violet?"

Evie frowned. "When she returned from Hollywood, yes. I tried to visit, but every time she gave me some kind of excuse. 'Oh, I'm feeling ill, come back later.' For weeks, she stayed indoors. I happened upon her once while she was grocery shopping, and she flinched like a skittish horse."

Evie paused to take a breath, and then shook her head. "I was thrilled to see her. I asked her about Hollywood, about her actress friends, but it was like pulling teeth. Normally she'd chat my ear off. Something wasn't right."

"Do you think Charles was hurting her?"

Evie closed her eyes. When she opened them, her gaze was sad. "We didn't speak about abuse in those days. Didn't call it by its name. I asked her if everything was all right at home, and she assured me that it was. But looking back, I wish I had done more. Charles was her only relationship, you see. I'd had a beau or two before I met my Frank. I don't think Violet knew that love wasn't supposed to feel like that . . . to feel frightening. She always wore long sleeves, up and quit her waitressing job as soon as she got married. But she loved that job."

Mari thought of the photograph she'd found of Abuelo, his arm around Violet's shoulder in her waitressing uniform.

"Did she befriend my grandpa when she worked as a waitress?"

Evie nodded. "I believe so. Violet was friendly with all the Beach Boardwalk performers. Ricky showed up one day, and he fit right in. Did you ever see him dive? He was incredible!"

Mari laughed. "No, he was in his sixties when I was born. I would have loved to see him dive, though. I have pictures."

"Hand me that cup, will you, dear? This talking is making me thirsty."

Reaching for a plastic cup on the bedside table, Mari handed it to Evie. The old woman placed her mouth on the straw, making a sucking noise. "That's better."

Mari held her breath. Then she asked the question she knew would be the hardest. But she needed an answer.

"Do you think Charles killed Violet?"

Evie brought a trembling hand to her chest. "She wasn't pushed from the cliff, if that's what you mean. Did Charles drive her to do it? Maybe."

They sat in silence, and Mari felt the weight of Evie's grief. How horrible, to have lost a friend to suicide, and to feel at fault. But what could Evie have done? Even with today's resources of crisis hotlines and women's shelters, many women returned to their abusers, only to end up dead.

"I'm sure you were a wonderful friend to Violet," Mari said, patting Evie's hand reassuringly. "Thank you for sharing your memories with me. Why don't you tell me about some of your happy times with Violet?"

Evie smiled. "There were so many. When the new Woolworth's opened in San Francisco we were over the moon. We went on opening day and bought matching leather wallets. I felt so cosmopolitan walking around that department store, and then on the train ride home, we shared a box of Cracker Jacks and laughed the whole way."

"That's lovely," Mari said, imagining young Evie and Violet giggling on the *Suntan Special* while it chugged through the Santa Cruz Mountains.

Closing her eyes, Evie lay back against the pillow. This amount of talking had exhausted her.

"Thank you," Mari said, turning off the tape recorder. "It was very nice to meet you, Evie."

"Wait," she said, her eyes still closed. "Your grandfather, Ricardo Cruz . . . he was a Mexican, right?"

"Yes?" Mari answered warily.

"Charles, Violet's husband. He despised Mexicans. I remember now, Ricky invited Violet and me to a party . . . at a bowling alley or some such place. I told him no, for Violet's own good. But she went. That was the night she left for Hollywood. I heard through the grapevine she caught a ride with Harry Goodman, a comedian she and Ricky were both friends with at the time."

Mari paused, thinking of the postcard in her grandfather's box of things. Had Abuelo helped Violet escape that night, unbeknownst to Charles?

Evie's eyes popped open. "Another thing. In the grocery store, Violet gave me a bag, and she was *adamant* I give it to Ricky Cruz. I told her I didn't know the man well enough, and she could give it to him herself, but she insisted."

"What was in it?"

"Clothing. She'd sewn a ladies' suit for his mother. The woman must've been petite, because the skirt and jacket were rather small. And the red fabric . . . so flamboyant! But Mexicans, they favor bright colors."

"His *mother*?" Mari replied, flabbergasted. Abuelo had left the strawberry farm in the Central Valley when he was fourteen, and hadn't seen his mother since then. He'd told Mari he sent his mother money hidden in a bag of flour for her tamales and tortillas, but what use would she have had for a red suit?

Evie's hands fluttered to her stomach, resting there. "Or perhaps it was Vera or Roxy whom she'd sewn the suit separates for. Those were Violet's Hollywood friends."

Mari frowned. "She wanted my grandfather to give a suit-dress to one of her Hollywood friends?"

Evie looked down at her hands. Then she looked up at Mari with hooded eyes. "I'm sorry, dear. I'm confused. This has all been quite a lot."

"Of course," Mari said. "I hope you can get some rest. Thank you for your time."

But as she turned to leave, she paused in the doorway. "Did you give the clothing to my grandfather?"

"The misses suit? Oh yes. I took the package to the post office. He had a box there. You know, the old post office downtown?"

Mari's heart skipped a beat. Had her grandfather kept a PO box that he'd never told anyone in her family about? She brought her hand to her lips, thinking of the brass key in her grandfather's trunk. There was one way to find out.

CHAPTER 21

Violet Harcourt

1940

Morning sun filtered through the white curtains, and I pulled the covers up over my head. Placing my cool fingertips against my cheek, I winced in pain. My body ached, and dark bruises covered my arms and neck like a rash.

A tear slid down my cheek. How many nights now had I endured beatings from Charles? I had lost count. The telephone jangled, the sound making me flinch. My heart clenched, knowing Evie was calling to check on me. Charles forbade me from answering the telephone or leaving the house, but I had heard him talking to my friend in his charming voice—the picture of a doting husband.

Listening to his heavy footsteps cross the living room floor, I waited. Charles answered the phone.

"Yes, hello, Evelyn. Unfortunately, she's still quite ill. No, please don't bring any food by the house. It's a stomach bug. Sure, call again tomorrow. Bye now."

I stared at the dark bruises mottling my arms, and the welts on my thighs. Last night, I had turned off my brain to get through what I once would have called lovemaking. This was not that . . . it was terrible.

Charles sat on my chest and smothered me with a pillow until I saw stars. I thought surely I would die. Fighting against him, I felt my breath trapped in my lungs until they burned. But at the last moment he released me. I'd fallen to the floor, clawing at the carpet as I gulped air.

Trembling, I sat up in bed, feeling a sharp pinch in my side. Perhaps Charles had broken one of my ribs. Since we'd returned to Santa Cruz, I'd tried my hardest to be the perfect wife. I wanted to love the fight out of him—to love him so much that he wouldn't hurt me any longer. I only spoke when spoken to. I cooked his favorite meals. But he found fault with everything—meals weren't served quickly enough; he believed I had been lusting after "that Jew screenwriter."

Wrapping my robe around my naked body, I rose from the bed and walked down the hall into the kitchen.

"There you are," he said, smiling as though last night hadn't happened. "What are you cooking for breakfast?"

I opened the cupboards, which were nearly barren, save for half a bag of sugar and a bag of flour. Opening the refrigerator, I peered inside. We had two eggs, a wilted head of lettuce and a quarter of a bottle of milk.

"I'll need to go grocery shopping. We're low on food."

He gave me a patronizing look. "I'll send one of the maids from the Oceano."

I swallowed, my heart sinking. Charles spent all day with me at home, making business calls from our phone. He stayed to "care for me while I recovered from my stomach bug." I wondered how long the arrangement would last.

Removing the final two eggs, I turned on the gas stove and cracked them into a pan. My stomach rumbled, but he would want to eat both. My throat tightened, thinking of little Olive, growing bigger. I needed to eat too.

"I'll be goddamned!" Charles said, slamming his fist down on the table.

I jumped, nearly dropping the spatula.

Cripes, what had I done now?

Charles stared at the morning paper, his dark brow furrowed. His large hand crumpled the pages. I looked out the kitchen window at the ocean waves, breathing in the scent of autumn. Damp leaves mingled with the sea spray. How many more weeks of abuse could I endure? I braced myself against the sink, too frightened to move.

Charles leapt up from the table. I cringed in anticipation, but he passed me and went straight to the telephone. The newspaper pages fell to the floor in a flurry. Bending down, I reached to gather them before he could reprimand me for the mess. Seeing the bold headline, my breath caught.

SEPT 16, 1940
PEACETIME DRAFT SIGNED; STATE GUARD CALL OCT 15. REGISTRATION IS ORDERED FOR 16, 500,000 U.S. MEN.

My heart began to pound. The United States would enter the war? My eyes raced across the text. President Roosevelt had signed the Selective Training and Service Act, the first-ever peacetime draft in U.S. history. All men between the ages of twenty-one and thirty-five were required to register. If drafted, a man would serve for twelve months.

A small swell of hope filled me. Charles was twenty-five. He was healthy. And by next month, he would be required to register. I had a window for escape. In spite of knowing the situation was awful, I silently thanked President Roosevelt. Charles's voice rose as he spoke to someone on the telephone.

"This is preposterous! How do I get out of it?"

I returned to cooking the eggs, eavesdropping on his conversation.

"Well, *you're* my lawyer, tell me what I ought to do."

I scrambled the eggs with a spatula while my mind wandered to the Tropical Gardens Nightclub, where I'd sold Chesterfields and Montecristos. Had I filmed my bar scene on the Paramount lot a mere few weeks ago? It felt like another lifetime.

I wondered if Roxy was dining at the Chateau Marmont, Schwab's Pharmacy or the Brown Derby. Perhaps she was eating a Cobb salad or tanning by the pool. I stared at the iron frying pan, pondering if my name would be in the credits of John Huston's film. But none of that mattered now. I thought of Vera's kindness, and how she'd showed me the ropes. Perhaps she'd go on to become an actress. I'd be lucky to still be alive in a year's time.

"I don't give a damn about the Jews!" Charles bellowed from the hallway. Hunching over the pan, I tried to make myself small. I turned off the gas and waited.

". . . If I need to pretend to be a goddamned Quaker then I will."

I slid the eggs onto a plate, and then I brought them to the kitchen table. Charles hung up the phone with a thud. Carefully, I set a clean fork and knife on either side of the plate, and then retreated to the sink.

Charles walked into the kitchen and glared at me. "Why are you standing there slack-jawed, you fat cow?"

His words felt like a punch to the gut.

"I'm sorry," I said, though I had no idea what I was apologizing for. Reaching for the soap and sponge, I began to scrub the pan.

"You're an idiot," Charles muttered. "No one else is ever going to want to be with you. And if you try to leave me again, I'll find you. You know that, don't you?"

Even if Charles returned to the Oceano and left me alone, I felt too frightened to run. He would stop at nothing to find me. I'd left him once, and now he was wise to the fact that I could do it again.

Taking a bite of egg, Charles made a face, and then spat it out. "These are cold."

"No, they can't be. I've only just served them."

He stood up, his eyes glassy with rage. "Are you telling me I'm wrong?"

"No," I said quietly.

But he backhanded me across the jaw and then knocked the plate of eggs onto the floor. I shielded my face from a second blow, my cheek smarting.

"You eat them," he said.

"Off the floor? Charles, please."

But he stood over me, waiting. My stomach rumbled. With tears trickling down my cheeks, I picked up the bits of scrambled egg and put them in my mouth.

"Don't use your hands."

Never had I felt so debased, eating food off the floor like a dog. That's how he saw me—as nothing more than a worthless mutt.

The days went by in a blur. More than once I heard knocking on the door, and saw Evie's face peeking through the window. I hid in the kitchen, knowing I would be dead if I opened it. I thought about taking my own life, to put myself out of my misery. But playing jazz tunes on the piano and thinking of little Olive growing inside me kept the dark thoughts at bay.

Charles returned to the Oceano, but there were men parked outside my home, watching me. An employee I didn't recognize stepped out of a black car and dropped a bag on the porch. Too frightened to open the door, I allowed the groceries to sit there all day in the sun. Charles hit me for my mistake. Oftentimes I feared he suspected I might be pregnant. But he said nothing of it. Soon I would begin to show. My window for escape grew smaller and smaller. Every day I prayed he would be forced to enlist.

The next morning, Charles seemed in a jovial mood. He smiled at me.

"We're joining a new church. A Quaker church."

"But we're Catholic," I said, thinking of our large wedding at St. Peter's.

His eyes narrowed. "Not anymore. You tell anyone who asks that we're Quakers and we always have been. I'm donating a large sum of money to the American Friends Service Committee. It's a U.S.-based Quaker aid society."

"That's very generous," I replied, confounded by this new behavior. Perhaps the guilt he felt about how he'd been treating me had driven him to a new faith?

He laughed. "Yes, I *am* generous. I'm selling the Oceano and moving my assets to an account in Switzerland. To the outside world, I am now a penniless pacifist."

Sell the Oceano? I knew I ought to keep my mouth shut, but I couldn't. "Why?"

He grinned like a cat that'd caught a canary. "My lawyer advised me to. As a Quaker, my religious beliefs are opposed to any kind of war. I shan't be forced to enlist. And I won't serve."

Was that possible? Surely anyone would see through this charade. But Charles was a man of wealth and power. His lawyer wouldn't have trouble convincing U.S. Army officials that he needed to remain on American soil. My heart sank.

"You thought I would leave you?" he asked, a frightening lilt to his voice.

"No," I whispered. "I know you'll never leave me."

"Good," he replied. "Because you're mine until death do us part."

After he left the house, I dropped to my knees and sobbed. Once again, he'd hinted that he intended to kill me. I had to act now. If I went to Evie, or to Mother, what could they do? Charles would find me there—he would harm them.

I thought of Ricky Cruz, and of the words he'd said the night I departed for Hollywood. *I won't ask you what's happening at home. If you're in trouble, I can help.*

Charles hadn't suspected Ricky when he helped me the first time. He wouldn't look to Ricky if I asked him for help again. And then I had the most outrageous idea. It was likely to fail in every way, but what did I have to lose?

Running to the sitting room, I uncovered my sewing machine. In the closet, I had bolts of unused fabric. My fingers trailed along the cloth, then settled on bright red rayon. Pulling the yardage from the shelf, I looked around for my scissors. Ricardo Cruz was my only hope if I wanted to stay alive.

CHAPTER 22

Marisol Cruz

2007

Mari walked down Front Street, past the homeless sleeping on the sidewalk, toward the marble and limestone landmark, the Santa Cruz post office. At nearly one hundred years old, it was the oldest continually operating state post office on the National Register of Historic Places.

Clutching the brass key in her palm, Mari could feel her heart beat faster. After speaking with Evie at the nursing home, she'd returned to Abuelo's trunk, finding the small key etched with the number 777. If it opened a PO box here, what would she find inside?

Stepping through the doorway, Mari admired the 1912 Renaissance Revival building, which had been modeled after a fifteenth-century foundling hospital in Florence,

Italy. Her eyes took in one of the colorful murals by the American artist Henrietta Shore. The lunette depicted farmers harvesting artichokes, which made her think of Abuelo, and his childhood picking strawberries.

There were four murals in total, which had been commissioned in 1935 by the federal government's Treasury Relief Art Project. President Franklin D. Roosevelt putting artists to work with the New Deal was the best thing to come out of the Great Depression. Henrietta Shore had painted the laborers with dignity, a quality the working class weren't always given.

Maybe the Santa Cruz Museum of Art & History would want to do something to celebrate the one hundredth anniversary of the post office? They could dedicate a plaque. Mari could already envision postal officials and local historians at the celebration . . . a celebration she organized.

She was getting ahead of herself. But in the past few weeks, she'd begun to feel different. Maybe it was confidence, "getting her groove back," but today Mari felt like she *could* be working for the Santa Cruz museum in five years' time. *Why not?* She'd won the Swanson Grant, after all.

"Hi," she said, approaching the clerk behind the desk. "I have a key which I believe belongs to a box here, registered to my grandfather. Do you have any post office boxes that have been in operation since 1940?"

The clerk nodded. "We do, indeed. Turn down the hall and take a left. You'll find our boxes in that room."

Mari did as she was instructed. When she stepped inside the room, thousands of antique PO boxes lined the walls. They were so beautiful, made of brass and marked with black numbers. She walked along the wall, searching for number 777.

She bent down, finding the small square box toward the bottom of the rows in the back corner. Her palm had become sweaty with the key clutched in it. She stuck it into the lock and twisted, letting out her breath. It was a perfect fit.

Swinging the door open, Mari peered inside. At first the box looked empty, but then something small and silver caught her eye. *Another key?* Mari removed it, staring in bewilderment at the small metal object. Her phone jangled with a notification.

Crap! She had ten minutes to walk to the Jupiter Café for her shift, and then she had to call back the dentist to confirm Lily's appointment, not to mention the ten million loads of laundry that needed to be done. As much as she wanted to find out what this key belonged to, her search would have to wait. Mari slipped it into her pocket, shut the door to the box and locked it. What secrets had Abuelo been hiding?

TRANSFERRING THE LAST load of laundry to the dryer, Mari listened as Lily giggled, watching an episode of *Maya & Miguel*. She tried not to let her daughter watch too much TV, but the show was funny and charming, plus it taught Lily Spanish words.

Swallowing, she felt a heavy knot in her stomach. The

city planning commission meeting was tomorrow night, and she'd rounded up neighbors who'd promised to attend. But that didn't mean she was ready to face Travis. Sometimes her rage toward him rose fast and furious as a tsunami. What if she hadn't been joking with her mom and she really punched him in the face? No one would take her seriously then, and she could kiss her grant goodbye.

Paulina walked into the laundry room, scooping up a basket of Lily's clothes, warm from the dryer.

"I'll help you fold these."

"Oh Ma, you don't have to."

"I want to." She smiled. "You've got a big day tomorrow."

"Thanks," Mari said. *"Te amo."*

"I love you too," Paulina said, picking up the plastic basket and carrying it into the living room. Mari sat down on the soft couch, lifting one of Lily's T-shirts. Lily giggled in front of the television, completely engrossed in her cartoon show. Dropping her voice to a whisper, Mari turned to Paulina.

"Ma, I found a key that belongs to a PO box downtown. It was in Abuelo's trunk. I know this sounds crazy, but I think he had a connection to Violet Harcourt, a beauty queen from 1940. She was Mayor Harcourt's father's first wife."

Paulina's eyes widened. *"Que?"*

"I found a picture of Abuelo with Violet. She worked as a waitress at the boardwalk. I think they were friends. I also found a postcard she may have written to him. I think she may have been in an abusive relationship, and I'm pretty sure he helped her escape to Hollywood. But when she returned, she committed suicide."

Paulina made the sign of the cross over her chest. "Abuelo never spoke about anyone named Violet. Are you sure he knew her?"

Mari nodded. "I visited an old woman named Evelyn Hastings who was friends with Violet. She remembered Abuelo. She said Violet asked her to give him a red dress suit for his mother, Great-Grandma."

Raising her eyebrows, Paulina cracked a smile. "Is she *loca*?"

"I don't think so. She seemed really with it."

"Why did you visit this Evelyn? Who is she?"

"I emailed her daughter, Karen, because I'm looking to interview old people for my grant project. Karen responded, and told me that Evelyn won the Miss California pageant in 1940. Evelyn lived in Santa Cruz during the summers, and I wanted to meet her."

Paulina picked up a pair of leggings and folded them in half. "So what did you find inside this PO box. Anything?"

"Another key."

"What?"

This time Lily turned around. "What are you guys talking about?"

"Nothing, honey," Mari said. "Watch your cartoon."

Reaching into her jeans pocket, Mari removed the small silver key. She handed it to her mother. Paulina opened her palm and stared at it, her brows scrunching together. She turned it over, pointing to the faded etching on the side. "Look, there's a number. I think this might belong to a safe deposit box."

"Like at the bank?"

Paulina nodded. "Your father and I have one. We keep some of Abuela's jewelry in there." Her eyes lit up. "You might want her wedding ring someday."

Mari smirked. "Don't get any ideas."

"When we cleaned out this house after Abuelo died, we moved everything to storage, sold stuff we didn't want or put it in the attic. He didn't have anything valuable, Mari. *Nada*. And he never told me about a safe deposit box."

"But if he had one . . ."

"Then it would be at the Bank of Santa Cruz. That's where he banked when he was alive. I still have some of his checkbooks."

"I'm hungry!" Lily yelled, hopping up.

Paulina slipped the key into Mari's hand.

"What do you want for dinner?" Mari asked, annoyed her conversation had been interrupted. But that was life with a kid, a nonstop series of interruptions.

"Spaghetti!" Lily announced. "With tomato sauce and cheese."

"Okay," Mari said. "Sounds yummy."

"I'll finish this," Paulina said, nodding at the laundry.

"Thanks," Mari replied, taking Lily by the hand. But as she filled a pot with water and turned on the stove, her mind spun. Travis Harcourt, Mayor Harcourt, Charles and Violet Harcourt—the past and present were colliding, and secrets were going to spill out.

THE ROOM WAS hot. So hot, Mari wished she'd put on an extra swipe of deodorant. She looked around the packed city council chambers and her heart fluttered. Fifty neighbors had shown up. And now they waited for Mari to speak, squished side by side in the tense atmosphere.

Council member Frank Ortega stood at the podium, frowning at the crowded room. He spoke into the microphone. "The planning commission will advise city council on matters pertaining to land use after receiving public input. Who would like to speak?"

With her heart pounding, Mari raised her hand. All eyes in the room were on her. She tried to swallow, but her mouth was too dry.

Someone handed her a microphone, and she took a deep breath. She found Jason's face in the audience, smiling at her encouragingly. Smiling back at him, her nerves abated.

"Good evening. Thank you for joining me tonight." She cleared her throat. "We are here to object not only to the condominium development scheduled for construction on Cowell Beach, but to the noise, congestion and traffic it will create."

People murmured in agreement.

Mari looked at the city council members. "For the home owners on Beach Hill and the surrounding area, blocked views of the ocean will hurt property values. This condominium will radically change the population of the neighborhood. Single tech workers with high incomes don't share the interests of our local families."

"That's right!" a man bellowed. "They'll want more liquor license permits and trendy restaurants, while we want good schools and community programs."

Mari smiled at the surprise on the city council members' faces. She'd started a Facebook page called "Save the Cowell Beach Gazebo" and had reached even more residents than she thought possible. This meeting was not going as city council had planned.

"Let's settle down," a council member said.

"Excuse me," a woman called out, looking over at Mari. "I'd like to speak."

Mari passed her the microphone.

"Hi. My name is Jan Selby and I'm a longtime Santa Cruz resident. I'm concerned that this condo development on the beach will set the tone for having condos all the way down the beach. What if beach access is restricted?"

"We can't have that!" another woman cried out. "Public access to the beach blocked? That's absolutely classist."

Vice Mayor Malia Echevarria stepped forward, an annoyed look on her face. "Public beach access will *not* be restricted."

"That's not true," a man piped up. "I live nearby, and just the other day I saw a fence go up around the perimeter. There were sandbags brought in."

"The fence is temporary," the vice mayor replied. "It will remain there until construction begins."

"So children will be at risk of stepping on nails?" a woman said, a toddler on her hip. "I'm a *mother,* and those kind of dangers are unacceptable."

Get the locals riled up, and you didn't know what you were in for. They were a righteous bunch. But Mari's hope faded the minute she saw Travis Harcourt take the podium. She'd worried he might show up, but then convinced herself he wouldn't. Now he was here, grinning at the room with that perfect white smile of his.

"Neighbors, friends. As you know, I grew up here in Santa Cruz too. I love this city. I would never do anything to hurt the community. I've already agreed to shorten the condominiums from eight stories to five, and to install solar panels."

Mari snatched the microphone back from Jan. "Because including solar panels allows for *expedited permitting*. This isn't about clean energy, it's about pushing your agenda through as quickly as possible."

"I'm sorry," Travis said, smiling condescendingly. "What's your name?"

For a minute, Mari's vision went red, and she thought about marching over, pulling back her hand and punching him hard in the jaw. But she took a deep breath in through her nose, and let it out through her mouth.

"Let's not play games, Travis. You know who I am."

A hush settled over the room as neighbors' eyes darted between them, sensing something dramatic about to take place.

He chuckled. "Neighbors, this condominium will *improve* the neighborhood. With the influx of new money, we'll have more to spend on our parks, schools and infrastructure. We're breathing new life into the community."

"At the expense of the old culture being erased and the gazebo being torn down and the destruction of everything that our older community members treasure!"

"The gazebo is a nonissue. It's barely standing. No one uses it. And I can promise you, my project has already received approval from the state's coastal commission, so nothing is going to stop it from going through."

Mari gritted her teeth. She'd spent hours looking at maps, documents and zoning laws, trying to find fault with Travis's permit, but he'd done everything by the book.

"Will the seawall cause erosion?" a woman asked.

"No," Travis replied. "We've already tested the soil."

Council member Frank Ortega rapped his gavel against the podium. "Thank you, community members, for voicing your opposition to this project. Meeting minutes will be recorded and posted online. Time's up."

Cries of protest sounded from the crowd, but he rapped his gavel again and said loudly, "Meeting adjourned."

"What happens now?" a gray-haired man asked, frowning at Mari.

She licked her lips, all the moisture gone from her mouth. "We have to keep fighting. We'll continue looking for flaws in the permit, look for opportunities to stop construction. But this could be a long process."

He shook his head. "We're the underdogs. I don't expect to win."

She sighed, her heart sinking as people shuffled out of the room. Looking around for Jason, she couldn't find him in the sea of faces.

Suddenly Travis was at her side, making her skin crawl. "Well," he whispered, smacking his chewing gum. "I didn't expect to see you again. Who the hell do you think you are, some kind of activist?"

Mari clenched her jaw. "I'm a Santa Cruz native just like *you*. Not to mention, one of the residents on Beach Hill whose views will be blocked."

He smirked at her. "You have no right to those views."

"You entitled piece of . . ."

"What?" He laughed. "You have no idea what I'm capable of. If you try to stall my project, I'll make you wish you hadn't."

"Travis, can I speak with you a moment?" Frank Ortega appeared next to them, stopping Mari from spewing the insults she wanted to hurl at Travis.

"In a moment," Travis said, chewing his gum obnoxiously. "Is my dad here yet?"

"Mayor Harcourt is on his way."

"Cool."

Mari rolled her eyes. Could he be any more flippant? When Ortega walked away, Travis lowered his voice. "Is this even about the development, or is it about the mistake *you* made four years ago?"

"*Mistake?*" Mari's throat tightened. She would not cry in front of him. "Our daughter is the love of my life. She's bright, funny, smart and better off not knowing what a complete asshole her father is."

"I never said I wanted to be involved," Travis said, shrugging his shoulders. "I thought I made that pretty clear."

"Clear as day," Mari replied, blinking back tears.

"Good," Travis said. "Then we're done here."

"No, we're not. I'll fight your development until you can't stand the sight of me anymore. I don't give up easily."

Travis smirked. "You don't get it, do you? My father has already approved everything. He's the one who told me to use solar panels and low-flow showers to keep it eco-friendly. It's *your* father you should be worried about."

"What the hell is that supposed to mean?"

All three council members watched them argue from across the room, Vice Mayor Echevarria frowning as she narrowed her eyes.

Travis cocked his head in their direction. "They're waiting for me. Take my advice. Stop fighting this. You're going to fail." He spat his gum into a foil wrapper, and then set it down on the folding table.

Mari looked at him in disgust. "Are you going to leave that there?"

He shrugged. "A janitor will clean it up."

Before she could get in the last word, Travis turned his back on her and walked away. A lump rose in her throat, and she clenched her hands into fists. So long as Mayor Harcourt approved the condo project, she wasn't likely to get anywhere.

Then she thought back to that day on the boardwalk . . . to the confused look on the mayor's face when he'd seen Lily. Mari's eyes darted to the used chewing gum, and her heart began to beat faster. Maybe it was time for Mayor Harcourt to know the truth.

CHAPTER 23
Violet Harcourt

1940

Taking a deep breath, I approached my husband. I'd been on my best behavior for the past week and had felt something shift in Charles. He had begun to trust me again. Setting my hand gently on his shoulder, I spoke softly.

"Charles, dear. Would it be all right if I walked to the grocery store? I know your employees have been so helpful with deliveries, but the neighbors may begin to suspect something is amiss if they never see me."

I willed my hand not to shake, even though I felt as if I were touching a snake that could bite me at any moment. He turned to me, his brown eyes warm.

"Violet, you haven't felt captive here, have you?"

"Not at all," I lied. "But Mother and Evie will begin to

wonder why they haven't seen me out and about. I look well, don't you think?"

My bruises had faded, usually a sign I would be due for more soon.

"One hour," he said, unfolding the paper. "And then I will see you back here."

"Of course," I said, my stomach lurching. I eyed the kitchen clock, praying that Evie hadn't changed her routine. She always did her weekly grocery shopping at noon on Saturday. I had to meet her for my plan to work. But I couldn't call her to tell her that I was coming or I would put her in grave danger.

Hurrying into the bedroom, I gathered my string-knit shopping bags and the garments I'd sewn in secret. I walked past Charles with a pleasant smile, even though I felt as if my heart might burst from pounding. "Is there anything in particular you'd like me to pick up?"

"Orange juice," he said, his eyes on the paper. "And steak."

My hand trembled as I touched the door handle. I angled my body away from him, praying he wouldn't notice my bulging pockets. "I'll purchase both."

Stepping out into the bright sunlight, I squinted my eyes. With the sea spray touching my face, and the scent of the September air in my lungs, I nearly cried tears of relief. I was *outside*!

I longed to run, but I forced myself to walk at a normal pace, my kitten heels clicking against the pavement. The neighborhood grocery store wasn't far, but I would need to hurry if I was to return within the hour. Reaching into the deep pockets of my dress, I retrieved the garments I had sewn. Then I stashed them into a string-knit shopping bag. Untying my white head scarf, I tucked it inside the bag as well.

As I approached Swan's Market, my palms began to sweat. I was greeted by advertisements for potatoes, and fresh country eggs at nineteen cents a dozen, which were painted on the window glass. It had been ages since I'd been shopping. I stepped inside, looking about the store for Evie. Housewives chatted near the produce, and an elderly grandmother with a cane stood by the deli counter, pointing at a ham hock.

I wrapped my gloved hands around a shopping cart, feeling like a foreigner in my own town. A man passed me on my right and I quickly averted my gaze, staring at the waxed floor. What if Charles had sent someone to follow me? I examined some canned goods, taking a deep breath in and letting it out. Placing a tin of beets in my cart, I looked around anxiously for Evie. I wouldn't have time to walk to her apartment or to the post office, and I didn't trust that I wasn't being watched.

As I rounded the corner, my heart sank to find the next aisle empty.

"Violet! Is that you?"

Gasping in fright, I brought my hand to my chest as Evie appeared behind me with her shopping cart. She glared.

"First you leave for Hollywood without saying so much as goodbye, and then you won't answer my calls? Now you look as if you've seen a ghost! Good grief, Vi, where in the dickens have you been?"

I longed to embrace my dear pal—to confide everything. "Oh Evie," I said, my heart aching at the hurt in her eyes. "I'm so terribly sorry. I've been a rotten friend."

"Yes, you have." She frowned. "Is everything all right? You'd tell me if you were in trouble, wouldn't you?"

I couldn't let Evie suspect a thing. Heaven knows what Charles might do to her. "I had an awful stomach bug, which kept me in bed for ages. I'm sorry I couldn't answer your calls."

"And Hollywood? Why wouldn't you tell me you planned to go?"

I shrugged. "I made a last-minute decision. I didn't expect Charles to say yes, but he did . . . so I caught a ride with Harry Goodman."

"What was it like?" Evie asked, falling into step beside me. "Did you meet anyone famous?"

I smiled. "I auditioned for a film with Humphrey Bogart. I got cast as an extra, 'the vixen at the bar.' Oh Evie, I wish you could have been there."

She grabbed my arm in excitement. "Hot diggity dog! Was Hollywood glamorous? What are the people like?"

I thought of Hollywood Boulevard: the fortune-tellers, the con men, the working girls and the vagrants wearing signs. Then I pictured the Beverly Hills Hotel and Bungalows with its crystal-blue swimming pool, beautiful people, and pink and mint décor.

"It's . . . different than I imagined, darker and brighter at once. I had a roommate named Roxy. Living there hardened her, I think. And I met another gal, Vera. She was sweet. She shared her lunch with me while we waited in the bus for extras."

Evie's eyes looked sad. "Sounds swell."

I took her hand. "None of those gals compared to you, of course! I missed you, Evie. I'm so sorry I didn't write."

Glancing at the clock on the wall, my heart beat faster. I hadn't much time to complete my shopping, if I were to make it back home to Charles.

"Enough about me," I said. "Tell me about the Miss America pageant. How was New Jersey?"

Evie smiled. "I didn't win. And the Jersey boardwalk isn't as beautiful as ours, but being there was such a gas. Frank loved Atlantic City. I was afraid I wouldn't get him to leave! We're lucky to have any savings left after how he gambled."

"It sounds wonderful," I said. The Miss California pageant felt like a lifetime ago, though it had only been in June. Taking the mesh bag from my cart, I thrust it toward Evie, trying to keep my voice light. "Doll, can you do me a favor?"

"Sure," she said, her amber eyes wide. "What is it?"

"Can you give this to Ricky Cruz? It's a present for his mother."

Evie laughed. "Why can't you give it to him yourself? I hardly know him."

I swallowed. "You know how Charles feels about Mexicans. He wouldn't find it proper. But Ricky's mother is poor. We're becoming Quakers, you see, and in the spirit of giving, I've sewn her something nice."

Evie scrunched her brow. "Quakers? *Heavens,* why?"

I shrugged. "Charles wants us to convert. Listen, if you don't feel comfortable giving the gift to Ricky in person, he has a box at the post office downtown."

"What number is it?"

"Seven seventy-seven," I replied. "Easy to remember."

Evie took the mesh bag. "Lucky sevens. Consider it done."

I breathed a sigh of relief. "Thank you."

She frowned. "You'll visit me, won't you? Now that you're well?"

"Of course. Let's get dinner together, the four of us, just like old times."

"At the Miramar Fish Grotto," Evie said, grinning. "Next week."

Picking up a carton of eggs and setting it in my cart, I memorized Evie's delicate features, her large amber eyes, tiny nose and rosy cheeks. "I've got to skedaddle. It was lovely seeing you, Evie. Please take care."

She laughed. "Don't act like this is goodbye forever. I'll see you next week!"

"Of course," I said, forcing a smile. *Oh Evie, if you only knew.*

I walked away with tears in my eyes. I would never see my dear friend again.

CHAPTER 24

Marisol Cruz

2007

"Mom, what are you *doing*?"

Mari gasped, nearly dropping Lily's pink hairbrush. "I'm cleaning your brush, honey." Lily narrowed her eyes. "Why are you putting my hair in a sandwich bag?"

"I ran out of trash bags," Mari said.

"Silly mommy!" Lily said, skipping out of the bathroom without checking the trash can, where a plastic liner hugged the sides snugly.

Breathing a sigh of relief, Mari checked the hairs she'd collected. Each one had a thick follicle and would work for the DNA test she'd ordered online. Along with Travis's used chewing gum, she had what she needed to prove his paternity.

Her stomach knotted. Could she go through with this?

Remembering his words at the city council meeting, that Lily was *"her mistake,"* she decided she could. Her daughter deserved so much better than him, and Mayor Harcourt deserved to know the truth. Also, what had Travis meant when he said she needed to worry about her own father?

Her phone pinged with a text from Jason. *Are we still on for our carousel ride tonight? Really excited to meet Lily.*

Mari smiled as she texted back: *Absolutely. See you soon.*

"Are you ready?" Lily asked, reappearing in the doorway. The pink soles of her sneakers lit up as she tapped her feet impatiently.

"Almost," Mari said, stroking Lily's head. "Grab your jacket and we'll go."

"Yay!" Lily squealed. "I'm going to ride the horsies! Can I have cotton candy?"

"Did you eat all your veggies?"

Lily nodded. "All my peas and carrots and even the broccoli, which I *hate*!"

Mari smiled. "Good girl. Then yes, you can have cotton candy."

MARI LEANED TOWARD Jason. "Sorry if Lily's a little much this evening. She's excited to meet you. And she's on a sugar high."

Lily shrieked as she ran down the wooden slats of the boardwalk, past the arcade games and the food stalls.

"Slow down, honey!" Mari called after her. But Lily kept running.

"Guess we should pick up our pace," Jason said, grinning as he began to jog. Mari's heart warmed as she plodded behind him. Lily had interrogated Jason, asking him if he was Mari's boyfriend, and what his favorite animals were. He'd explained that he was Mari's *friend* and that his favorite animal was a dog, but also unicorns. This thrilled Lily to no end, because she didn't know of any men who loved unicorns.

"We're gonna ride the carousel!" Lily cried. "The horsies have jewels! Jason, will you ride next to me?"

"Hey," Mari said, frowning. "You don't want *me* to ride next to you?"

"No!" Lily said. "Jason."

Jason smiled, and then bent down to whisper loudly in Lily's ear, "I think we should let your mom ride next to us. When you do something nice for somebody, one of the carousel horses turns into a unicorn at night."

Lily's eyes widened. "Really?"

"Really."

"Will he grow wings and a horn and fly away?"

Jason nodded. "He'll fly over the ocean, over your house and all over town, and then he'll come back and *pretend* to be a wooden carousel horse. But you and I will know that he's really a magic unicorn."

Lily clapped her hands in delight as Mari bought a strip of paper tickets from the vendor. While they waited for their turn on the carousel, she smiled at Jason.

"For a computer guy, you have quite an impressive imagination."

He grinned. "I guess I'm just a big kid."

As the carousel slowed to a stop, Mari helped Lily up and watched as her daughter looked around in awe.

"Which horse are you going to pick?"

"That one. Wait, no. The purple one!"

The hand-carved merry-go-round brimmed with beautiful horses; it had brought children's seaside dreams and fantasies to life for a hundred years. After Lily picked her horse, touching its carved flower garland and stroking its long, real horsehair tail, Mari and Jason settled into the saddles of the two horses beside her.

"I'm excited," Jason said. "I've never ridden this carousel."

"You're in for a treat," Mari said. "Charles Looff completed his first carousel at Coney Island in 1875 and went on to create several more around the country, including this one. It's really special. I used to ride it with my *abuelo* when I was Lily's age."

Lily leaned toward Jason. "My great-grandpa was a famous diver. Did you know that? I didn't know him but I've seen pictures of him in our house."

"Your mom told me," Jason said, smiling at Mari.

The music from the antique organ began to play as the carousel started to spin. Mari's horse rose upward on its metal pole, and she felt her heart swell. Jason was a natural with Lily. Even though she'd asked him to call himself a "friend," she felt ready to introduce him as her boyfriend soon.

"That's a cool façade," Jason said, pointing at the Ruth & Sohn band organ, protected by a pane of glass.

"It's German, and super-rare, from 1894. The façade is definitely in need of refurbishment, though," Mari said, looking at the peeling paint. Women blowing trumpets in strapless green gowns framed a mechanical conductor, who wore gold knickerbockers and a green jacket. His wooden arm waved a baton in time to the music, while cherubs with harps watched overhead. "I think I could talk to Carol at the museum about restoring it."

"How's the grant project going?" Jason asked, the globe lights of the carousel illuminating his face. He looked so handsome, his strong forearms flexing as he held on to the pole attached to his horse.

"The city council meeting felt like a roadblock." Mari sighed, heat rising under her skin as she thought about Travis. "But I'm meeting with the two artists I've chosen to work with for my grant project tomorrow. They're students at UC Santa Cruz."

Jason smiled. "How did you choose them?"

"They had incredible portfolios. One did an ethnographic study of families in the region, living in the beach flats. You know, their cultural interests, preferences . . . dreams. She used their discarded household items to build these beautiful sculptures."

"Mom," Lily shouted. "Stop talking!"

Mari laughed. Her four-year-old certainly had a way with words.

"Sorry," she said.

Jason reached out and held her hand. "Don't apologize.

I love your passion. And I think your idea for creating a diorama of the gazebo is really cool."

With Lily distracted by the spinning carousel, Mari enjoyed the warmth of Jason's hand on hers, and the knowledge that this was developing into something special.

"**WOW, YOU HAVE** a really beautiful view," Mari said, looking out Jason's apartment window at the UC Santa Cruz soccer field, surrounded by redwood trees, the Pacific Ocean shimmering in the distance. She'd agreed to go back to his place for a glass of wine after they'd dropped off Lily with her mother.

Now her mouth felt dry and her stomach filled with butterflies. She hadn't slept with anyone since Travis, meaning she'd practically become a virgin again.

"Thanks," he said, handing her a glass of Malbec. "I'm really lucky I got into employee housing. You can't beat the view from campus."

Mari sipped the wine, which was fruity and delicious. It eased her nerves a little bit. "You were great with Lily today."

"Well, she's a great kid. You've done a fantastic job raising her. She's funny and smart. How does she know all those vocabulary words?"

Mari laughed. "Some are from me. My mom does a good job of teaching her new words too. She's the director of Lily's preschool."

"It was really cool meeting your parents," Jason said, his eyes meeting hers.

Mari's mom and dad had been all *too* eager to come to the door when she and Jason had dropped Lily off. They'd invited him over for dinner before Mari had the chance to mouth *no*. Her mom was already bragging about her homemade enchiladas while her dad was shaking Jason's hand heartily.

"They liked you," she said, setting down her wineglass.

"You think so?"

Mari rolled her eyes. "Would my mom have invited you to dinner next week if she didn't? I think it's obvious."

Stepping forward, Jason set down his wineglass and wrapped his arms around Mari's waist. He tilted his head, resting his forehead against hers. "I'm really happy I met you. Thank you for opening up to me."

She closed her eyes, breathing in the scent of his cologne. Walls she'd had up for years were slowly coming down. Jason's lips met hers. She kissed him softly at first, then passionately. He walked her backward toward the couch, and soon she was lying against the cushions, his weight on top of her.

Taking a break from kissing, she looked into his warm brown eyes.

"I'm sorry. It's been a really, *really* long time since I've been with someone. I have no idea what I'm doing."

Jason smiled, pushing a wayward strand of hair from her face. "Well, I'm so distracted by how pretty you are it doesn't really matter what you're doing." He glanced down at his pants. "Just don't hurt me and we'll be fine."

Mari laughed. Once again, Jason used his humor to put

her instantly at ease. She grinned. "I don't know. I might break it."

"Okay," he said, hopping off the couch. "The night's done. I'll call you a cab."

"Come here," she said, giggling as she pulled him into a kiss, toppling a few of the couch cushions onto the floor. "I promise I'll be gentle."

As they kissed and undressed, she didn't feel self-conscious about her stretch marks or her breasts, which had sagged a bit since giving birth, and she didn't think about Travis, the loads of laundry at home that needed to be done and the mile-long checklist in her head. In the moment, she felt free, safe and loved. Closing her eyes, Mari let herself fall for Jason. The freedom of letting go was exhilarating.

"HOW WAS LAST night?" Paulina asked, winking at Mari. "You got home late."

Mari's cheeks prickled with heat. Jason had asked her to stay over, but that would have given her parents proof she and Jason had slept together—one of the drawbacks of living at home. Instead, she'd left at midnight, grinning like a schoolgirl when he'd kissed her goodbye. She'd forgotten how good sex could be. Or maybe it had never been that good before? Either way, she couldn't wait to do it again.

"It was nice," Mari said, looking at her plate of scrambled eggs.

"Just *nice*?"

"It was wonderful. Okay? No more questions."

Paulina pointed the spatula at her. "I like him. We didn't talk long, but I got a good feeling. I think he might be a keeper."

"You do?"

Paulina nodded. "Lily talked about him all night. He told her the carousel horses turn into unicorns when you do something nice for somebody."

"I know," Mari said, smiling. "I think he's a keeper too."

"Is he coming over for dinner next week? We'd love to have him."

"I think so," Mari said, filled with excitement at the thought that she was inviting her *boyfriend* over for dinner. "What night?"

"Friday," Paulina said, setting down her spatula. "I'm going to cook Abuela's enchiladas. I hope he likes Mexican food."

"Everyone likes Mexican food," Mari said, drinking the rest of her coffee. "And if he doesn't love your enchiladas, I'll dump him."

Paulina laughed. Then her eyes grew serious. "Are you going to try that key in the safe deposit box at the bank today?"

Mari nodded. "I won't be gone for long. Are you okay to watch Lily?"

"*Si,* but then I'm meeting my friend Rubia for lunch."

"I'll be back within an hour. When does Dad get home?"

"After four. He's working today."

Mari carried her plate over to the sink and rinsed it off.

She kissed her mom on the cheek. "Thanks, Ma. I'll let you know if I find anything."

WALKING DOWN LOCUST Street, Mari took a deep breath as she spotted the columned façade of the Bank of Santa Cruz. It was an imposing marble structure, similar to the architecture found in downtown San Francisco.

She stepped through the glass doors, looking around at the tellers, and the security guards in uniform. *What if there was something inside the safe deposit box that she didn't want the bank employees to see?* According to California law, the bank would be required to make photocopies of everything removed from the box.

"Good morning, can I help you?" A smartly dressed man walked toward her, wearing a gold name badge that read CARL.

"Yes," Mari said.

She'd done some research online, and even though she was in possession of a key, California law also stated that she needed to bring Abuelo's death certificate in order to access his safe deposit box, and proof of her own identity. She'd gotten the signed certificate from her mother and she reached into her handbag to retrieve it.

Mari swallowed. "I'm here to access my grandfather's safe deposit box. He's deceased, but I brought the required paperwork."

"What's your name?" Carl asked.

"Marisol Cruz," Mari answered. "I have the key and his

death certificate, along with my birth certificate and driver's license."

"May I see them?" Carl asked.

"Sure," Mari said, digging in her bag and handing him her identifying documents.

"And the key?"

"Here," Mari said, placing the key in his palm. She handed him the death certificate, and felt a pang of sadness.

"One moment," Carl said. Taking the items, he disappeared through a door, and began tapping away at a computer behind the glass partition.

Mari checked the time on her phone. Already half an hour had passed since she'd left home. And the walk back would take fifteen minutes. She didn't want to make her mom late to lunch with her friend. As much as she desperately wanted to unlock this box today, maybe it wasn't meant to happen.

Carl returned, a sympathetic smile on his face. "I'm sorry to hear about your grandfather's passing."

He handed Mari the key and her driver's license, along with a form. "Please fill this out. It states that you've removed the contents of the safe deposit box for observation only, and together we've recorded the belongings of the deceased in our bank records."

"Okay," Mari said, taking a pen from Carl.

After completing the form, she returned it to him. Her mouth felt dry as she followed him. He unlocked a door at the back of the room, and then turned down the hallway.

They emerged into another room, smaller than the first, lined with metal boxes. Now Mari's palms had become clammy.

"Here's your grandfather's safe deposit box," Carl said, pointing to a rectangular metal box in the wall of identical boxes. "Would you like me to open it? There's a viewing chamber to your right, if you'd like some privacy."

Mari looked at the cubicle he had nodded toward. "Okay," she said, her voice coming out in a squeak.

Carl inserted the key, removing a metal box from its shelf in the wall. He handed it to her. "Here you go. I'll be right outside. Then when you're ready, we can record the items together. All right?"

"Sure," Mari said, her heart pounding. She carried the box into the cubicle and sat down in a chair. *This was it.* Swinging the lid open, Mari peered inside. She gasped. In the dim light sparkled a pair of clip-on earrings. Carefully removing one, she held it in her palm. The Art Deco earring swirled delicately upward like a silver branch, a cluster of diamonds framing a brilliant sapphire. These had belonged to Violet.

A paper in the back of the safe deposit box had been folded in a small square, neatly as origami. Mari unfolded the note. It had become worn with age and creased many, many times, small enough to fit inside a matchbook. Mari worried it would disintegrate in her hands.

She covered her mouth as she read Violet's plea.

After a few minutes had passed, Carl cleared his throat. "Miss Cruz? Are you ready to document the items?"

"Yes," Mari said, her voice faint. "Just a minute."

Without thinking, she slipped Violet's note into her pocket. She took a deep breath, opened the cubicle door, and returned the box to Carl.

"There's a pair of diamond and sapphire earrings inside."

"That's all?"

She nodded, Violet's note burning a hole in the pocket of her jeans.

CHAPTER 25

Violet Harcourt

1940

My fingers trembled as I crumpled up the Butterick pattern. I'd sewn both two-piece ladies' suits in red rayon, one a size smaller than the other. The peplum jacket would provide the illusion of a womanly figure. I set fire to the paper, using a poker to nudge it toward the back of the fireplace. With a September chill in the air, I'd complained to Charles of the cold all day, so he wouldn't suspect a thing.

Tonight, he was meeting with his lawyer at the Hotel Palomar in town. I'd overheard their phone conversation weeks ago, noting the date and time. This window of opportunity allowed me to risk everything, to reach out to Ricky with my plea for help.

Edging toward twilight, the darkening sky reminded

me I ought to leave. My heart sank, thinking of Evie and how I had lied to her again. I remembered what a gas we had when we'd traveled to the Woolworth's in San Francisco, purchasing matching wallets. Had that only been two years ago? I had difficulty recalling a time when Charles didn't control my every move. I swallowed, praying she'd brought the bag of clothing to Ricky. If Ricky didn't arrive tonight . . .

I needed to be strong, for Olive. Would I hurt her? The impact would inflict less damage than Charles could. I had no other choice.

Opening my Woolworth's wallet, I stared at the Social Security card printed with the word "Specimen" and a nine-digit number. The sample had always been there, but the night I began sewing, I hoped it would serve a vital purpose.

For the past week, Charles and I had eaten supper in silence, save for the newscaster's voice on the crackling transistor radio. I enjoyed FDR's "Fireside Chats" and his calm, collected demeanor, but now with the escalating threat of war, Charles had become paranoid. He called his lawyer daily about the draft, asking how to manage his hidden assets overseas. The stress wore on him, and with it, his patience with me diminished. I could sense his rage building.

The pink scar on my wrist shone in the dim light, a reminder of Charles's cruelty. If I failed to escape this time, there would be no second chances. Picking up my sewing shears, I walked into the bathroom.

Standing in front of the bathroom mirror, I looked at my pale reflection. *Breathe.* The sun would set in an hour, and I didn't have a moment to waste. A faint purple bruise began to show beneath my right eye, a parting gift from Charles. Removing the bobby pins from my curls, I watched my long auburn hair fall in waves over my shoulders. The scissors felt cold in my hands.

I pressed my lips together. I'd always loved my hair, taking pride in its shine and scarlet richness. But I felt numb as I snipped, watching it tumble into the sink. When I finished, the bob grazed my jawline, making my blue eyes appear larger. I gathered the hair, tossing it into a paper bag from the supermarket.

Tearing open a cardboard box, I took out a tube of black hair dye, applying it from my roots to my newly shorn ends. Evie hadn't noticed the Valmor dye in my shopping cart, hiding beneath a carton of eggs. My eyes watered from the sting of the chemicals and my nose twitched from the terrible scent.

For crying out loud!

I grabbed a piece of toilet tissue and wiped up a drop of goop that had fallen on the sink before it could stain. Oh, why hadn't I thought to wear an old pair of evening gloves? The tips of my fingers were turning purple. Glancing at the clock on the wall, I swallowed. It was nearly seven-thirty.

Sticking my head beneath the faucet, I rinsed my itching scalp. The water ran a muddy purple, and I grabbed an old towel. I stopped, holding my breath when I thought I heard

Charles turning his key in the lock. But it was only a trick of my imagination. Patting my hair dry, I felt the lightness of my new cut—the freedom of it. I mopped the water from the bathroom floor, and then hurried outside.

The street was quiet. As discreetly as I could, I lifted the lid of a trash bin two doors down, discarding the wet towel, the paper bag with my chopped hair and the empty tube of hair dye, along with its box. The skirt I'd sewn hugged my growing belly, the red peplum jacket hiding the small swell. Opening the side door of my home and darting inside, I walked into my bedroom. I took a white chiffon scarf from a drawer and wrapped it around my head, tying it beneath my chin. With my new haircut and color completely concealed, I exhaled.

Seven-thirty.

Checking my reflection in the vanity, I put on a swipe of red lipstick, and then my black sunglasses. But the purple of my fingertips . . .

My stomach lurched as if I were waiting at the peak of the Giant Dipper roller coaster. Shaking my head, I slipped on a pair of white gloves. There was no time for detail. Charles could be driving home this very moment. I clenched my teeth, touching the bruise on my cheek. He wouldn't harm us anymore. This time, I would escape for good.

ADRENALINE PUSHED ME out of the house. I walked briskly along the footpath, carrying my large handbag as if it were a bomb. My eyes darted toward every car that passed. Charles was likely having me followed. However, being watched was all part of the plan. Onlookers would witness my fall from grace.

The sun hung low in the sky. Purple shadows stretched long over the pavement, the branches of the cypress trees gnarled and menacing. In less than half an hour, everything would fade to darkness. Walking faster, I held my breath.

A pair of boys walked down the road, perhaps thirteen years old. Looking at the sidewalk, I attempted to pass without drawing their attention.

"Good evening, Miss. Do you have a cigarette, perchance?"

"I'm afraid I don't," I replied, my voice trembling.

Turning on my heel, I walked away quickly. If I appeared distraught, that would aid my story. But the fewer people I spoke with, the better. The winding footpath brought me closer to the bluffs overlooking the ocean. I swallowed. A couple ambled down West Cliff Drive, out for an evening stroll. I felt guilty about the horrible sight they were about to witness, even though it wouldn't be real.

The stone arches of Natural Bridges came into view. I slowed to a stop. Climbing over the guardrail, I looked to my left and to my right. The couple in the distance had noticed me. My heart began to pound as I walked toward the cliff's edge. The ocean roared in my ears. I gasped as I looked at the choppy water below, my saddle shoes sending a cascade of pebbles toppling over the brink.

A yellow triangular sign with the words WARNING, NO ENTRY, HAZARDOUS CONDITIONS stood to my right, clearly marking the spot. The road was empty of automobiles at the moment, but a car could round the corner and pull over if I were spotted. Taking a step closer, my breath hitched. Waves crashed against the rocks like a battering ram, relentless and strong. I could feel the couple watching me as I leaned over the edge, trying to catch a glimpse of the sandy shelf below.

The sun dipped toward the horizon, taking the last rays of light with it. I stared into the dizzying depths of the cold, swirling blue water below. Voices called in the distance. I had no time to deliberate.

I thought back on Ricky's words, and the sincerity in his eyes that fateful night when I drove Harry Goodman's Oldsmobile through the fog.

If there's anything you need, I'm always here for you. You promise you'll come to me if you're in trouble?

I had come to him. I couldn't see Ricky, but I trusted he would save me. With my heart pounding, I shut my eyes.

And then I jumped.

CHAPTER 26

Marisol Cruz

2007

Mari stared at the note in her hands. She'd left the bank in a trance, Violet's letter stashed in her pocket like she was a criminal. But really, the letter had no monetary value, and she hadn't wanted to explain its significance to Carl. Now she read it again in the privacy of her bedroom, taken aback by the secret Abuelo had kept his entire life.

Mari's eyes pricked with tears. How terrified Violet must've been, pregnant and alone. She clenched her teeth, her suspicion that Charles was an abusive husband now confirmed. And Abuelo—had he risked his life to save Violet? Or had he left her alone, to take her life out of desperation?

Mari stood. Could Violet *still* be alive? She would be an old woman now, in her late eighties. Mari flipped open her laptop, and then drummed her fingers against the keyboard. Where to start? Closing it again, she walked into the kitchen, hoping her mom had come home.

Ernesto sat at the kitchen table, drinking coffee and reading the paper.

"Hey, Dad. Is Mom home yet?"

"Not yet, *mija*. She's still out with her friend. What's up?"

Mari bit her lip. "Not much."

She wanted to tell her father everything about Abuelo, but she didn't want to upset him. Her claiming Abuelo had risked his life to save Violet—a woman her grandfather had never spoken of—might be interpreted as an insult to Abuela's memory. From Violet's note it appeared they were only friends, but Abuelo was incredibly loyal to her.

Lily would be done with dance class in an hour, and then after picking her up, Mari had to work the night shift at the Jupiter Café. Since she'd started working weekends at the boardwalk, Wanda had given Mari the worst shifts, probably out of spite.

Remembering the trunk of Abuelo's things, Mari decided it seemed as good a place as any to start.

"Hang on a sec."

After darting into her bedroom, Mari rummaged in the closet where she'd stashed the trunk. She flipped the lid open, taking out the contents. With the vintage postcards and trinkets cradled in her hand, Mari returned to the kitchen. She set them down on the table. "I was looking through Abuelo's things, and I was wondering if you could tell me more about his travels as a young man."

Ernesto smiled, picking up the first postcard, the Ferry Building.

"Papa loved San Francisco. He told me how glamorous it was back in his day. He took Abuela out to dinner and to jazz clubs in the Fillmore District."

Mari smiled, envisioning how wonderful the historically black neighborhood must've been before it was ruined by urban renewal in the 1960s.

"What about this one?"

She handed him the drawing of the Empire State Building in New York.

Ernesto laughed. "He was so proud of traveling to New York. It was the first time he ever flew on a plane. He took Abuela for their fifth wedding anniversary. She told me he prayed during takeoff and his knuckles were white as a sheet. He was scared outta his mind! But determined to show her the Big Apple."

"That's romantic," Mari said, envisioning her grandparents walking around Central Park and looking at the lights of the Brooklyn Bridge.

Ernesto snorted. "Romantic? *Creo que no.* He didn't have much money then, so they stayed with a cousin in Queens. The house had fleas."

Mari brushed her arm, her skin crawling. "Ew! How do you know that?"

"Because he told me. He tried to plan the perfect trip, but there they were on a pullout couch, itching all night. They were young, though, and they laughed about it."

"That's love," Mari said, her heart warming as she

imagined traveling somewhere with Jason. He was definitely a glass-half-full type of guy, and she could see him making the most of a crappy situation. He'd probably ask her to dance in the rain.

"How about this?" Mari said, handing her dad a key chain in the shape of Texas, painted with the Texas flag.

Ernesto winced. "He went to Houston for a diving competition. But when he won, no one clapped. Said it was the worst racism he ever encountered. Of course this was the forties. He said some guys in cowboy hats threatened to kill him."

Mari clenched her fists. "That's horrible."

"They followed him around in their pickup truck, yelling insults and throwing beer cans. But he never gave in to their taunts, didn't fight them. Probably the reason he came home safely."

"I wish he would've punched them."

Ernesto laughed. "You have your mama's fire. Don't get on *her* bad side."

Mari giggled. When Paulina snapped, her tongue was sharp as glass.

"And when did he go here?" Mari asked, pushing the vintage postcard of the Wrigley Building across the table. It showed the Michigan Avenue Bridge at sunset, the famous building set against a brick cityscape.

Ernesto furrowed his brow, squinting at the postcard. "He never went to Chicago."

"Are you sure?"

"Absolutely. He *loved* to talk about his travels. When I

was a kid that was all he ever talked about. I can tell you every detail of that trip to New York and that trip to Texas, but he never mentioned Chicago, not once."

"Maybe someone sent it to him."

Her father turned the postcard over. It was blank, like the others. "You're right. This one has a stamp. The others don't. See?"

Mari snatched the postcard from him, looking at the stamp and postmark date: October 1, 1940—a few weeks after Violet's death was reported in the papers. After reading Violet's letter, it all made sense.

"Thanks, Dad," Mari said, taking the postcard.

"Wait, where are you—"

But she walked straight to her bedroom, her body humming with adrenaline. Violet had sent a postcard once before, from the Brown Derby in Hollywood. Had she sent a blank postcard from Chicago to tell Abuelo she was safe?

Violet wouldn't have used the name Harcourt, obviously. Maybe she'd chosen her maiden name, Sweeting.

Opening her laptop, Mari typed "Violet Sweeting, Chicago 1940."

Nothing came up.

Evie had mentioned that Violet made new friends in Hollywood. She might've used the name of someone she knew.

Mari typed "Evelyn Sweeting, Chicago 1940" into the search engine and waited. *Nothing*. She tapped her chin, remembering the first name of one of Violet's Hollywood friends Evelyn had mentioned. *Roxy!* But aside from a pin-ball machine called the Roxy, her search yielded nothing.

Mari struggled to remember the other name. Evie had mentioned her trip to San Francisco with Violet, buying matching wallets from Woolworth's . . . oh, what was the other girl's name?

"Vera."

Mari smiled, then typed "Vera Sweeting, Chicago 1940." A marriage certificate appeared in the image search. On July 7, 1944, Vera Sweeting had married Eugene Stanek in Cook County, Illinois.

Vera had written in her age as twenty-four, which would have been Violet's age at the time. Eugene Stanek was twenty-five.

A knock sounded at the door and Mari startled. She wasn't expecting anyone. But after the city council meeting, maybe a disgruntled neighbor had decided to drop by to share his or her frustration. She needed to schedule a meeting with the mayor. Hopefully he would hear her out. Building condos on the beach was wrong for the community, and in his heart he had to know that, whether it was his son's project or not.

"You gonna get that?" Mari called to her dad.

"No," he grunted. "It's probably solicitors."

Mari stood, smoothed her jeans and walked down the hallway. Spying a thick head of hair peeking through the window glass, her mouth parted in surprise. Opening the door, she smiled. "What are you doing here?"

Jason stood on her front porch, a bouquet of sunflowers in his hand. "These are for you."

"They're beautiful," Mari said, taking them. "But what's the occasion?"

"I saw them at the farmers' market and thought of you. I know you love yellow, and I wanted to stop by. I hope that's okay."

"Hmm," Mari said. "Kind of stalkerish, don't you think?"

Jason grinned. "Yep. I have your face printed on a pillow that I snuggle with every night, and a doll made out of your hair."

"Gross," Mari said, giggling as she leaned in to kiss him.

Jason stroked her cheek. "Can I come inside?"

She glanced over her shoulder. "My dad's home, so no funny business."

"I wouldn't dream of it."

As she opened the door, Mari realized she hadn't cleaned her room, and there were piles of laundry everywhere. She cringed a little at the crumbs and unwashed dishes in the kitchen. But that was Mom life—the chores never ceased.

"Sorry, it's messy," Mari said, leading Jason down the hallway.

"Who's that?" Ernesto called from the kitchen.

Mari dropped her voice to a whisper. "Ignore him."

"It's okay," Jason said. "Let's go say hi."

"Ugh," Mari said "Okay."

"Hi, Ernesto," Jason said, stepping into the kitchen. "It's great to see you again."

Ernesto looked up from his paper. "Jason! I didn't know you were coming by."

"I was in the neighborhood."

"He brought me flowers," Mari said, smiling. "Aren't they pretty?"

"Si," Ernesto said. "Your *abuela* loved sunflowers too."

Mari filled a vase with water and set the flowers in the center of the kitchen table. "They brighten up the room."

Jason smiled. "My grandmother loves them too."

"Come with me," Mari said, taking Jason by the hand. "I have to show you something."

Ernesto raised an eyebrow, but he returned to his newspaper.

"Now he definitely thinks we're up to something," Jason said, as Mari tugged him down the hallway. "Wait," he said, pausing in front of the black-and-white photograph of Ricky. "Is this your grandfather?"

Mari nodded. "When he was young."

Jason looked at Ricardo Cruz in midair, his body poised in a V shape as he plunged headfirst toward the ocean. "He did some pretty daring tricks, didn't he?"

"You have no idea," Mari said, eager to tell Jason about her discovery. "Come in here. I found something online I want to show you."

Jason stepped into her bedroom, looking around.

"Nice. So this is your room?"

"Ignore all the stuffed animals and the laundry baskets. I share it with Lily."

"Oh, so this tiara isn't yours? I think it'd look sexy on you."

"Very funny," Mari said, throwing a pillow at him.

Jason sat down on her floral bedspread, checking out her bookshelf. Mari picked up Violet's note. "Remember how I told you that my grandfather knew a beauty queen who committed suicide in 1940?"

Jason scrunched his brow. "Violet Harcourt?"

Mari smiled. "Good memory."

Jason reached out his arm and stroked her waist. "I can remember facts spoken by those beautiful lips. Come here."

"Not yet," Mari said. "I have to finish telling you the story. It'll blow your mind. Read this note."

She handed the paper to Jason and watched his eyes widen and then narrow as they darted across the page.

"Holy shit."

"I found it in a safe deposit box at the bank along with the diamond and sapphire earrings Violet describes in the letter. I think my grandfather saved her life."

"This," Jason said, pointing at the note, "is incredible. Are you going to tell anyone? This could be a huge story."

"I know," Mari said, sitting down next to him and balancing her laptop on her knees. "I'm planning to tell Carol at the museum, but I need the *whole* story. I did a little digging, and I think Violet might have survived and moved to Chicago."

"No way."

"She'd be eighty-seven this year. Obviously, she had to change her name. I went off a hunch and Googled her maiden name along with the name Vera. And look what I found."

She tilted her laptop toward Jason so he could see the enlarged marriage certificate on the screen. "Vera Stanek of Illinois. All I have to do is search census records and find an address to see if she's still alive."

His face fell.

"Where did you find this?"

"Online."

Jason stood up, his hands shaking. "This is some kind of joke, right?"

Mari reached for his hand. "What's wrong?"

Jason pulled his hand away, his face twisted in a grimace.

CHAPTER 27

Violet Harcourt

1940

As I fell toward the ocean, tears blurred my vision and the cold wind stung my cheeks. It all happened so fast. A split second later, I hit the ledge below. In the same instant, I saw the red of my peplum jacket catch the wind, continuing to drop toward the ocean. Ricky was wearing it along with the red skirt I'd sewn for him. I wished I'd had a moment to thank him . . . but no words escaped my lips.

Quickly, I rolled beneath the rocky overhang. In the dark grotto hidden under the outcropping of sandstone, I watched the tail of his white head scarf whipping in the breeze. The ocean swallowed him whole. I covered my mouth.

My stomach twisted, noticing how the surf at Natural Bridges was far more violent than down by the boardwalk. Placing a hand over my belly, I counted the seconds: *10 . . . 20 . . . 30 . . . 40 . . . 50 . . . 60.*

"Please be all right," I whispered to Olive, hugging my stomach. I'd only dropped about six feet, and I prayed the impact hadn't hurt her.

The sky faded to black, and I squinted my eyes. There was no movement beneath the waves. My heart clenched. What if I had persuaded my friend to kill himself in my desperate attempt to escape? I'd watched Ricky Cruz perform his daring stunt diving act enough times to believe he could survive the fall. But he hadn't resurfaced.

Oh God. I had made a terrible mistake.

Then I saw something. A slip of red fabric bobbed in the water. I gasped. *The jacket.* Beside it floated the white chiffon scarf, like a ghost gliding atop the surface. The earth above me shook with approaching footsteps. I pressed my back against the cave wall and held my breath. Sand and dirt sprinkled my hair. I flinched when the man spoke. His words were labored, as if he'd been running.

"Dear God, did you see her jump?"

"Christ. She hit the cliff on the way down. My wife screamed when she saw it. Bounced off the rock like a checker, went straight into the water. I told my wife to ring the police, to run to the nearest house and see if they have a telephone."

"Do you reckon she'll survive?"

"I doubt it. She hit the rock hard. Besides, there aren't any fishing boats at this hour. There's no one to throw her a life preserver."

"Jesus, Mary and Joseph."

The earth shook again as the men walked away. I broke out in a cold sweat, my eyes scanning the coastline. Ricky had cleared the jagged rocks below, but the water was cold, and the tide strong.

Ricky, where are you?

Then I noticed a dark form creeping slowly around the cliff's base, much farther down the beach. I nearly cried out in relief, recognizing the lean man, naked save for a pair of striped skivvies. My friend had survived.

"Thank you," I whispered.

I could never repay Ricardo Cruz for his act of bravery. I'd given him my diamond and sapphire earrings, which had belonged to my grandmother, sewing them inside the red dress along with my note. They were meant to bring me luck on my wedding day. *Something old, something blue.* I hoped Ricky would use them in whatever way helped him find prosperity in his own life.

In the darkness of the cave, I unbuttoned my red peplum jacket and shimmied out of my skirt. Shivering in my brassiere and girdle, I fumbled in the dark for my handbag. I opened it, taking out a simple blue-collared dress. After changing, I folded up the red jacket and skirt, tucking them into my handbag. Removing my white head scarf, I stuffed it inside the bag, and then pushed the clasp together, hiding the evidence.

A crowd would gather shortly, eager to gawk at the cliff's edge where a distraught woman had taken her life. People were drawn to the macabre—it was human nature. Sirens wailed in the distance, reminding me I had to move. With my purse slung over my shoulder, I clawed my way up the cliffside, the toes of my saddle shoes finding footholds in the rock.

"We're going to be all right," I whispered to Olive, my gloved hands digging into the earth. I hauled myself up, swinging my leg over the guardrail. Brushing the dirt off my dress, I stood on the footpath, wondering what a fright I must look. My knees were scraped from the fall and my arms scratched. As the sirens drew closer, I walked down West Cliff Drive in the direction of the lighthouse.

Ambulance lights flashed as the emergency vehicles rounded the bend at Steamer Lane. The sirens wailed, louder and louder. My breath came in ragged gulps, my arms and legs pumping as I started to run. I crossed the street, eager to avoid the group of people who had started to gather on West Cliff Drive.

Women with rollers in their hair stepped out of their houses in their bathrobes, looking around to see what the commotion was all about. Whispers carried on the wind. *Have you heard? A suicide.* Ducking my head low, I walked with my eyes on the ground, terrified someone would recognize me. My train would depart from the boardwalk in twenty minutes. And news would reach Charles in no time.

I thought of Charles sitting at the hotel bar, his face grave as someone told him that his beloved wife had died. Hot tears pressed against my eyelids. I had robbed him of the opportunity to kill me, but I didn't feel vindicated—only sad. Perhaps in his delusion he believed he loved me, and he'd weep with grief.

My heart clenched, thinking of Mother and Evie. My death would hurt them terribly. But so long as Charles lived, I could never tell anyone the truth. To the world, I *was* dead. Violet Harcourt would be remembered in infamy. When I'd dreamed of seeing my name in print, this wasn't what I had imagined.

Spotting the Giant Dipper, I felt the knot in my stomach loosen slightly. The train waited at Casino Station. I took off my sunglasses, fearing they would make me too conspicuous. Then I wiped off my red lipstick, using my thumb. Reaching into my purse and opening my compact, I looked at my reflection. With my short black hair, makeup-free face and dirt-smudged cheeks, I appeared to be a woman down on her luck.

As I approached the boardwalk, I imagined how a single, working-class woman might walk, how she might feel. Closing my eyes, I pictured her. She was from Louisiana. Her husband had died. She was in her forties, tired and hardened.

I opened my eyes, fully embracing my character. Fear of being recognized fell away as I, all weary bones and grit, approached the station agent. I unclasped my purse and fumbled for the ten-dollar bill I had pilfered from Charles. Sliding it beneath the glass, I grunted in a smoker's voice with a Southern drawl, "San Francisco."

"Round-trip?"

"One-way."

The ticket agent took my money and handed me a ticket, along with a handful of change. "Train departs in ten minutes."

Instead of thanking him, I hobbled toward the train platform. If questioned, perhaps he would state my hair was gray instead of black. Memory could be tricky that way. I'd heard of factories seeking women now that news had spread of men enlisting and being called in the draft. From San Francisco, I could get on a Greyhound bus that would take me to Gary, Indiana. I didn't know a soul in the Midwest. Charles, if he suspected I was alive, would never look for me in a factory town.

My eyes pricked with tears. I took one last look at the boardwalk, the bumper cars, the carousel, the Skee-Ball machines and the sky glider chairs. Would this be the last time I set eyes on the Pacific Ocean, breathing its familiar scent of fresh sea air?

With its eerie whistle, the train shot a white plume of steam into the night sky, reminding me I had to keep moving. My heart pounded in rhythm with its pistons. *Had Ricky made it home safely?* How cold he must've been, emerging from the water without someone to throw a blanket around his shoulders.

"All aboard!"

I jumped as the conductor bellowed instructions, ducking my head while passengers moved toward the train coaches. Allowing the crowd to push me forward, I climbed aboard, my eyes searching for an unoccupied seat at the back. A woman in a fur coat laughed, leaning her head against the arm of a blond man.

Though it terrified me to expose my face, with my short black hair and plain dress, I hoped to blend into the background. How strange to think I once craved the spotlight—dying to be recognized as a great beauty on the silver screen. Now I yearned for only one thing—to provide a better life for my daughter.

Placing a warm hand over my stomach, I took a deep breath. I couldn't feel her move yet, but I could sense Olive's presence. She had given me courage tonight. No matter what challenges lay ahead, I would never be alone. She was with me every step of the way. And for her, I would be strong.

"Last call for San Francisco!" the conductor hollered. The steam whistle sounded, high and shrill. I held my breath as the locomotive rumbled in place, waiting for the doors to close. Any minute now, the train would depart.

Without warning, two policemen boarded the car. They'd found me. The ruse was up.

Passengers whispered to one another as the cops walked down the aisle, flashing their badges. I turned my face toward the window. *What would I say to them? Would I go to prison?*

"People say it's Mr. Charles Harcourt's wife," one burly policeman said to the other. "Two boys saw her walking in the direction of Natural Bridges around seven-thirty. Said they asked her for a cigarette."

"You sure it was her?"

"A neighbor saw her leave the house in a red dress and a white head scarf. Said she looked frightened. Matched the boys' description. Violet Harcourt. Only twenty years old. Real pretty too. She won the beauty pageant in June."

I shut my eyes. *They knew my name.*

"Her fella owns the Oceano? Hell, what more could she want? My wife's still on my ass because I haven't paid the gas bill."

"These are tough times. I can't speak for a motive, but you know how moody women are. So she's sick in the head, so what?"

"Cripes. So it's a suicide?"

"Looks that way. A few folks saw her jump. Still no body, though."

Too frightened to look up, I wondered if the other passengers had turned around in their seats, if they would point at me. I heard their hushed whispers.

"Give it till morning. She'll probably wash up down the beach."

"Christ, Fred. Children don't need to see a dead body. Maybe we oughta close the boardwalk?"

"Train's clear of the husband. I don't think he's trying to skip town. Check with the chief, see if they found him."

The two officers turned around and then disembarked the train. I looked down at my hands, my palms slick with sweat. They hadn't mentioned Ricky's name. They were looking for Charles.

Suddenly the train rumbled to life, and we were moving. *I had gotten away with it.* Pressing my face against the window glass, I watched the boardwalk grow smaller in the distance, the lights of the Ferris wheel illuminating the night sky. The police officers stood outside the Plunge, smoking cigarettes.

When the train passed over the San Lorenzo River Bridge, a tear of relief slid down my cheek. Taking off my dirty gloves, I stared at my purple fingertips, my ring finger free from its cumbersome diamond.

This time, I hadn't left a note for Charles. My wedding band and engagement ring on the nightstand told him he didn't own me anymore.

Until death do us part.

In death, I had finally found my freedom.

CHAPTER 28

Marisol Cruz

2007

Jason looked at the marriage certificate, then back at Mari. "Gene and Vera Stanek are my grandparents' names."

"Jason," Mari said, but she was at a loss for words.

He crossed his arm over his chest, and then put one hand to his mouth, staring at the ground. "They got married in Cook County, Illinois. How old did you say Vera Stanek would be?"

"Eighty-seven."

Jason stared at Mari, and then shook his head. "My grandmother lives in Naperville, Illinois. She's eighty-seven years old."

"But your last name is Doyle. Jason Doyle." Mari realized how stupid she sounded, but she couldn't process what was happening.

"Stanek is my mom's maiden name."

"Have you seen pictures of your grandmother when she was young?"

"She hates to take pictures. We hardly have any."

"Here," Mari said, taking the laptop from him. She typed "Violet Harcourt, 1940" into the search engine and waited for Violet's beauty pageant image to load. Gently pushing the computer toward Jason, she pointed to the screen. "That's Violet."

Jason squinted at the screen. "I can't be sure. It could be her. Wait . . . no, those are definitely her eyes." He dropped his head into his hands. "Are you telling me that my grandma was an abused woman? That she had a secret life?"

"I don't know. You'd have to ask her."

"She said she grew up on a farm in Oregon." He once again covered his mouth with his hand. "But . . . she was pregnant. No, that means if it's her, she was pregnant with . . . my mother."

He pushed the laptop away. "I can't—this is too much."

Mari's throat was so tight she could barely breathe. It all made sense. Jason grew up in Chicago. He said his grandmother never talked about her life before the war.

"Jason, wait."

"What?"

She looked at him, wishing she could touch his unruly brown waves. Suddenly she became aware of how much she cared for him.

"Listen, I'm so sorry for dumping this on you. You don't

have to speak to your grandma about this—especially if it would upset her."

His eyes narrowed. "So you didn't tell anyone?"

"Not yet. I wanted to tell Carol at the museum, but I haven't emailed her."

"Would you mind keeping it to yourself for now?" Jason rubbed his hands through his hair. "Jesus . . . what if Gene isn't really my grandpa? Am I related to the Harcourts?"

Mari tried to swallow. "I don't know."

"That would mean *Travis* is . . . is what, my cousin or something?" Jason grimaced. "I can't take this."

"Jason," Mari said, her voice wavering. "I'm sorry. I had no idea. Hey, where are you going?"

But he had already wandered out of the room in a confused daze, muttering something about his grandmother.

"Jason," Mari called after him. The front door slammed shut and she drew her elbows in, pressing them against her ribs. She'd told Jason about his beloved grandmother's painful past—a past Violet had gone to great lengths to keep hidden—and dropped the bomb that could decimate his family. It was no wonder Violet's words had shaken Jason. Mari looked again at Violet's note, her desperate plea for help.

Dear Ricky,

You once told me that if I was in trouble, you were here to help. I am ashamed to admit this, but my life is in danger. As *you might have guessed, my husband Charles is a violent man. I fear that he will kill me.*

If you've found this note inside the jacket pocket of the ladies' suit I've asked Evie to give you, then you are my last hope of survival. Charles will never stop searching for me until I am dead. I'm begging you to help me, so he thinks I have taken my own life.

I've sewn this jacket and skirt in your size. There's a cave just beneath the yellow warning sign at the cliff's edge on West Cliff Drive (near the intersection of Auburn Avenue). On Friday, September 24th, meet me there at seven PM. Wear these garments and wrap this white scarf around your head. Don't let anyone see you.

At sunset, I shall jump from the cliff wearing an identical outfit. The moment I land on the ledge below, you must jump the remainder of the way. I recognize I'm asking too much—it's a thirty-foot drop and the water is dangerous, but you're the only person I know who can survive the fall.

You once told me you could hold your breath underwater for two minutes. It's enough time to convince the world I've drowned. I can never repay you for my life, but I hope the diamond and sapphire earrings from my grandmother will bring you luck.

Ricky, I admire you so much for following your dreams, and for helping me when I left for Hollywood. My only dream now is to live. I am pregnant with Charles's child, and I want nothing more than to bring her into the world, safe and sound. I know I'm asking too much, but I pray in my heart you will help me again. Thank you for listening, and for being there, always.

Your friend,
Violet Harcourt

"WHAT TIME IS Jason coming over?" Paulina asked.

Mari sighed. "He's not coming."

Paulina set down her tray of enchiladas. "Why not?"

Mari looked at the dinner table, set with their best china. Ma had put so much effort into making a nice family meal.

"I told him something upsetting."

Jason had texted her after his abrupt exit, to tell her he was flying home to Chicago for a few days. Mari's stomach knotted at the thought of him confronting his grandmother, but he said he wanted to talk to her in person.

Paulina dropped her voice to a whisper. "Are you guys okay?"

"Yeah," Mari said, thinking back to the text exchange. Jason had assured her he wasn't mad, only shaken. "He had to fly back home last minute. He's really sorry he couldn't make it tonight."

Lily came skipping into the kitchen. "Smells yummy! When can we eat?"

Mari smiled at her daughter. "As soon as we say grace."

Ernesto walked into the room. Her father looked out of sorts. He ran a hand through his hair until it stuck up at all angles, and his eyes had dark circles underneath them. Something was upsetting him—Mari could tell.

"Well, this looks wonderful," he said, smiling at Lily. But the smile didn't reach his eyes.

Mari took her daughter's hand on one side and her mother's on the other. She closed her eyes.

"*Bendícenos Señor,* bless this food which through you in your goodness we receive. Bless the hands that prepare bread for the hungry. Amen."

"Amen," Lily said. "Yummy, yummy in my tummy."

As Mari ate, she watched her father. Normally he'd be scooping up extra helpings of enchiladas, flirting with her mom and making Lily laugh. But he was silent at the dinner table, slowly eating the food as if it tasted like cement.

"Where's Jason?" Lily asked, as if on cue.

"He's in Chicago."

"Why'd he go there?"

"He went to see his family."

"But *why*?"

"Because that's where he's from," Mari said. "Sometimes people visit their families."

"We don't," Lily said, chewing loudly. "Our family lives *here*."

Mari smiled. "That's right. Aren't we lucky?"

Paulina had noticed Ernesto's strange behavior as well, and she reached for her husband's hand. "*Mi amor*, is everything all right?"

He looked up, surprised. "Yeah. Fine."

Now Lily was interested too. "What is it, Abuelo?"

"Nothing," he said, standing up from the table and taking his plate. "Work stuff."

Mari watched her father walk into the kitchen. She bit her bottom lip.

"I'm done," Lily said, pushing her plate away. "Can I play?"

Mari nodded. "Sure. Go ahead."

As Lily skipped down the hallway toward the living room, Mari picked up her family's plates and carried them over to the sink. Paulina followed her. Ernesto sat at the kitchen table, his head in his hands.

Paulina placed a hand on his back. "What's wrong?"

He looked up with bloodshot eyes. "Immigration authorities came by my office today. They asked to see my papers."

Mari scoffed, heat rising under her skin. "*What?* But you were born here!"

"*Si.* They realized they'd received a bad tip. But you know, some of my guys, they're undocumented."

Paulina rubbed her husband's back. "You think ICE will come back?"

He rubbed his face with both hands. "I don't know."

Mari swallowed, her heart plummeting into her stomach. What if there was an ICE raid on one of her father's construction sites? Those workers had families—children to support who'd have no one to take care of them if their parents were arrested.

"Why now?" Paulina asked, her brows drawing together. "Who would tip off Immigration? You've been running your firm for ten years."

He shook his head. "I don't know."

"This happened today?" Mari asked.

Ernesto nodded. "I'm going to get all my I-9 forms in order, just in case. But some of my guys, you know, they provide false information."

"It's okay," Mari said, her stomach knotting with the knowledge that it could mean thousands of dollars in fines for her father, and devastating consequences for his undocumented workers. "We'll contact an immigration attorney. There are nonprofits that your workers can go to and get help."

Paulina squeezed her husband's shoulder. "We'll get through this."

After finishing up the dinner dishes, Mari gave Lily a bath, read her a bedtime story and tucked her in bed. Then she lay awake, tossing and turning, too anxious to sleep. Her phone pinged with a text.

She smiled, hoping it was Jason, texting her good night. Her stomach clenched when she saw the unfamiliar number—then realized it wasn't entirely unfamiliar; she had it stored in her phone once, a long time ago.

I told you not to mess with me. Looks like daddy is going back to Mexico.

Mari clenched her phone so hard, she thought it might break. Travis Harcourt had gone too far. Angry tears sprung to her eyes. She wasn't going to take any more of his crap. Two could play at this game.

"I'M HERE TO meet with Mayor Harcourt," Mari said, straightening her shoulders as she spoke to the mayor's secretary. She'd put on her best blouse and a pair of gray slacks and black flats—the closest thing to business attire she had.

Like the days when she functioned on less than three hours of sleep during Lily's first year, Mari had woken up this morning with superhuman strength. She would channel her hurt and anger into action.

"Do you have an appointment?"

"No," Mari said. "But this is urgent."

The woman disappeared down the hall, and then returned, a smile on her face. "He has fifteen minutes before his next meeting starts."

Mari followed the woman down the hall, grateful Santa Cruz was small and community-oriented enough that she had the opportunity to speak with the mayor in person. Taking a deep breath, she followed the secretary through a glass door into Mayor Harcourt's light-filled office.

"Good morning," he said, standing up from his chair.

Mari shook his hand firmly. "Good morning."

"So," he said, smiling. "How can I help you?"

"Do you remember me, from the museum booth at the Beach Boardwalk Centennial Celebration?"

"Yes," Mayor Harcourt said, his eyes twinkling. "I knew you looked familiar. You sold a record number of raffle tickets."

"Right," Mari answered. "I'm a resident of Beach Hill, and I've collected signatures from over forty neighbors opposing the Cowell Beach condominium development. Not only will the condos change the character of the beach, but also the historic gazebo will be destroyed. We're not okay with this."

Mayor Harcourt nodded. "I understand your concerns. But the developers have agreed to shorten the condominium construction from eight stories to five, so views won't be obstructed. Beach access will remain public. And the building will be in compliance with all of our green building standards—one hundred percent eco-friendly."

"That's great," Mari said, looking down at her hands. "And I appreciate all the effort the developers have put into meeting our community needs, but you see, the gazebo has a special significance to me."

Mari reached into her purse, removing a drawing of the gazebo that Lily had made. In pink and purple crayon, it showed a couple holding hands underneath the gazebo roof. Up above, she'd drawn stars in blue, and thanks to Jason's story, a flying unicorn.

"My daughter is four. She drew this picture of her great-grandparents dancing at the gazebo. Their names were Ricardo and Maria Cruz. It was where they met, and where they had their wedding reception. It's a special place to our family."

Mayor Harcourt smiled as he stared at the drawing. Then his brown eyes met hers. He waited silently, listening—really listening.

Mari took a deep breath, and then let it out.

"Back when Mexicans were characterized as gangsters—you know, with zoot suit riots and all that—the gazebo was a safe space. Oftentimes, Mexican Americans were denied entry to traditional dance halls and venues, where they wanted to hold *quinceañeras* or wedding receptions. The owners would make up reasons why they couldn't rent the space, but there was no reason other than racial discrimination."

He sighed. "Have you thought about contacting local preservation groups? They might be able to help shoulder the costs of relocating the gazebo. Of course, you'd have to purchase a new plot of land for it."

Sure, they could go through the trouble of figuring out

how to relocate the gazebo, and make everyone happy. But this was personal.

"No," Mari said. "The gazebo belongs where it is." Her heart began to thud again and her hands trembled as she prepared to drop the bomb. "The reason I'm here, though, isn't the gazebo. It's your son, Travis."

The mayor raised his eyebrows. "You know my son?"

"I do. We shared a history class at UC Santa Cruz."

Her hands shook as she reached into her purse, pulling out the envelope from the DNA testing center where she'd submitted Lily's hair and Travis's gum.

"And he's the father of my daughter."

The mayor laughed, then looked at her as if he'd been splashed in the face with a bucket of cold water. "I'm sorry. What did you say?"

Mari pushed the envelope toward him. "We spent the night together in college, the summer of our graduation. He had a big party at his house on West Cliff Drive. He said you purchased it for the water polo team."

The mayor's face drained of color as he pulled the paper from the envelope and looked over the series of letters and numbers. At the bottom of the page in bold it stated: ***Probability of paternity: 99.9998%***

His eyes narrowed. "How did you get this?"

"Travis spat out a piece of gum and stuck it on the table at the city council meeting," Mari said, a sharp edge to her voice. "I submitted it with some hairs from my daughter's hairbrush. I'm sorry to go to such extremes, but, you see, I told Travis he was going to be a father four years ago. He wanted nothing to do with Lily."

Mayor Harcourt let out a deep breath, and then rubbed his eyes. He turned to Mari, the friendliness in his voice gone. "Why should I believe your story?"

"I understand. It's a shock. Listen, I have a year's worth of emails that I sent to your son, with pictures of Lily attached. I begged him to meet her, told him I would take full financial responsibility, I just wanted her to know her dad." Mari's voice broke on the word "dad." She covered her mouth with her hand.

The mayor reached for a box of tissues and pushed it toward her. His eyes softened. "Take one."

Mari did. Then blew her nose. She laughed at the ridiculousness of the situation. "Honestly, I wasn't ever going to tell you about her. But then Travis threatened my father. Immigration authorities showed up at his construction firm." She pushed her cell phone toward the mayor. "Here, look at this text message."

His eyes widened, and then narrowed.

Mari smirked. "Is that how you want your son treating people? By the way, my father is a U.S. citizen."

The mayor said nothing. His jaw set in a hard line. He'd recognized his son's phone number. Sure, she could have faked the text message, but Mari hoped the mayor could tell she being was one-hundred-percent honest.

Eventually, he cleared his throat. "Santa Cruz is proud to be a sanctuary city. We don't want any of our residents to feel unsafe here."

Mari stood up. "Your son has made it clear he wants no involvement in my daughter's life. But he needs to leave me alone. If my father's construction firm receives any more threats, or visits from ICE, I'll be contacting you."

As she turned to leave, Mayor Harcourt looked shell-shocked.

"Wait."

Mari turned around. "Yes?"

"Here's my personal email address," he said, frowning as he scribbled on the back of a business card. "If you could forward me those emails where Travis said he wanted nothing to do with . . . his daughter . . ."

Mari nodded. "Of course."

She took the business card from him, exhaled a deep breath and stepped away from his desk. Mayor Harcourt's cheeks colored. "Can I keep the drawing?"

"Sure."

The mayor might not be ready to accept that he was Lily's grandfather, but Mari already felt lighter. She'd told the truth. And right now, that was all she could do.

CHAPTER 29

Violet Harcourt

June 1943

My overalls clung to my body in the sticky summer heat. Unlike Santa Cruz, where the coastal breeze smelled like sea salt and sunshine, Gary, Indiana, stank of dead fish and soot, the summer air thick with humidity. The town was made up of old brick factory buildings, belching black smoke into the sky. A pang of longing hit me—my dream of sandy beaches and blue water.

A shrill whistle sounded as I walked toward the steel plant, signaling an end to our break. In this industrial town nestled against the shores of Lake Michigan, I'd found new strength and purpose. Three years ago, I'd stepped off a Greyhound bus with nothing to my name save for a cotton dress and a pair of saddle shoes. I'd been frightened and alone. Now I had friends and a steady paycheck—a new life, a safe haven.

Securing employment in my condition had been difficult; initially I'd concealed my pregnancy under loose dresses and thickly knit cardigans. The supervisor of women employees, Mrs. Stoner, came to know me as the other gals at the factory had—as Vera Sweeting, a farm girl from Oregon. I constructed my story like a Hollywood character: I had been put in my unfortunate position by a young farmer, the baby conceived in a barn, then I'd been sent away in shame by my family, who had disowned me.

"Hallo, Vera!"

I waved to the woman who'd called out, Agata Mirzljack, a Croat with two young children, her face obscured by goggles. My heart swelled, thinking of my precious Olive, who enjoyed playing with Agata's children, Ana and Jacob. Rosy-cheeked and delightful, my daughter had become my world. With my blue eyes and Charles's dark hair, she was the most beautiful baby, born on an April morning, her lungs strong. I'd cried tears of joy, seeing her perfect, angry red face, and vowed to protect her forever.

The end of my pregnancy had been difficult, that first winter in Indiana brutal. The temperature had dropped to twenty degrees, blizzards blowing icy-cold wind through the gap beneath the windowpanes in my boardinghouse. I'd thought of my fine coats in Santa Cruz, collecting dust in a closet. Or perhaps Charles had discarded them.

Upon my arrival in Indiana in September, I obtained work as a secretary in the steel plant, submitting my employment paperwork with the number on the "specimen" Social Security card from my Woolworth's wallet. That January, when I could no longer conceal my growing bump, I feared Mrs. Stoner would let me go. But she kept me on, rolling her eyes when I waddled from office to office.

I'd been so skittish my first year, even after seeing my death reported in the papers. Looking at my smiling pageant photo, I no longer identified with that starry-eyed girl. No matter the similarities in our faces, I knew she was gone. And slowly, I became Vera. I continued to dye my hair black and to keep it short. These days, it was covered by a scarf, and like the other gals, I had no need for frivolity.

Putting on my hard hat, I looked around at the women who'd become my companions. Since the bombing of Pearl Harbor, everything had changed. When I started here, I was one of a few girls. Today, laborers in dirty overalls cleared the tracks outside the factory of debris, all of them female. Some had husbands overseas, some had children, and others were unmarried. But all of us sweated near the blast furnaces, directed giant ladles of molten iron and poured red-hot ingots. We were black and white, Polish and Croat. We were women of steel.

Waving at Agnes and Emmy Lou, I fell in line behind them, walking into the factory. Sweat trickled down my back as I entered the burning heat of the boiler room. Flapping belts and buzzing welding guns grew louder. The furnace blazed, and women wearing protective masks and goggles welded steel parts, sparks crackling.

"Say, Vera," Emmy Lou called over the noise. "Do you remember your first day here as a riveter, when Agnes razzed you?"

Agnes laughed. "Ha! You didn't know up from down."

I smirked, pulling on my protective gloves. "You asked me to get you a left-handed hammer, and I looked for it in earnest for a good ten minutes."

We took our seats in an assembly line, drills in hand. The movement came naturally to me now, easy as breathing. Attaching rivets to sheets of metal, we worked on what would become an aircraft sent to fight the Nazis. With sweat dripping down my brow, I felt pride in the strength of my arms, the same pride reflected in the grit and determination of every face in the room. To think we'd been considered the weaker sex.

I remembered how I'd complained to Emmy Lou, a college girl from Iowa, of factory heat on my first day.

"It's no hotter than a kitchen," she'd responded, her smile bright as her pink lipstick. Back then I'd sat next to Klara, a grandmother from Hungary with reddened, chapped hands. My heart had broken, fearing the work was too much for her. But Klara was stronger than an ox, a fact she reminded me of often. Now she spent her days looking after my Olive, who was a rambunctious toddler and kept Klara on her toes.

A familiar sadness settled in the pit of my stomach

when I thought of my mother. Though she wasn't a warm woman, I pictured her holding Olive in her arms, a smile on her face. I had robbed her of that opportunity, and I had broken Evie's heart. Did Evie have her own children now? Surely she did—she and Frank would make lovely parents. And Ricky, had he met a sweetheart? Did he have a family of his own?

I'd mailed him a postcard during my first trip to Chicago with Agnes and Emmy Lou. The city had dazzled me with its bright lights and smartly dressed women in hats and furs. The soaring skyscrapers and jazz joints were such a welcome break from the dreary landscape of Gary. At first, I'd been too frightened to mail the postcard, but I wanted to send Ricky a sign I was all right—I had made it to a safe destination.

The noise of the factory drowned out my thoughts. I pushed the sadness back into a corner of my heart and locked it away, focusing on the task in front of me, drilling. In two hours' time I would see my precious Olive. And she would run to me with her chubby arms outstretched, and I would know in my heart that I had made the right choice.

When the whistle sounded again, signaling an end to our workday, I wiped the sweat from my brow and removed my gloves. My muscles ached as I walked with Agnes and Emmy Lou toward the bus stop. Jiminy Cricket, I was dog-tired. Drilling from dawn until dusk with only a short lunch break had taken its toll on me.

"I'm spent," I said, clutching my purse. "I hope there's hot water tonight. Last week the shower was on the fritz."

"Remember how you used to moan about the humidity?" Agnes said, nudging me in the ribs.

"Well, Oregon sounds cool and lovely," Emmy Lou interjected. "You can't blame the gal. What's your hometown again, doll?"

"Eugene," I replied, a lie I had repeated so many times, it had become my truth. "The Emerald City. I miss its lush green grass and trees."

"Then you're not a Hoosier," Agnes said, lighting a cigarette.

"Because she misses her hometown? Agnes, not everyone can be an Indiana native like you. We're all Hoosiers. We take pride in where we live and what we do."

The factory chimneys billowed smoke into the rust-colored sky, and the sticky air smelled like tar. My heart ached for the rush of the ocean and the tingle of cool sea spray against my face. Would Santa Cruz fade from my memory, like a place I'd once seen in a dream? Even if I never returned, it would live in my heart forever.

Paying our toll, we boarded the bus. Emmy Lou and Agnes chatted as we passed rows of wood frame houses with covered porches. I remembered my first time riding this bus route to our boardinghouse. Emmy Lou had told me about the different neighborhoods. "This here's the East Side," she'd said. "It's a nice place. You've got the West Side and south of the train tracks is South Side, near Ninth Avenue. There you've got your Negroes and your immigrants, lots from Poland and Russia."

I'd become accustomed to the bustle of downtown Gary,

a small strip with the Palace Theater, a few churches and the grocery store, where Negro women in smart hats chatted and did their shopping. I enjoyed the mix of people, who were different from the familiar faces I'd known all my life in Santa Cruz.

The bus stopped on the corner of Fifth Avenue and Arthur Street, and we stepped out, walking toward the tall brick boardinghouse. Its lobby smelled of stale coffee and cigarette smoke, but it was clean. Other female factory workers who lived here had children as well, and Olive loved to run up and down the hallway with her playmates, shrieking with delight.

Though it would be nice to have a place of our own, at twenty dollars a month, our single room at the boardinghouse was what I could afford.

Emmy Lou checked her mailbox, then came away teary-eyed, finding it empty. "It's terrible, isn't it? Not knowing when our boys will come home?" Her blue eyes met mine. I touched her arm, wishing I could take away her pain. She'd shown me a photograph of a handsome man in uniform, her beau, George, who'd been sent to Europe to fight. She sniffled. "I pray to God every night to keep him safe."

My stomach turned, thinking of Charles. He had remarried, a socialite named Grace Vanderkamp, and I'd felt sad instead of relieved. I'd seen their wedding announcement in a California paper, which I'd purchased for twenty cents from the newsstand downtown. A firm isolationist, he had managed to dodge the draft, still hiding behind his false Quaker pacifist status. My friends in the factory were braver than he was.

When the girls had gone, I unlocked the door to my room on the second floor. At least my tired legs didn't have to climb more than one set of stairs.

"Mama!" Olive bounded toward me, her dark curls bouncing and her chubby arms outstretched. My heart filled with love. I knelt down and opened my arms, pulling her into a tight hug.

"My darling! How I've missed you."

I kissed the top of her head, breathing in the scent of soap. Klara stood, gathering the wooden-colored blocks they had been playing with.

"She was good girl today. Ate her cabbage soup."

"Good girl," Olive repeated. "I eats it all."

"Of course you did," I said, hugging her close. My sweet, spirited little girl—I longed to give her the world. In our cramped and narrow room, we shared a bed. I'd brightened the brick walls by taping Olive's drawings up, and I kept a vase of sunflowers by the window. I'd purchased yellow fabric with a daisy print and sewn curtains to replace the dirty beige ones that smelled of stale smoke.

I thought of my former wardrobe: designer heels, red silk and green velvet dresses, mink coats and stylish hats. My vanity with its oval mirror held drawers of pearl necklaces, gold bracelets and ruby rings. Charles could have given Olive anything she desired, and I had deprived her of that. But what I lacked in wealth, I made up for in love. My daughter would know I loved her fiercely.

I cracked open the window to let in some air, despite the oppressive humidity. Cars honked on the street below, and the bus hissed as its doors opened.

"Good night, Klara," I said. "We'll see you in the morning."

Klara waved at Olive. "Bye-bye, honey."

"Come here," I said, patting the bedcovers next to me after Klara had shut the door. Olive hopped up and giggled as I tickled her.

"Did you have fun today?"

"Uh-huh. When we go lake, Mama?"

"Soon."

The blue ache of nostalgia colored my thoughts when I remembered the sounds and smells of the Beach Boardwalk. How Olive would delight in dipping her toes in the Pacific Ocean, in riding the bumper cars, in touching the horses on the Looff Carousel. I'd taken Olive to the shores of Lake Michigan last weekend, but they weren't the same, though beautiful in their own way.

"Do you know how much I love you?"

"To the moon," she said, opening her arms wide.

"That's right," I said, kissing her forehead. And as I sat there with my daughter cuddled in my arms, the city sounds faded away, along with the ache in my muscles. This moment was enough. This was perfect.

THE AIR-CONDITIONING ALONE was worth the price of admission. The scent of buttery popcorn filled the theater lobby, and to be in the darkness for a few hours, my thoughts pulled far away from the war, was definitely a welcome escape. With Klara babysitting, my friends had managed to drag me out.

Emmy Lou turned to me. "Vera, why don't you sit down? Get us a group of seats together and we'll be back with the popcorn and soda pop."

"You sure?"

"Yes, go on. Today's half price because the film is not a new release. Look how full the theater is!"

"All right," I said, realizing I hadn't even asked what film we were seeing.

I made my way down the aisle, my eyes trying to focus in the darkness, the rows of seats already mostly full. Under the flickering film reel, faces stared at the screen. *Cripes.* What were my chances of finding three seats together?

My eyes came to rest on a sandy-haired man who sat alone toward the end of the aisle. He had an empty seat to his right, and two empty seats on his left. He hadn't slung his coat over the back of the chair next to him to claim it, like many moviegoers had. I took a deep breath and strode over.

"Excuse me," I said softly. "Is this seat next to you taken?"

"No, ma'am," he said, his blue eyes shining. He had quite a pleasant face, handsome, really—and I was grateful he couldn't see the color of my cheeks in the darkened theater. I hadn't thought about anyone that way in years.

"Oh, thank you," I said. "I'm awfully sorry to trouble you, but would you mind moving over one? You see, I'm with two girlfriends, and we'd like to sit together."

"No trouble at all," he said, picking up his hat and coat.

"Thank you," I said, setting my purse and cardigan down on the seats next to me, to save them for Agnes and Emmy Lou.

I settled next to him, aware of the squeak in the seat and the weight of my body. In the darkness, it felt strangely intimate to be in such close proximity to a man. I could smell the crisp scents of his cologne and his hair pomade. Both were sweet, and slightly spicy. I liked the smell, very different from Charles.

"Are you sure I can take all three?" I asked. "You're not waiting for anyone?"

He shook his head, an embarrassed look on his face. "No, no, I'm alone."

"Oh," I said, regretting that I had asked a foolish question. I hadn't meant to make the poor fellow feel bad.

He chuckled. "You must think I'm odd, going to the pictures alone. As one of the few young men in the theater, I already feel odd enough. Trust me, my mind is as much with our brothers at war as yours. But why not see a picture show? We all need a little escape sometimes, don't we?"

Whether it was the darkness concealing our faces or the earnestness in his voice that prompted me to ask such a bold question, I couldn't say. But I felt like I knew him, and that I could speak to him as a friend. "Why aren't you at war?"

He shrugged. "Flat feet. It's a damn shame, because I would be honored to serve my country. I teach music at West Side High School."

"Music?" I leaned in closer. "What instrument do you play?"

"Piano. I teach classical, but I love jazz."

"Really? Who's your favorite musician?"

"Duke Ellington."

"You don't say. He's my favorite musician too."

It had been so long since my fingers had touched piano keys or my voice had warbled in song. To think I had won the Miss California bathing beauty pageant, that I had moved to Hollywood and been featured as an extra in a film. I felt much older than my twenty-three years. Motherhood and working in the factory had aged me.

He smiled. "I like the tone of your voice. Are you a singer? You remind me of that jazz tune 'Summertime.' Do you know it?"

It was the song I'd sung at the Miss California pageant.

"Yes," I said. "It's a lovely tune."

"Sorry. I haven't even asked your name."

"It's Vera," I said, extending my hand. "I'm a factory girl. I work at the steel plant, installing rivets for the aircraft going to war."

His warm hand enveloped mine, sending shivers through me. In my peripheral vision, I saw Agnes and Emmy Lou making their way down the aisle with the soda and the popcorn, looking for me. But I didn't want them to arrive just yet. Because that would mean my conversation with this man would end. And I didn't want it to.

His eyes met mine, twinkling in the darkness.

"I'm Eugene," he said, his smile kind. "That's swell.

You gals are amazing. And it's a real pleasure to meet you."

"Likewise," I answered, my heart skipping a beat.

The music started and the curtain rose. Emmy Lou and Agnes pushed past me, settling to my right. Noticing that I had been speaking with Eugene, Agnes nudged Emmy Lou in the ribs. They both giggled. My cheeks burned.

"Sorry," I whispered. "These are my friends Agnes and Emmy Lou. This is Eugene. He was kind enough to give us these three seats."

"Lovely to meet you," Emmy Lou said, her eyes brimming with mischief. She'd tried to set me up several times over the course of the years we'd known each other, but I'd turned down her offers to attend dances and potlucks.

The screen crackled and the music cranked louder, drowning out their giggles. I ate a handful of buttered popcorn, enjoying the opportunity to sit in silence. But when the title flashed across the screen I gasped, nearly knocking over the paper popcorn bag and our sodas.

"What'sa matter?" Agnes hissed, leaning over.

"Nothing," I whispered. "I thought I saw a rat."

"Did you?" Emmy Lou asked, picking up the hem of her skirt, her eyes widening as they darted to the floor.

"No. I imagined it."

As the girls settled down, I stared at the screen as if it were a portal to another time. This was the John Huston film I had auditioned for, where I'd shared a scene with Humphrey Bogart. I'd never seen it.

Agnes and Emmy Lou whispered throughout the film, giggling and swooning at the handsomeness of the male actors, and gasping when they wondered if Humphrey Bogart's character was in fact a killer.

I was aware of Eugene's hand resting only inches from mine. It was as if I could feel the warmth of his skin, soothing me. Even without touching, I felt his presence. I held my breath, waiting for the bar scene, to see if I would see myself on-screen, an auburn-haired beauty in a red dress.

Then I appeared in black-and-white, my waves sultry, obscuring my face. I couldn't breathe. I couldn't move. I watched myself staring into the gin glass and remembered everything—Roxy, Tommy, Benny Bronstein, the Tropicana, the Beverly Hills Hotel and Bungalows, the lavish party at Ernst Lubitsch's mansion.

"She's beautiful," Eugene whispered in the darkness. "But not as pretty as you."

I turned toward him. *"What?"*

"Forgive me if I'm being too forward," Eugene said, leaning in close to me. "But I would love to take you out sometime. Would you let me take you out?"

The scene changed, and my former self vanished as if she'd been nothing more than a mirage. If Emmy Lou and Agnes had recognized me, they hadn't reacted. They sat with their heads together, whispering and munching on popcorn.

"Yes," I said, a sense of calm coming over me. "I would like that."

"Wonderful," Eugene said, smiling.

Eugene.

I liked the sound of his name. It sounded like the ocean waves. Like home.

CHAPTER 30

Violet Harcourt

2007

Sun poured through the large, arched window in the family room, warming my aching bones. I practiced tai chi in the park every Sunday with my elderly friends, but I could feel myself slowing down. At eighty-seven, I figured death could come for me at any moment. But I didn't fear it. I had lived a wonderful life.

"Gene," I called, watching my husband as he sat in the kitchen. "Stop feeding that dog table scraps. He's getting fat."

My husband ignored me, handing our dachshund another piece of bacon. Kielbasa lapped it up gratefully, wagging his tail. I smiled, realizing my dear doggie boy was getting gray around his muzzle, also entering his final years.

"You spoil him," I said loudly.

"As he should be," Gene called back, sipping his coffee.

I looked at the back of his head, dotted with liver spots and completely bald except for a ring of wispy white hair. This year marked our sixty-third wedding anniversary—I loved the man more and more each year.

After I quit working in the steel factory in Gary, we'd lived in an old brownstone in Chicago's Wicker Park. Division Street was known then as "Polish Broadway," there were so many Polish immigrants, and Eugene had felt right at home. His loud and large family had embraced me, his new wife, with open arms. And I'd finally begun to shed my ghosts. Vera Stanek's identity fit me like a second skin.

Taking jobs in Chicago had been good for us both. Eugene taught music classes at the local high school while I taught private voice lessons in our home. In the evenings, we'd danced to records in our living room, our hearts pressed together. For every painful memory I wanted to erase, Eugene planted a new one like a seed waiting to bloom.

Do you remember when you burned the curtains because you insisted on lighting all fifty candles on my birthday cake? Do you remember when we made love on a blanket under the stars? Do you remember when I kissed you in the rain?

My husband was a treasure. Kielbasa was the sixth dog we'd owned, from a long line of dachshunds. Our brick Dutch Colonial in the suburbs of Illinois had been filled with children's laughter, the tearing of wrapping paper at Christmastime. First there was Olive, and then Edward, our son. Gene agreed to adopt Olive as his own, and we changed her last name to Stanek.

As she grew older, she began to look more like Charles, her hair a rich chestnut color whereas Edward's was strawberry blond. When she was old enough, I told Olive the same lie I had told Gene—her father had died at war. In truth, Charles was very much alive, and for many years I looked over my shoulder wherever I went.

"Such a nervous girl!" Gene's mother would lament, clucking in her thick Polish accent. "Nerves not good for health."

I looked at our wood-burning fireplace and smiled, remembering the Christmas stockings that hung there. Our first dachshund, Dottie, had eaten some tinsel off the tree when Olive was five and Edward was two. I'd burned the cookies that morning, and spent the whole time fretting whether the damn dog would be all right.

A knock sounded at the door, startling me.

"Gene," I called out. "Are we expecting visitors?"

He shuffled his newspaper. "What?"

"Heavens," I muttered, walking toward the door.

No matter how many times I nagged him, Gene didn't like to wear his hearing aids. I'd urged him to get the implant, but unlike me, Gene felt wary of new technology. I prided myself on my understanding of the computer—my grandchildren had explained the Internet to me. What a marvel it was! I had my own Facebook page and followed my grandkids on their adventures. Of course, they were young adults now, older than I was when I married. But times were different.

"Who is it?" I asked, my hand resting on the brass knob. My front door had a window carved into the oak, but I'd shrunk in my old age and couldn't make out the face of the person on the other side, only a shock of thick, brown hair.

"It's me, Grandma."

I pressed a hand against my chest, a smile spreading across my face. Then I pulled the door open. "Jason! What are you doing here?"

My heart flooded with love, looking up at the strapping young man my grandson had become. He had Gene's kindness and the most beautiful brown eyes I'd ever seen. He bent down and wrapped me in the most delicious hug. I pressed my arms against his strong back and held him close, feeling small in his arms.

"Surprise! I decided to visit."

"I thought you weren't coming home until the holidays. This is a welcome surprise indeed. Come in!"

I ushered him inside, still unable to believe how tall he'd grown. How old was he now? Twenty-eight? How time had flown.

"Is Pops home?" he asked, running a hand through his messy hair.

"He's in the kitchen. He'll be so thrilled to see you."

Jason smiled, but his eyes held sadness. My smile faltered. *Oh dear. What could be troubling him?* But when he looked at me, his eyes brightened. "You look beautiful, Grandma. You haven't aged a day."

I laughed. "You're too kind. Are you hungry? Can I fix you a sandwich?"

Jason grinned, tugging the collar of his flannel shirt. "No, Grandma, don't trouble yourself. If I get hungry, I can make myself a sandwich."

"Let me do it," I said, walking toward the kitchen. "It keeps me young."

Every morning, I put on a swipe of red lipstick, and noted how my smile hadn't changed. The multitude of wrinkles around my eyes and mouth came from years of laughter. I wouldn't have it any other way. And now that Eugene and I weren't getting by on tins of beans and plates of rice like we did during the war years, I made an effort to eat healthy—fruits and vegetables. Eat your colors, as the doctor said.

"Look who's here," I said, clapping my hands together as Jason followed me into the kitchen. Gene looked up from his paper, and then broke into a wide smile.

"Is that you, Jason? Holy moly, I thought you weren't coming home until Christmas. It's still summertime, isn't it?"

"No, Gene," I deadpanned. "It's December. Go shovel the driveway and put the lights up like I asked you to."

"Oh hell," Gene said, laughing until he coughed. "She loves to tease me."

Jason laughed too, a wonderful sound, deep and contagious. He gave his grandfather a hug, but there was something in his posture—I could tell he was unsettled.

"How's your new job?" Gene asked, patting Jason on the back. "Do you like living in California? We sure do miss you."

Of all places, Jason had found a job in Santa Cruz. I'd nearly had a ministroke when he'd told me where he was moving. My heart ached to set my feet in the sand, to dip my toes in the Pacific Ocean, but I'd never returned.

"It's going well," Jason said. "I love California. Great weather, great people."

"Have you met anyone special?" I nudged him in the ribs.

"Actually, yes," he said, his brown eyes meeting mine. "And if it's okay with you, Grandma, I'd like to talk to you in private."

My stomach flipped, the way it would when I'd reached the peak of the Giant Dipper roller coaster, before it tumbled downward at full speed. I hadn't ridden that rickety old thing in over sixty years, but I still remembered the sensation.

"Sure, dear. Let's go into the sitting room."

"What, I'm not invited?" Gene said, setting down his coffee.

Jason patted him on the shoulder. "I need to talk to Grandma alone. Sorry, Pops."

My slippers padded across the hardwood floors as I walked toward the living room. I settled in the window seat overlooking the garden. Jason sat down next to me, the wood creaking beneath him. He'd gotten a bit of a suntan, and it suited him.

"So what is it you want to tell me?" I asked, placing my hand on his. "You've met someone special?"

He looked down at our hands, and then up again, his eyes serious.

"I have. Her name is Mari. Marisol Cruz."

"Lovely name. Is she a Spanish girl?"

"Her family is Mexican American. They've lived in Santa Cruz for generations." He took a deep breath in, and then let it out. "Grandma, have you kept a secret from me? About your life before the war?"

My heart began beating so fast. Was this the beginning of a heart attack? But I took a deep breath in and counted: 2, 4, 6, 8. My heart slowed its beating when I let the air out.

"Why do you say that, dear?"

Jason shook his head. "Grandma, this isn't easy for me. I need you to tell me the truth. Did you know someone named Ricardo Cruz? Did he save your life?"

I shut my eyes, my heart flooded with memories of that night. The fear, the desperation, then the exhilaration of riding that train to freedom.

He knew.

I opened my eyes. "Yes."

Jason blinked rapidly. "It's true, then? You were a beauty queen married to a man who tried to kill you? Was your name Violet Harcourt?"

Over the years, I'd slipped into the comfort of living life as Vera Stanek. I didn't want to step out into the harsh cold world beyond that. It would mean I had harmed those I loved most by lying to them.

"Yes," I whispered. "I haven't heard that name in a long time."

I wanted to hug him, to tell him that it was okay to cry, but his jaw set in a hard line as he fought his emotions.

"Jesus," Jason said, rubbing his face. "How did you do it?"

"I used my Social Security card from Woolworth's. In 1938 a wallet manufacturer decided to show how well a Social Security card would fit in a wallet. A sample card was included with each wallet, printed with the actual number of the company president's secretary. It worked when I used it as my own."

"What?" Jason said. "No way."

"It's true. You can search it on the Google."

He pulled his phone from his pocket.

"Well, I never. Do phones have the Internet now?"

"Yep. They're called smartphones." He typed away, and then his eyes widened. "Grandma, this article says that by 1943, five thousand seven hundred and fifty-five people were using the secretary's Social Security number."

I smiled. "That card was the wrong size and had the word 'specimen' printed on it, but I wasn't the only person who used the number. In fact, I was quite relieved when I found out I wasn't alone."

A crease formed between his thick eyebrows. "So that's how you were able to remarry?" He dropped his voice to a whisper. "Does Pops know?"

"You'd be surprised what comes out after sixty-three years of marriage."

His eyes widened. Someday he would learn to love and trust someone as deeply as I trusted Gene. It had taken me ten years before I told my husband my secret, but one evening after a bottle of wine, the truth came spilling out. He'd hugged me and held me close, promising he wouldn't tell a soul. And decades later, he remained true to his word. In private he called me his gal from the movies, though he knew I was more at home mucking around in the garden.

"It was a painful time," I said, my voice breaking. "I didn't have anywhere to turn. I was in a bad marriage, and I tried to leave when I moved to Hollywood to become a film actress. But Charles, my first husband, he came for me."

Jason squeezed my hand. "Grandma, I'm so sorry you went through that."

I pushed the image of Charles, fists raised, to the back of my mind. I'd made a choice to let the pain go, to wake up every morning with a smile on my face, to befriend other positive people, to cherish every moment, to snuggle my dogs, to appreciate my time digging in the garden, the sun on my shoulders.

I smiled at him. "It's all in the past."

His face clouded over. "But Mom. Is she . . . is she?"

I nodded. "She's his daughter."

Jason grimaced.

"And Pops, so he's not . . ."

I gripped Jason's hand. "Jason, look at him. You're practically wearing the same flannel shirt. Pops might not be your flesh and blood, but in his heart and in yours, he is your grandfather. You know that."

Jason's eyes filled with tears. He wiped his cheeks with the back of his hand. My heart broke for him. "I know this is a lot to take in. We never meant to hurt you. We thought it was easier this way."

"How?" Jason asked. "Everything I've known my entire life is a lie."

"That's not true," I said, rubbing his hand. "My love for you, your mother's love for you, and Pops's love for you, that's the truth. It's the only truth that matters."

"Shit," Jason said, covering his face with his hands. "I'm sorry, Grandma. I didn't mean to swear. This is so overwhelming for me."

I rubbed his back, like I used to when he was a little boy who couldn't stop crying after he'd taken a fall and scraped his knees. But then I began putting the puzzle pieces together. "How did you know the name Ricardo Cruz?"

"He's Mari's grandfather."

"The girl you're dating? Oh my word." I blinked back tears. "Ricky Cruz was a dear friend. I wondered over the years if he told anyone the truth about me, but I don't believe he ever told a soul."

My heart ached to reach out to my old friend, to thank him again.

"How is Ricky?"

Jason's face fell. "Oh, I'm sorry. He passed away."

"Oh dear," I said, pressing a hand to my chest. I should have expected as much. So many of my friends had passed over the years, Gene and I hardly had any left. But that didn't make the news any easier. I had lost my chance.

"But his family?" I asked, looking up at Jason. "He married and was happy?"

Jason smiled. "Yes, very happy. He bought a house on Beach Hill in Santa Cruz that his kids and grandkids live in. Mari has told me so many stories about him. It sounds like he lived a full and wonderful life."

"How did Mari find out about me?"

"She discovered the note you wrote Ricky. She's actually been following your story for a while. She found your obituary—God, that's weird to say—in an old magazine, and got hooked on figuring out what happened to you."

I laughed. "And here I thought I could disappear."

Jason frowned. "Why didn't you come forward? Try to get Charles arrested?"

I pressed my lips together. "I feared the legal consequences of what I'd done. I wanted a normal life for your mother. And a second chance for myself."

"I see." He rubbed his chin. "When Mari showed me your note, and told me that Violet Harcourt was you, I freaked out."

"Understandable."

"I panicked, left her house in a huff. Mari works for the Santa Cruz museum and wants to tell your story. But I told her it isn't her story to tell."

My stomach knotted, and I pressed down the familiar fear of being discovered—a fear that had haunted me my entire life. But Charles was dead now. Would anyone really send an old woman like me to jail if I came forward with the truth?

"Grandma?" Jason asked, his eyes concerned.

"Sorry, dear, I was thinking." I smiled. "Do you love her?"

His eyes twinkled. "Yeah. I do."

"And have you told her yet?"

"Not yet. I've thought about texting her to let her know."

"Psssht." I waved my hand. "We'll have none of that hogwash. A young man should not communicate his love by text."

Jason laughed. "Okay. Should I call her?"

I gripped his arm, suddenly filled with a giddy sense of excitement, like I was a young girl riding my bicycle down West Cliff Drive with the wind in my hair.

"I have a better idea."

CHAPTER 31

Marisol Cruz

2007

"Order up for table seven!"

Mari looked at Manuel, sweating beneath his hairnet as he called out another breakfast order, his face red as a tomato.

They had been slammed this week. Students had their families in town, and everyone had decided the Jupiter Café was where they wanted to have brunch.

Picking up the hot plate of hash browns and eggs, Mari carried it over to table seven.

"Hash browns and eggs?"

The girl in front of Mari wrinkled her nose. "Are those *scrambled*? Gross. I did *not* order scrambled. I ordered sunny-side up."

"Are you sure?" Mari asked, sweat dripping down her

back as she looked around the restaurant. They were understaffed, thanks to Wanda. Glancing at her notepad, Mari saw "scrambled eggs" written in her neat penmanship.

"Yeah, I'm sure," the girl scoffed, looking down at her long acrylic nails.

"Sorry," Mari said, biting back her frustration. "We'll make it right this time."

As she walked away, the girl turned to her friend and said, "I won't be tipping *her*." Then they both erupted into giggles.

Gritting her teeth, Mari returned to the kitchen.

"What's the problem?" Manuel asked.

Mari shook her head apologetically. "She wants sunny-side up."

He threw up his hands and then muttered a string of curse words. His bad mood permeated the air.

"Hey." The new waitress with a pierced lip and blue hair walked up to Mari. "I think I screwed up. I switched table eight and table four. Can you help me?"

Mari took a deep breath, summoning her last drop of patience. Today could not get any worse. "Sure. Just give me a minute."

"How's it going in here?" Wanda asked, appearing in the kitchen, her eyes wide behind her rhinestone glasses. She frowned. "Looks like those folks need coffee. What's the holdup, Marisol? *Andale, Andale*!"

"I'm on it," Mari said, anger creeping up her neck. She began to reach for the coffeepot, but stopped midway.

What *was* she doing here? Time seemed to stand still as she realized she'd spent the last four years doing exactly this—yielding to Wanda's demands and smiling at rude customers.

Was she too afraid to put herself in the position of wanting something bigger, because she might fail? Sure, the hours of waitressing had suited her schedule, and the pay was steady, but working at the museum booth had shown her she could do more.

Mari spun around. "You know what, Wanda? I speak *English.* You don't need to tell me to *andale.* I'm moving as fast as I can."

Wanda curled her lip, her bright red lipstick creeping into the wrinkles above her mouth. "Are you giving me attitude?"

"No. I'm pointing out that we're understaffed because you didn't hire enough servers this week. And we're *all* doing the best we can. In fact, *you* could help us by bringing that coffee to those folks yourself."

"Listen here, missy. You're lucky to have this job."

Mari took a deep breath, and then straightened her shoulders. "I'm going to stay until the end of my shift, because I'm not leaving Manuel and Bridget in the lurch. But then you're going to mail me my last paycheck. Because guess what? I *quit.*"

Turning her back on Wanda, Mari stormed out of the kitchen. Manuel raised his eyebrows, and then smiled ever so slightly before returning to the sizzling stovetop.

Bridget followed her, wide-eyed. "That was badass."

"Thanks," Mari said. "We'll fix your order. I'm only going to be here for a few more hours, so pay attention, okay?"

UNTYING HER APRON, Mari smiled. She hung it up on a hook for the next waitress to wear. Punching her time card for the last time, Mari enjoyed the satisfying thump of the stamp. Some of the kitchen staff wanted to get beers, but she declined.

Mari waved goodbye, then stepped out the back entrance into the parking lot. It was a beautiful summer evening, the sky still light and the air warm. Smoothing her short blue dress, Mari hoped she'd never smell like greasy French fries or onion rings ever again. Her future wasn't certain, but she knew she could do more than waitress—she had her museum position on her résumé now.

It was scary to have terminated her main source of income, but hopefully it would light a fire under her to find a new job as soon as possible. Something she really wanted this time—a career that would make her daughter proud.

Mari walked across the parking lot. The driver's-side door opened on a silver Honda, and Jason emerged, holding a bouquet of pink roses, orange tulips, purple orchids and yellow sunflowers. Mari blinked, trying to make sure she wasn't hallucinating. Then she brought her hand to her mouth. "You're back already? Why didn't you text me that you were coming?"

Jason smiled. "Because I wanted to surprise you."

He looked so handsome in his flannel shirt, his brown eyes sparkling. He'd only been gone for a few days, but she'd really missed him.

"How did you know when my shift ended?"

"I called your mom."

"Well, don't tell her yet, but I quit."

"*What*? Just now?"

Mari laughed. "Yeah. It was time."

"Come here," Jason said, wrapping his arms around her. "Congratulations."

She hugged him tightly, breathing in the scent of his cologne. Then she kissed him slowly on the lips, savoring the moment.

Jason handed her the bouquet of flowers, which she took, burying her nose in their soft petals. They were so beautiful.

"What's the occasion?"

He swallowed, his eyes locking on hers with an intensity she hadn't seen before.

"Well, I wanted to tell you that I love you."

Looking into his warm brown eyes, Mari felt a rush of emotion. Her heart pounded with a mixture of nerves and excitement. Then she said the three words she'd never uttered to anyone, except members of her family.

"I love you."

"Whew," Jason said, breaking into a giant grin. "I was scared for a moment there you were going to tell me to get lost."

"Never." She nodded at the silver Honda. "Did you buy a car?"

"It's a rental. Come around to the passenger side. There's someone I want you to meet."

Mari's stomach dropped as she saw a petite woman sitting in the passenger seat, her short hair dyed brown and neatly curled.

"Is that who I think it is?"

Jason pulled open the passenger-side door. The woman looked at Mari and her whole face lit up. Even in her eighties, she was still beautiful. Her blue eyes twinkled and her red lipstick illuminated her lovely smile. She extended a dainty hand.

"You must be Mari. I'm Vera Stanek. But you may know me as Violet."

Mari took Violet's hand in hers. "It is *such* a pleasure to meet you. I can't believe I'm meeting you in the flesh!"

Violet laughed. "I'm not the queen of England, dear. I'm a little old lady from Illinois. Help me up so I can give you a hug."

Mari pulled Violet up from the passenger seat. She was so petite, and looked frail. But when Violet wrapped her arms around Mari, her hug was powerful. Mari closed her eyes and breathed in the floral scent of Violet's perfume. When she pulled away, Violet's eyes shone with tears. "You look like your grandfather."

A lump rose in Mari's throat. "I do?"

Violet stared at her. "You have his eyes. Ricky Cruz was

a brave man. He saved my life many years ago. He's the reason that I'm here today."

Mari blinked back tears. "Thank you. He left your note in a safe deposit box at the bank. I only discovered it recently."

Mari loved the papery feel of Violet's warm hands as they clasped hers.

"My dear," Violet said. "There is so much I want to tell you. But first, can we walk along the beach? I haven't seen the Pacific Ocean in a very long time."

MARI WATCHED VIOLET, standing in the sand, her eyes closed. She faced the ocean, the wind in her hair and the breeze on her face. Waves crashed against Cowell Beach, rushing toward Violet's toes. When the cold water reached her ankles, she didn't flinch. Instead, she smiled up at the sun, tears streaming down her face.

"She looks so happy," Mari whispered.

Jason smiled. "She is."

Violet stretched out her arms. "I'm ready now. Help me, please."

Mari took Violet's arm on one side, and Jason took the other. They supported her as they walked across the sand back to the stairs leading to the boardwalk. Violet breathed heavily after the slow climb, and Mari helped her onto a bench.

"Are you okay, Grandma?" Jason asked. "Let's put your shoes back on."

Violet patted his arm. "I'm all right, dear. Thank you."

As Jason bent down and helped Violet back into her loafers, she pointed at the roof of the arcade.

"Ricky's zip line extended all the way from the top of that building down to the end of the pier. He dangled by one ankle and one wrist. Donny Pierson held him like that, and then they would both plunge into the ocean. It was wild."

"I love that you got to see my *abuelo* perform." Mari took a deep breath. "How did you know he would help you that night?"

Violet stared at the waves. "I didn't know for sure. But your grandfather had already helped me once, when I left for Hollywood. I was frightened to drive because it was dark and foggy, but he told me I could do it."

Mari's heart ached, wishing she could hug Abuelo one last time. "That sounds like him. He was always encouraging me. I took a summer position at the Santa Cruz museum because I wanted to honor his memory."

Violet clasped Mari's hand. "I want to thank you, with all of my heart. I so desperately wanted to thank Ricky that night, but I didn't get the chance."

"You must've meant a lot to him."

"He was always willing to help a friend in need. He had a heart of gold." She looked toward the boardwalk. "This place brings back so many memories. I never thought I would see it again. Santa Cruz still feels like home."

Mari looked at the gazebo and sighed, knowing it would be demolished soon. "There's nowhere else like it."

Violet pointed at the shops dotting the Beach Boardwalk. "My friend Evie and I used to get milkshakes from Marini's. I loved the maraschino cherries. Is Marini's still in operation?"

"It is," Mari said. "Both the boardwalk location and another storefront on Pacific Avenue." She looked at Jason for reassurance. "And Evie, your friend, she's still alive."

Violet brought her hand to her heart. "She is?"

Mari nodded. "She lives in a nursing home in San Jose."

"You met her?"

"She helped me solve the mystery of how you escaped. She told me you'd sewn a dress suit for my grandpa to give to his mother."

Violet smiled. "Oh heavens, I did say that, didn't I?"

Mari laughed. "Knowing my great-grandmother worked on a strawberry farm in the Central Valley where she'd have no use for a suit, and that my father hadn't seen her in years, I knew something was odd."

"I was so frightened," Violet said, her eyes distant, as if she were lost in thought. "I needed Evie to give Ricky the skirt and jacket for my plan to work. I didn't know if she would. What did she tell you that helped you unravel the mystery?"

"That she left it at his post office box. I never knew he had one, but I had a brass key in an old trunk of his. I decided to try it at the post office downtown."

"Is that where he left my note?"

"No. Inside was another key. It opened his safe deposit box at the bank. Your note was in there, along with a beautiful pair of diamond and sapphire earrings."

"Oh," Violet said, her face falling. "I had hoped he would use them to help himself. He didn't sell them?"

Mari shook her head. "He never liked taking charity from people."

"Let's get going," Jason said. "It's getting cold. I don't want you to get sick, Grandma. We should get back to the car."

"All right," Violet said, taking his hand. She nudged Mari. "Isn't he a caring boy?"

Mari smiled. "Yes, I think so."

Violet frowned. "Do you think it would give Evie a terrible fright if we visited her? I'm not sure it's the right thing to do. To make her think she's seen a ghost."

Mari bit her lip. "I think we should. Evie has some regrets about not doing more to help you, when you were married to Charles."

For a minute they walked in silence, the weight of the past heavy between them. Violet spoke first, her eyes sad. "It wasn't her fault. I never confided in her."

MARI GINGERLY TAPPED on the door to Evie's room at her San Jose nursing home, Violet behind her, clutching Jason's hand.

"Evelyn," she called. "Can I come in? It's Mari."

Evelyn wore a yellow sweater and sat in a wheelchair facing the window. Mari's heart sank. Perhaps she wasn't feeling well today.

Mari spoke again. "I visited you once before. Your daughter, Karen, told me about you. We spoke about your beauty pageant days."

Evelyn spun around in her chair, looking at Mari.

"Sorry, dear. I only heard half of what you said. I was watching a blue jay in the garden outside."

Mari nodded. "Do you remember when I came to visit you? We spoke about Santa Cruz in the 1940s and your friend Violet."

Evie wheeled herself closer to Mari. "Yes, I remember that, dear. It made me quite emotional. I still miss her, even after all these years."

"Evie, I want you to take a deep breath. The truth is, I've brought Violet here to see you."

Violet stepped into the room, her hands clasped in front of her heart.

Evie brought a trembling hand to her mouth. "Vi, is that you?"

Violet nodded, tears in her eyes. "Yes."

"But it's not possible!"

With Jason guiding her by the arm, Violet walked over to Evie, then placed a hand lovingly on her friend's shoulder. "I'm so terribly sorry for what I put you through. I didn't die that night. I escaped on a train north to San Francisco. I've thought about you so many times over the years."

Evie stared at Violet for a long time. "You look like your mother. Did you know that? I'll be damned. Is this really you?"

"It's really me."

"But everyone saw you jump—" Her voice broke. "That day in the supermarket, I ought to have said something."

She shook her head. "I saw how frightened you were and I let you go. I should have asked you if Charles was hurting you."

Violet squeezed Evie's shoulder. "Please don't blame yourself. I didn't have the guts to tell you about Charles. Do you remember the bag that I gave you that day?"

"Vaguely. What was it? Wait . . . a red ladies' suit."

Violet nodded. "*You* helped me escape. It was a skirt with a peplum jacket I'd sewn for Ricky Cruz to wear. He jumped off the cliff, pretending to be me."

Evie stared up at Violet, wide-eyed. "But that's bananas!"

Violet laughed. "It *was* bananas. I was desperate. I didn't want Charles to hurt you, and I feared he would if I confided in you. But you executed my escape plan perfectly by bringing the garments to Ricky Cruz."

"I left the bag at the post office."

Mari cleared her throat. "And he got it. Because of you, Violet escaped."

The old friends clasped hands, staring into each other's eyes. Evie began to smile. "Well, I never. Here we are. For sixty years, I've believed you were dead, and now you're standing here in front of me. I'm spooked!"

Violet's eyes glistened. "Oh Evie. I longed to write to you. Did you have a good life? Did you and Frank have children?"

"Yes," Evie said, smiling proudly. "We have a daughter and a son. We tried for more, but it wasn't in God's plan. Dear Frank passed away five years ago. He worked at his auto dealership until he was seventy-seven. He loved talking to customers."

Violet laughed. "That sounds like Frank."

Evie nodded at Jason. "Is this your grandson, Vi?"

"Yes. Isn't he handsome?"

Jason extended his hand to Evie. "It's a pleasure to meet you."

Mari smiled, looping her arm around Jason's waist. "He's my boyfriend."

"Wonderful," Evie said, clapping her hands together. "You make a lovely couple." Then she beamed at Violet. "Do you remember when you taught me the secret to your egg salad recipe?"

"Mustard!" they said in unison. Then they burst into laughter.

"Do you remember what you told Mr. Warner at the pageant office?" Violet asked, gripping Evie's hand.

"You mean about *Uncle Frank*?"

The two old women were laughing so hard they had tears in their eyes.

"Uncle Frank!"

Mari smiled, leaning against Jason. She breathed in the scent of his cologne, and loved the feel of his soft flannel shirt against her skin. Her cell phone jingled in her purse, and she reached in to retrieve it.

"Mari Cruz."

The man cleared his throat. "Hello. This is Mayor Harcourt. I mean, Tom."

"Oh," Mari said, her shoulders tensing. "Hi."

"Listen. I got your phone number from your supervisor at the museum. I hope you don't mind."

Mari patted Jason's arm, mouthing that she'd be in the hallway. Once she stepped outside, she held the phone close to her ear. "No, it's fine. What's going on?"

The mayor's voice was soft. "I've done a lot of thinking these past few days." He didn't sound like the mayor at all, but like someone trying to make amends. "I wanted you to know that I read every one of your emails."

"Okay?"

He cleared his throat. "Do you have time to meet me this week? It doesn't have to be at my office. I can get you a coffee at Peet's. Unless, of course, you prefer Starbucks."

Did the mayor just offer to buy her a coffee?

"Sure," Mari said.

"Great," Mayor Harcourt replied. "I would really love to talk to you in person."

CHAPTER 32

Marisol Cruz

"Welcome, everyone, to our Santa Cruz Beach Boardwalk holiday celebration!" Mayor Harcourt's voice projected from the same stage where he'd stood six months earlier—only this time his feet stirred up a dusting of fake snow. Sprigs of holly and redwood decorated the Ferris wheel and the sky glider chairs overhead, lending their woodsy scent to the sea air. More than the scenery had changed since the summer, when Mayor Harcourt had announced his son's construction project.

Mari sipped her hot apple cider, and Jason wrapped his arm around her shoulders, hugging her tight. He looked so handsome in his beanie and heavy flannel. No matter the season, she could kiss him all night long.

"Thank you all, who've gathered here on this foggy

and chilly evening. I think it's fair to assume you're all locals."

The crowd laughed, and Mari chuckled too. The boardwalk had been transformed with sparkling fairy lights and a Christmas tree decorated with beach balls.

Jason rolled his eyes. "You Californians think sixty degrees is cold? You'd *never* survive a Chicago winter."

"Shhh," Mari said, tugging his arm. "Tom is still speaking."

It was weird how easily his name rolled off her tongue. The day they'd met for coffee, Tom had looked at her with sincerity in his eyes, and told her that reading her emails had broken his heart. He was pulling the funding for Travis's project.

Travis Harcourt hadn't raised the money himself—he was not the successful businessman he pretended to be. Every cent for the project came from his private trust fund, controlled by his father. But Tom Harcourt had decided there were two people more deserving of that money . . . Mari and Lily.

"Tonight," Tom said, smiling at Mari, "I'm proud to unveil the newly restored gazebo. Thanks to the tireless work of our young historian, Marisol Cruz, the gazebo will be preserved as a historic monument, honoring Santa Cruz's rich Chicano and Latino cultural heritage."

The crowd clapped, and Mari smiled, tears in her eyes. The gazebo had been reinforced with new wooden beams, all of the Victorian gingerbread details salvaged. With a fresh coat of paint, globe lights strung from the rafters, and a colorful mural depicting members of the Latino community, the gazebo welcomed visitors.

It was an exact replica of the diorama Mari's artists had created—only this time, it was life-size. Violet had agreed to record her story, and for the remainder of the Beach Boardwalk Centennial Celebration, the art installation had been on display at the museum booth, drawing curious visitors. With increased local interest in the gazebo from both the diorama and Violet's story of Ricky Cruz, ultimately it was saved from demolition.

Now the diorama and Violet's recording had become a permanent installation at the Santa Cruz Museum of Art & History, along with a plaque on the wall: *Mari Cruz, 2007 Swanson Grant recipient.* But it was Violet's words, honoring Ricardo Cruz, that brought tears to Mari's eyes. In her story, Abuelo was the hero, and the gazebo an important part of the boardwalk he loved.

"I'm so proud of you," Jason whispered, sending a shiver down Mari's neck. He kissed her flushed cheek.

Mayor Harcourt smiled. "And now, for the ribbon cutting!"

Mari handed Jason her cider and walked past the gathered members of the community to the stage, where Tom presented her with a large pair of ceremonial scissors.

Her mouth felt dry looking out at the sea of faces. She'd never been a fan of speaking to crowds, but she recognized many of the neighbors who'd attended the city council meeting. Mari felt elated to share this accomplishment with them.

She cleared her throat.

"Thank you all for coming out tonight to celebrate the unveiling of the gazebo. As the saying goes, it takes a village. I could not have accomplished this without your support. My grandparents danced here underneath the stars over sixty years ago. And tonight, we'll do the same. Happy holidays!"

Mari snipped the red ribbon and the crowd erupted into applause. She thought of her *abuelo* smiling down on her and wiped a tear from her eye. The swing band began to play "In the Mood" and Mari couldn't help swaying her hips to the rhythm. It was impossible to feel sad listening to such an upbeat song.

Lily skipped toward Mari, followed by Mari's parents, and she wrapped her arms around Mari's waist. "I love you, Mama."

Mari's heart filled to the brim. "I love you too, sweetie."

Lily turned to the mayor. "Will you dance with me?"

"Of course," he said, taking Lily's hand and spinning her around. Though Mari and Tom had agreed not to tell her that he was her biological grandfather until she was older, Lily had come to know him as a friend. For every occasion where Travis wasn't present, Mayor Harcourt showed up in spades. Over the past few months he had attended each of Lily's dance recitals and every kindergarten play, clapping enthusiastically.

Mari frowned, thinking of how Tom's relationship with his son had become strained in the wake of what he'd learned about Travis. But as Tom put it, Travis needed to learn to stand on his own two feet. Travis had taken a job at a tech company in San Francisco. Tom was no longer paying his rent.

"Dance with me?"

Mari turned around to see Jason, who took her by the hand.

"Of course," Mari replied, laughing as he dipped her. They danced to the brass band, skipping and shuffling, swaying their hips to the music.

"My turn!" Lily cried, grabbing Jason by the hand.

Mari smiled, watching them dance together, her heart swelling with happiness. Over the past months, Jason had become a father figure to Lily. He helped her with school projects, drove her to dance practice and read her stories every night. Sometimes they fell asleep together on the couch, heads touching. It was strange to think that they were related—Jason's grandfather being Lily's great-grandfather. But Charles Harcourt's cruelty had gone to the grave. In this family, there was only love.

The band played on, swing and mariachi and salsa. Mari found herself laughing and spinning around the dance floor with different partners. Her mom and dad had some serious moves. In fact, they were getting a little too cozy, Paulina giggling as Ernesto whispered something in her ear, cupping her butt with one hand.

Jason laughed. "Look at the two of them, still so in love. You might need to wear earplugs tonight."

Mari slapped his arm. "Ew, Jason. I don't want to think about that!"

After dancing to a few more songs, Jason pulled her to the side, wiping the sweat from his brow. "I need a break. Walk with me for a minute?"

"Sure," Mari said, taking his hand.

The ocean rushed in her ears, the sea breeze cooling her flushed cheeks. Even in December, Santa Cruz was stunningly beautiful, the fog hanging over the ocean like a cloak. The damp air smelled like seaweed and brine, like home.

Once they had walked a ways down the beach, Jason paused. Mari looked at the sparkling lights of the boardwalk in the distance, illuminating the night sky. Breathing a sigh of contentment, she thought about how much she had to be grateful for. She'd accepted a full-time position at the Santa Cruz Museum of Art & History, as an assistant curator. She'd become closer to Violet and Gene, who'd invited her whole family to visit them for the holidays, and she looked forward to meeting Jason's parents too.

Mari and Jason often met up on their lunch breaks during the week, now that they both had nine-to-five schedules, sometimes on the UC Santa Cruz campus, overlooking the ocean, sometimes downtown, closer to the museum. Once, as a joke, they went to the Jupiter Café. Mari had giggled and buried her face in Jason's jacket when Wanda glared at her. But she savored every cheese fry, and then left Bridget a hefty tip.

"You're beautiful tonight," Jason said, pushing a strand of Mari's hair behind her ear. "You think I'm cheesy, because I say it too often, but I love you."

Mari smiled. "I love you too."

Jason's eyes grew serious. "I ended the lease on my apartment. It'll be up at the end of this month."

"*What?* Why?"

"It's not big enough for three people. And I've spotted a few places that would be perfect for you, Lily and me. What do you think?"

Mari bit her lip. She'd become so accustomed to sharing her bedroom with her daughter, to having her mom and dad down the hall. But she was turning twenty-seven, and it was time to fly the nest. Her heart fluttered at the possibility.

"I think it sounds wonderful."

"Good," Jason said, squeezing her hand.

He reached into his pocket and took out Violet's diamond and sapphire earrings. "My grandma wants you to have these."

Mari sucked in her breath. She'd returned them to Violet when she'd come to visit over the summer. "Oh no, I couldn't possibly. They're too valuable."

"What if I told you they're for a special occasion?"

"Like what?"

"Well, they're something blue."

"I don't get it."

He laughed, and then rubbed his face. "Oh man, I'm already nervous. You're not making this easy for me."

Before she could put two and two together, Jason got down on one knee in the sand. Mari's throat tightened and her eyes welled with tears. Reaching into his pocket, he removed a gray velvet box. He opened it, and inside sparkled an oval-cut diamond ring, the delicate Art Deco–filigree setting perfect for her.

"In case you were wondering why I've only taken us to cheap places for lunch and why I never want to go to the movies, this is the reason. Thank you for putting up with me, and never complaining that we only eat pizza slices."

"Jason," Mari said, a tear sliding down her cheek.

He smiled. "Mari, I love you so much. I've loved you from the moment you talked to me about *The Kite Runner* and then ran away. I vowed that day I would never stop chasing you. Will you marry me?"

Mari laughed. "Yes."

Jason slid the ring onto her finger, and they kissed, the music of the brass band carrying on the breeze, and the lights of the gazebo shining in the distance. Mari felt her *abuelo* and *abuela* smiling down on her as they danced among the clouds. Violet had taught her an important lesson: a broken heart could heal, and love made a family.

The past didn't matter now, only the future.

ACKNOWLEDGMENTS

Thank you again to my wonderful editor, Lucia Macro. This novel would not be what it is without your suggestion that Violet pursue an acting career in Hollywood. I must admit, initially I wasn't drawn to the glamour of Hollywood in its Golden Age, but delving into research (and exposing Hollywood's dark underbelly in contrast to all the glitter) turned out to be so much fun. Thank you for believing this story is "magical." You are a joy to work with.

To my agent Jenny Bent—there is no better literary agent in all of New York (or the world for that matter). Thank you for your emails, your phone calls and your texts from Frankfurt at 2 A.M. You are my tireless advocate and you make me laugh. It is a pleasure to work with you. Thank you also to Denise Roy for your keen eye and talent for discovering the heart of the story. I appreciate your insight in shaping this novel into a book that I'm proud of.

To my fantastic team at William Morrow—thank you. A

big round of applause for my copy editors (who helped me hide all evidence of repetitive blushing and hand trembling) and to my designer, Elsie Lyons, who created two beautiful covers. To Amelia Wood in marketing and to my publicist, Michelle Podberezniak, I appreciate how hard you work to connect me with readers and book sellers!

To my critique partner Sally Hepworth, thank you for reading this novel in its many iterations over the years and for being the brilliant writer that you are. Your feedback is a gift. Another Hollywood trip is definitely in order!

To Anna Evans, thank you for reading early drafts of this novel and for your constant support. You are such a talented writer and your time is coming, I know it. To Niki Robbins, my favorite beta reader: thank you for loving the "old" *Boardwalk Summer*. I promise you will love this version too. To Nayelli Dalida, thank you for volunteering to check my Spanish and for reading a final draft of this novel.

To Sarah Dodd, Katie Flynn, and Jennifer Dean, thank you for volunteering your professional knowledge in the fields of psychology and law. Alas, like Hollywood, publishing can be tough. The character my questions pertained to was cut from the novel. But your advice was excellent nonetheless.

To my mom, thank you for providing me with inspiration, the vintage Hollywood calendar and books to help me with my research. You have always fostered my creativity. To my sister Carolyn, thank you for reading an early draft of this novel, but more importantly, thank you for always listening to me. Don't start charging by the hour for phone calls!

To my mother-in-law, thank you for inviting me to speak to your book groups. What fun they were to talk to!

To my husband, Will. Thank you for comforting me during times of stress and for watching Hazel when I disappear for hours to write. You and Hazel are the loves of my life (and Bernie too of course—dog hair, drool and all).

Finally, to my readers: thank you for your emails, your Facebook messages and your blog posts to let me know that my writing has touched you in some way. I have my dream job because of you and I can't thank you enough.

To the dreamers: never stop dreaming, never give up.

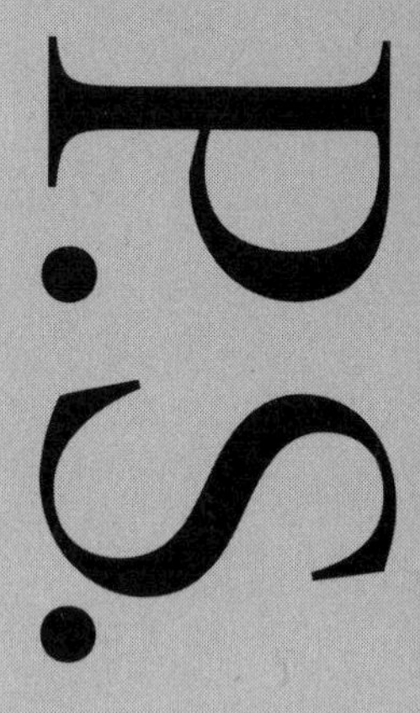

About the author

About the book

Insights,
Interviews
& More . . .

About the author

Meet Meredith Jaeger

Erika Pino Photography

MEREDITH JAEGER was born and raised in the San Francisco Bay Area. A graduate of the University of California, Santa Cruz, she worked for a San Francisco start-up before publishing her debut novel, *The Dressmaker's Dowry*. She lives outside San Francisco with her husband, toddler and bulldog, where she now writes full-time.

Behind the Book

In April 2014, while I was reading SFGate.com, the *San Francisco Chronicle*'s online newspaper, a headline struck me: "Santa Cruz Beach Boardwalk's Lively History Lives On." Ten years earlier, I had graduated from UC Santa Cruz with a degree in modern literature. My college years remain some of my fondest memories, and the charming seaside town of Santa Cruz still holds a special place in my heart.

Reading about the history of the Santa Cruz Beach Boardwalk, the state's oldest surviving amusement park, I remembered the thrill of riding the Giant Dipper as a child. The 1924 roller coaster is still a rumbling, rattling, shriek-inducing good time. This past summer, my husband and I took our one-year-old daughter to the boardwalk to ride the historic 1911 Looff Carousel. The Ruth & Sohn band organ piped classic amusement-park tunes, and the hand-carved horses delighted her. ▸

Ruth & Sohn band organ built in 1894. Photo credit: the author

Behind the Book *(continued)*

Giant Dipper roller coaster, 1993. Photo credit: Fritz Jaeger

Looff Carousel, 2017. Photo credit: the author

The log ride (with Giant Dipper in the background). The author, her father and younger sister, 1993. Photo credit: Carol Nyhoff

Although the boardwalk has enchanted children for generations, it didn't occur to me to set a novel in Santa Cruz until I read a line of the article that gave me chills. It described a windowless office above the Cocoanut Grove Ballroom, crammed with boxes of boardwalk memorabilia collected over a century.

I pictured that cramped room in my mind. Instantly, I saw my character Mari coming into contact with one of these artifacts, Violet's obituary, and unraveling a seventy-year-old mystery. Reading about a 1940 stunt that took place at the boardwalk, the "Slide for Life," solidified my plot. Don "Mighty Bosco" Patterson and his twelve-year-old assistant, Harry Murray, performed it. The two men zip-lined 750 feet, from the top of the casino to Pleasure Pier. Patterson hung by his knees, dangling Harry Murray by one ankle and one wrist. They dove into the ocean seconds before their trolley slammed into the pier. Eventually, the state banned the stunt for being "too hazardous for minors." Harry Murray was replaced by Marion Blake, a female performer.

Harry Murray served as my inspiration for Ricardo Cruz. I respected the courage it took for this young boy to perform such a dangerous stunt. But California is home to more than ten million immigrants, with Latinos outnumbering Anglos as the largest ethnic group. I decided to honor California's rich Chicano heritage by making Ricardo Cruz an immigrant ▸

Behind the Book *(continued)*

from Mexico and his granddaughter, Mari, the novel's protagonist.

Don "Mighty Bosco" Patterson hangs from the cable on a speeding trapeze, with the young Harry Murray suspended below, 1940. Photo credit: Santa Cruz Beach Boardwalk Archives

Don "Mighty Bosco" Patterson with the young Harry Murray, 1940. Many versions of this stunt were performed until 1945. Photo credit: Santa Cruz Beach Boardwalk Archives

The view from Beach Hill where Mari lives. Photo credit: the author

Violet's inspiration came from a photograph of the first ever Miss California pageant, held in Santa Cruz in 1924. I hadn't known that "bathing beauties" once stood on the very beach where I'd studied in college, sashes over their woolen swimsuits. Although the 1940 Miss California pageant was held in Venice, California, I changed the location to Santa Cruz for my novel. In 1947, the pageant returned to Santa Cruz and was held there annually until 1985. ▸

First Miss California contestants, 1924. Photo credit: Santa Cruz Beach Boardwalk Archives

Behind the Book *(continued)*

The first Miss California was eighteen-year-old Faye Lanphier of Alameda, who beat out Santa Cruz's own Mary Black. Faye was crowned on the beach bandstand in front of thousands of admirers. Then she danced the night away with flappers at the Cocoanut Grove Ballroom. The streets were lined with flags and fifty thousand gladioli framed a stage overlooking a lily pond, creating a Court of Blossoms. Many locals opposed the competition, believing the ladies wore too much makeup and showed too much skin. But Hollywood soon changed those attitudes.

Actress Ann Blyth as a mermaid with lifeguard Lester Eisley. Blyth was at the boardwalk filming Mr. Peabody and the Mermaid, *1948. Photo credit: Santa Cruz Beach Boardwalk Archives*

Even during the height of the Depression, the boardwalk remained popular with its music, ballroom, beach and easy transportation. The *Suntan Special* train carried passengers to and from Oakland, San Jose and San Francisco. In 1932, the train delivered over three thousand people each Sunday to Santa Cruz, where the brass of the beach band greeted them. In the opening scene of *Boardwalk Summer*, the beach band plays while Violet takes the stage, then Charles disembarks the *Suntan Special*.

Contestants on the 1948 Miss California pageant runway, which extends from the bandstand into the crowd. Photo credit: Santa Cruz Beach Boardwalk Archives

I imagined the boardwalk in Violet's day—people dancing to big bands such as Benny Goodman's, Artie Shaw's and Tommy Dorsey's; eating ice cream and hot dogs; frolicking in the Plunge (a heated indoor saltwater pool) and ▸

Behind the Book ***(continued)***

watching Plunge Natatorium Water Carnivals with performances by Olympic swimmers, acrobats and divers. I pictured Violet swept up in the excitement of her pageant win, wanting nothing more than to pursue her dream of Hollywood stardom.

Poster advertisement for the Plunge Water Carnival, 1936. Photo credit: Santa Cruz Beach Boardwalk Archives

The Story of Hollywood by Gregory Paul Williams was invaluable to me, providing details of the restaurants, hotels, talent agencies, gossip columnists and clubs that were popular during Hollywood's Golden Age. *The Santa Cruz Beach Boardwalk: A Century by the Sea* is another wonderful book containing a treasure trove of information and photographs that aided me in researching *Boardwalk Summer.*

Members of the Plunge Water Carnival Water Ballet group, 1941. Photo credit: Santa Cruz Beach Boardwalk Archives

When a screenwriter sexually assaults Violet, promising her a big break, his behavior highlights a problem still faced by actresses in Hollywood today. Countless allegations of sexual assault, rape and sexual harassment have been made against powerful movie producers, media moguls and directors, with brave women and men coming forward to tell their stories. This long, ugly history has existed since the dawn of the casting couch. Our cultural endemic goes ▸

beyond Hollywood, and in order to change these sexist attitudes, we must start with educating our children about what behaviors are acceptable or unacceptable.

One of the issues I struggled with when writing *Boardwalk Summer* was figuring out how Violet could start a new life under a new identity. Then I discovered a fascinating fact—the social security card goof of 1938. On the ssa.gov website, there's an article titled: "Social Security Cards Issued by Woolworth."

In 1938, the wallet manufacturer E. H. Ferree Company of Lockport, New York, decided to promote its wallet by showing how well a social security card would fit inside. A sample card was inserted in each wallet and the company vice president thought it would be a smart idea to use the actual social security number of his secretary, Mrs. Hilda Schrader Whitcher. Her number was 078-05-1120.

Department stores all over the country sold the wallet. Discovering this abused social security number was my "aha moment" when it came to solving my problem. In 1943, nearly six thousand people were using Hilda's number.

The fictional Mary's Chicken Shack, where Violet worked as a waitress before she met Charles, is inspired by many real-life concession stands that existed on the boardwalk for years. One of the long-standing Santa Cruz businesses mentioned in the novel is Marini's Candies. It opened on the boardwalk in 1915 and sold saltwater taffy, caramel apples and peanut brittle. Fourth generation Marinis run the business today. Stop by for a sweet treat if you're in Santa Cruz! The 1308 Pacific Avenue location is where Jason and Mari have their second date.

Mari works as a waitress at the Jupiter Café, inspired by its real-life counterpart, the (vegetarian) Saturn Café, where I ate frequently in college. Even my husband, an avid meat-eater, is a fan of their "Chicken" Avocado Club sandwich.

Saturn Café 145 Laurel St. Santa Cruz, CA. Photo credit: the author

Like Mari, I also revisited McHenry Library on the UC Santa Cruz campus when researching this novel, and I felt pangs of nostalgia for my life as an undergrad. Although I wish I'd gotten serious about novel writing back in ▸

Behind the Book ***(continued)***

college (as the saying goes, Youth is wasted on the young!), I'm grateful every day to have my dream career as an author and to share my love of California history with my readers.

This brings me to the heart of *Boardwalk Summer.* Two ambitious young women are forced to make the difficult choice between family and career. Although women today are blazing their own trails and attempting to have both (myself included), the balance is never easy. I hope that Mari and Violet inspire women everywhere to go after what they want in life. It's never too late to follow your dreams.

The author on West Cliff Drive, Santa Cruz. Photo credit: Carolyn Jaeger

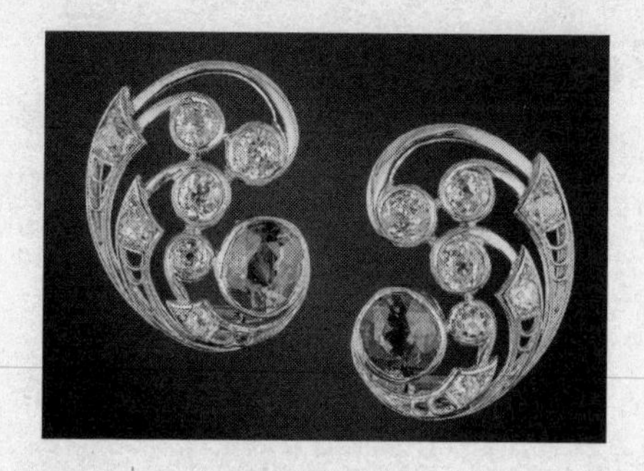

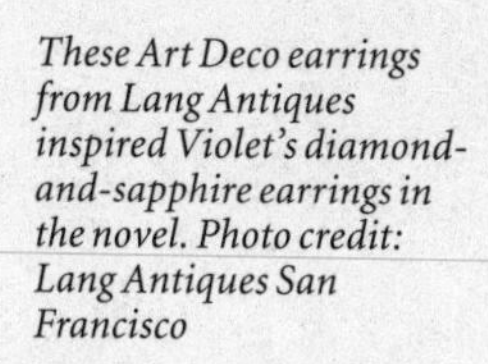

These Art Deco earrings from Lang Antiques inspired Violet's diamond-and-sapphire earrings in the novel. Photo credit: Lang Antiques San Francisco

Natural Bridges State Beach. Photo credit: the author

Reading Group Guide

1. Do you think that Violet made the only choice that she could when she escaped from Charles? According to the National Domestic Violence Hotline, on average it takes a victim seven attempts to leave an abusive spouse or partner before they leave for good. Why do you think this is?
2. How does Charles Harcourt fit the psychological profile of an abuser? Do you think that his wealth and power made him even more of a threat to Violet?
3. Mari and Violet are both young mothers who make difficult choices. Do you think that Mari was right to give up graduate school? Do you think that Violet regretted giving up her acting career? Are women today able to "have it all," or are they forced to choose between rearing children and pursuing a successful career?
4. Anti-Semitism is expressed in Violet's story line along with anti-Mexican sentiments. How have these negative attitudes toward minorities in the United States resurged recently, and why?
5. How do Violet's priorities change over the course of the novel, and what is the catalyst for those changes?

6. Mari is intent on saving the gazebo because it is a historic structure and it has personal significance to her. How do you feel about historic preservation? Does it impede city development, or is it a good thing?
7. Ricardo Cruz saves Violet Harcourt's life. What did you think of their friendship? Were you surprised that it was platonic?
8. Do you believe that Violet should have confided in Evie about Charles? How did withholding the truth affect their friendship?
9. Why did Violet continue to keep her identity a secret even after Charles's death? Do you think she was wrong to tell her husband, Gene, the truth about her past, but not her grandson, Jason?
10. Did you admire Mari for how she talked to Lily about different types of families, or would you have handled this sensitive topic differently? Should she have told Lily the identity of Lily's father?
11. Violet and Ricky both came from homes where their parents thought that dreams were foolish. Do you think that this strengthened their bond? Are there any dreams that you believe are too impractical to chase? Why? ▸

Reading Group Guide ***(continued)***

12. Violet lies about being married in order to compete in the Miss America pageant. Mari says of the pageant, "Just one more opportunity single mothers were denied." Do you agree with Mari? Is the rule that a contestant must be "unmarried, not pregnant and not the adoptive or biological parent of a child" unfair?

13. Of Hollywood, Violet says, "It's . . . different than I imagined, darker and brighter at once." Do you think that Violet's perception of Hollywood changed after she arrived? What is your impression of Hollywood during its Golden Age?